"Rarely do you encounter a work of literary fiction, brilliant in its execution and engaging in its indelible characters, that is also a romp, a grand entertainment. *Goyhood* is all of that—its language rich and precise, its people irresistible, and its marvelous story a literal joyride."

— Steve Stern, author of *The Village Idiot*

"A high-octane debut overflowing with heart, *Goyhood* swerves the line between devilry and virtue, humor and heartbreak. Buckle up for this one."

— Elyssa Friedland, author of *Last Summer at the Golden Hotel* and *The Most Likely Club*

"From Ocean Parkway to Bourbon Street, *Goyhood* is a classic American road novel with an ultra-Orthodox twist. Hold on to your kishkes. This book is a rollicking exploration of grief, love, brotherhood, and the American South that isn't afraid to ask the tough questions as it cannonballs into the deep end of Jewish identity."

— Michael David Lukas, author of *The Oracle of Stamboul* and *The Last Watchman of Old Cairo*

"Combining razor-sharp wit, memorable characters, and seemingly effortless prose, *Goyhood* is a true delight."

— Lynda Cohen Loigman, author of *The Matchmaker's Gift* and *The Two-Family House*

"The high-octane jaunt through America's South that follows Rabbi Belkin's shocking discovery is a volatile mix of *Shtisel* and a Burt Reynolds-style car-smasher."

— Paul Goldberg, author of *The Yid* and *The Dissident*

"What do you do when you find out you've been living a lie? Road trip, of course! Part Marx Brothers, part Malamud, Kerouac by way of Philip Roth, this brisk and witty picaresque mixes laughs, tears, and enlightenment in equal measure. It's a delightful ride, so grab a yarmulke and buckle up."

— Mark Sarvas, American Book Award-winning author of *Memento Park* and *Harry, Revised*

"With its refreshingly quirky indie movie sensibility, Reuven Fenton's *Goyhood* is an entertaining and deftly-paced novel of the meaning of family and faith."

— Adam Langer, author of *Cyclorama* and *The Salinger Contract*

GOYHOOD

A NOVEL

REUVEN FENTON

central
avenue

2024

This is a work of fiction. Names, characters, places and incidents either are the
product of the author's imagination or are used fictitiously and any resemblance to
actual persons, living or dead, business establishments, events or locales is entirely
coincidental.

Published by Central Avenue Publishing, an imprint of Central Avenue Marketing Ltd.
www.centralavenuepublishing.com

Published in Canada
Printed in United States of America

1. FICTION/Jewish
2. FICTION/Coming of Age

GOYHOOD

Cloth: 978-1-77168-368-5
Ebook: 978-1-77168-369-2

1 3 5 7 9 10 8 6 4 2

Keep up with Central Avenue

To Drs. Brocha and Anne Fenton

GOYHOOD

— PROLOGUE —

IT WAS A HEAT WAVE THE LIKES OF WHICH NEW MOAB HADN'T SEEN SINCE 1938, WHEN THIRTY-THREE RESIDENTS DIED AND scores more were hospitalized with sunstroke. Modern cooling staved off a second onslaught, but outside, flowers wilted, lawns yellowed and garden rodents burrowed deep underground to sleep it off.

On his third straight day indoors, twelve-year-old David Belkin got up at noon. He found a party-size bag of Doritos and turned on *The Bold and the Beautiful*. He stayed on through *The Young and the Restless* and *As the World Turns*. Fourteen minutes into *Guiding Light*, he had an epiphany: if he was going to fry his brain anyway, he might as well do it as God intended.

He stripped down to his shorts, took a tablespoon from the kitchen and went out the back door. The air was like vaporized cooking oil, coating his throat and nasal passages. Undeterred, he sat cross-legged in the shade of the pecan tree and set about prying at the cracked clay with the spoon. It was a labor, and pretty soon sweat beads clung to the brown fuzz on his chest and lower back. The spoon got slippery, so he took it by the head and chipped away with the handle.

The screen door clattered and he looked up as his brother Marty, younger by forty-three seconds, came down the porch steps. The twins had the same high foreheads, Roman noses, and light chestnut hair, but David was built like a linebacker, with a brick-red skin tone. Marty was slight and fair, with prominent blue veins on his temples. His normally keen eyes had a strange, vacant look, and he was walking like someone with rheumatoid arthritis.

"What's wrong?" David asked.

Marty tried to grin at his brother, but grimaced instead. He leaned over the rail and threw up in a patch of tall weeds. David spectated for a few seconds, then got back to digging. Marty, when it was all out of him, straightened up and wiped his mouth with his forearm.

"Better now?" the elder asked.

"I think so. I ate some bad tuna salad."

"We have tuna salad?"

"Not anymore." Marty hoisted up his saggy shorts. Pink was coming back to his cheeks, elasticity to his spine and shoulders. He jutted his chin at the shallow divot by his brother's bare foot.

"How's that going?"

"Go get a spoon and help me."

"Nah."

The elder twin got back to work while the younger trekked across the yard, a badland of red clay patched with bermuda, crabgrass, nutsedge and clover. He circled the rusted trampoline that their mother got for free off a newspaper listing and climbed over a split-rail fence onto the neighbor's property. A geriatric hound dog named Reynolds lay face up under a sycamore tree, tongue grazing his lower eyelid. There was a length of cable hooking his collar to a trolley run between two trees. Marty got to his knees and rubbed the dog's belly.

"How you doin', big guy?"

Reynolds started panting. His ears pulled back and he raked the air with his paw. His uninhibited pleasure soothed Marty's soul after what he'd just witnessed through the open door of his mother's bedroom, an image he'd never get out of his head. For a happy little while, boy and dog were content to laze in the shade, listening to the hypnotic buzz of cicadas and inhaling the peppery odor of pine sap.

Until a growl generated from deep in the back of Reynolds's throat. His ears stiffened and he sat up, pointing his snout at the Belkin house. Marty didn't need dog ears to hear it too. His insides started churning again.

"Booyah, got a fat one!"

David was on his knees, smiling at something in his cupped palm. Reynolds stopped growling and trotted to the fence. He stuck his head between the rails to greet the elder Belkin, who rewarded him with a face rub. David thrust his prize out at Marty. It was a doozie alright—fat and red with a formidable clitellum, writhing to form the letters C and S.

"Beauty," Marty said.

David stroked it affectionately with his fingertip before lowering it to the dog's snout. "Bon appétit, boy." Reynolds sniffed it and rejected it with a nasal exhalation.

"He's got enough worms in him already," Marty said.

David laughed, then side-armed the creature into the grass. "I'm bored. And hot as balls."

The moans and cries from inside the house were getting louder. "Let's get out of here," Marty said.

"How 'bout we go to the quarry?"

"Too crowded."

"There'll be girls," David said.

"How 'bout the pine barrens?"

The elder thought about it. "Can we get ice creams first?"

"Duh."

"Deal. Lemme just wash this mud off my hands." He started toward the porch steps.

"Stop!"

David spun around. "Jesus, what?"

"Use the hose."

"That's what I was gonna do, dumbass."

While David washed up with the garden hose, Marty grabbed the little

Igloo cooler next to the porch. They took turns drinking cold water from the hose until they could hold no more. Their Schwinns, bought for ten dollars apiece at the Salvation Army, were propped against the side of the house. Marty's crankset was stuck permanently in high gear, and David's tires had as much tread as a pair of blue jeans, but the bikes got them where they had to go. Tied to the back of Marty's seat was a dream catcher he'd made out of woven willow sticks, dental floss and wild turkey feathers.

They stopped at Otto's corner store for some five-for-a-buck ice cream sandwiches. Then they headed south on Dixieland Highway, traversing a suburban gridscape of crackerbox Capes and colonials. They dodged broken bottles and potholes and rises of buckling concrete. Shade trees were scarce and the sun was malevolent, but before long they were in the next town, Moab, where mature oaks shaded the road and the pavement was smooth enough to roll a Matchbox car on. The homes were Greek Revival, the lawns thick, uniform and immaculate.

Moab, formerly New Moab, was a well-heeled community founded by plantation owners before the Civil War. Post–World War II, in the magnanimous spirit of the time, the town incorporated a swath of vacant land north of the border and subdivided it into tracts of affordable housing for ex-GIs. The natives received their new neighbors with detached gentility—at first. Over time, chocolate overtook vanilla as the dominant skin shade uptown, and the gentry started lobbying for secession. Their state representative argued the matter before the Georgia General Assembly in 1984, and won. The northern municipality got to keep the name New Moab; the southern dropped the "New"—but did keep the entire business district and all of its tax revenue.

Little of which vexed the Belkin boys, who were only twelve, and white. They stopped at the Central Plaza movie theater to check out posters for *Beverly Hills Cop III*, *The Flintstones* and *Speed*. The next stop was McTaggart's Antiques, whose window display featured tin busts of General Lee and Stonewall Jackson, and a bayonet authenticated to have felled Union Major

Lucas McTeague at Bull Run.

They moved on. At the corner of Virginia Avenue and Dixieland, Marty came within a whisker of knocking over a brunette in a tracksuit exiting the automatic doors of CVS.

"Watch it!" she shouted.

David twisted his torso to flick her the bird. When he faced forward again, his eyes bugged. His brother had come to a dead stop in the middle of Virginia Avenue. He slammed his brakes, barely avoiding a fender bender. "The fuck, man! You almost killed me."

"Check it out," Marty said. He was staring across Dixieland in the direction of Ebenezer Missionary Baptist Church.

"What about it?"

"Not Ebenezer. Further down." David's eyes followed the line of his finger. Next door to the church was the parsonage, and next to that an old yellow house with a gabled roof, dormer windows and a porte-cochère. The boys had cycled past the house a hundred times, but there was something different now. A glossy banner over the front door read "Chabad of Moab." On the front lawn stood a towering steel candelabrum with eight branches rising diagonally from the stem.

"What is that?" David said.

Marty didn't answer. He was thinking about a movie he'd watched on a Sunday afternoon not long ago. The movie was a chore to sit through, tedious to the point of debilitating, and he never would have hung in there if not for the sublime introductory sequence—paradoxically the most riveting seven minutes of cinema he'd ever seen. In it, a big black rectangle called the Monolith appeared on Paleolithic Earth and brought intelligence to a tribe of man apes to the tune of Richard Strauss.

The candelabrum, too, had arrived unannounced, unexplained and impertinent to time and place. And it, too, was in his head. What did that mean—in his head? He couldn't explain it any better than the apes. Did it speak to him? No. It brought. Yes, *brought*, and Marty . . . *received*, he supposed, through a sixth sense that was neither auditory nor cognitive but some melding of the two.

"Did you get that?" he asked.

"Get what?"

"That feeling."

"What are you talking about?"

"Not a feeling. More like a—"

"That thing's taller than Shaq," David observed. "What is it, some kind of sculpture?"

"No, it's a . . . what do you call it? What Jews light on Hanukkah."

"Jews?"

Marty snapped his fingers three times. "You know. They have them in the Hallmark commercials at Christmastime."

"Yeah, I dunno. Should we get going?"

"What do you think it's doing here?" Marty asked. "Hanukkah's in December. And I've never heard of any Jews living in Moab."

"I bet there's some," David said. "Jews are loaded."

A car horn blared at the intersection, and the boys hurried to the corner. David pedaled on; Marty did not. He reached into his back pocket and pulled out a flattened box of Chesterfields. He shook one out and stuck it in the corner of his mouth. From a front pocket he pulled a camo-colored Zippo that he'd stolen last summer from an Army Navy store.

David, vexed, turned around and came back. He looked from the candelabrum to his brother's face, and back to the candelabrum. He did recall the Hanukkah lamps in the Hallmark commercials, but those had been ornately patterned and accented, with branches that arced up gracefully. This one was all utility, straight lines and right angles. He eyed the Igloo hanging on Marty's handlebar, wondering how its contents were faring.

"Come on," he whined.

Marty took a final puff, flicked the cigarette away and blew a smoke ring at his brother's face. He gave the candelabrum one last look, making a mental note to knock on the door of the yellow house on the way home. He had questions.

THEY CROSSED FORREST Street, Vance Boulevard and Lee Avenue, and into Moab proper. Here embodied an idealized American South that Hollywood extolled in the likes of *Steel Magnolias*, *Fried Green Tomatoes* and the soon-to-be-released *Forrest Gump*. Ancient live oaks canopied Dixieland Highway. Behind them stood august antebellum estates ensconced on swaths of St. Augustine grass, their gardens lush with lilacs, roses and camellia bushes.

The boys pedaled at a leisurely pace under the leafy overhang, each in his own thoughts. David fantasized he was on his way home to one of the estates, a Black mammy waiting at the door with a slice of apple pie à la mode and a glass of lemonade. Marty tried in vain to put into proper English the almost-but-not-quite physical sensation he'd felt at Virginia and Dixieland. The feeling lingered irrespective of distance, as though an angler had hooked him and was letting the line unspool for a while.

They hid their bikes in some wild barley outside the pine barrens, a forty-acre wilderness at the southern outskirts of Moab. Marty took the Igloo and they went in. It was wonderful among the tall pines. The air smelled of conifer resin and the sweet yellow needles that crackled under their feet. They stopped to pick wild raspberries, still mostly green and mouth-puckeringly tart.

After half a mile, they arrived at a clearing in which stood a huge cuboidal chunk of granite covered in lichen. Generations of kids called it the meteor because of how it loomed alone in the center of a treeless section of woods. The boys scrambled easily up a sloped side and sat pretzel style on a shallow depression. The cool stone mollified their sun-and-mosquito-ravaged legs.

David picked up a square foil wrapper torn halfway down one side and grinned naughtily. Marty plucked it out of his fingers and spun it away. He opened the Igloo and flipped it over. David was relieved to see the rectangular confections weren't fused into a molten lump. They ate with gusto, heedless of the freezer-burn aftertaste, and when they were done, scooped up the sodden paper wrappers and put them in the cooler.

Marty smacked his lips and lay on his back. David smacked his lips and lay beside him. They stared at the electric-blue sky garlanded by a wreath of tree points. Marty took out the Chesterfields and stuck one in the corner of his mouth. His thumb was on the wheel of his Zippo when he heard a flap of wings. He looked up just in time to see a powder-gray bird duck into a cluster of pine needles.

Lanius ludovicianus, he thought. Loggerhead shrike.

"Feels like we're on the Moon of Endor, doesn't it?" David said.

Marty lit the cigarette, took a drag and handed it to his brother, who did likewise. Something at their six o'clock caught David's eye.

"Hey, what's that?" he asked, pointing to the crook of a branch high in a loblolly pine. Wedged in there was something resembling a pillow with all its down bunched in the center.

"Good eye, Ese," Marty said. "Wild turkey."

"Wild turkeys can fly?"

"You bet. During the day they're on the ground eating seeds and berries. But they like to roost high up in trees so that predators can't get 'em while they're sleeping."

"Why's it sleeping during the day?"

"Dunno. The heat, maybe."

They passed the Chesterfield back and forth and watched the birds tree-hop.

"How come you like birds so much?" David asked.

"I just think they're neat."

"You think you might wanna be like a bird scientist when you grow up?"

"An ornithologist."

"Yeah."

"Maybe," Marty said. "How 'bout you?"

"Do I wanna be an ornithologist?"

"No, what do you want to be, period?"

"Don't care, as long as it makes me rich."

They luxuriated in their full bellies and the cool granite on their skin, and the never-gets-old smell of pine resin. "Really makes you think," Marty said.

"What does?"

"The big old sky."

"What about it?" David asked.

"If there's more to life than just living."

"What do you mean?"

"I don't know. Like, maybe each of us is assigned a mission at birth, and life's about figuring out what the mission is and then doing it."

David thought about it. "Like Luke Skywalker."

"Basically."

More silence passed before David, apropos of nothing, said, "I think you'll make a great dad someday."

AS THEY PEDALED home, a heaven-sent breeze rustled their hair and cooled their sweat. At Dixieland and Virginia, Marty wanted to knock on the door to the yellow house and ask about the candelabrum. David griped that *Saved by the Bell* was on in ten minutes. Marty folded.

When they pulled up to their house on Bragg Street, they saw a man standing at the front stoop with his back to them. One foot rested on the bottom step. The other was swallowed by crabgrass and seed-head dandelions. Their mother, Ida Mae, stood in the doorway in her pink bathrobe—the belt cinched tight, thank God—and her peroxide hair in a messy bun. She chatted with him while sipping from a red Solo cup.

There was an archetype of man that came to see their mother. He wore some variation of band T-shirt, dungarees and work boots. He had ropey forearms and black crescents of dirt under his fingernails, and, remarkably often, a cigarette angled on his ear like a pencil. This was not that man. This man wore a suit, a wide-brimmed fedora and oxford shoes, all black. He weighed all of maybe one hundred thirty pounds.

David thought, *He's got to be barbecuing in that suit.*

Marty thought, *Child Protective Services.*

But Ida Mae seemed at ease, and when she saw her boys she smiled and beckoned them over. The man turned around. He had an astonishing beard— a ZZ Top masterpiece that ended three inches above his navel. It made him look wise beyond his years, which probably numbered no more than twenty-five. A certainty struck Marty like a lightning bolt: this was the man responsible for the candelabrum.

The twins left their bikes on the curb and crossed the yard to meet the stranger. "Boys," Ida Mae said, "I'd like you to meet the new rabbi of Moab. He just arrived two days ago from New York with his wife and baby boy."

"Girl," said the man.

David gawked at the beard with his mouth slightly ajar.

"Quit staring and introduce yourself," Ida Mae said.

"I'm Dave."

The rabbi shook his hand. "My name is Yossi Kugel. It's a pleasure to meet you, Dovid."

"David."

"Did you know that your namesake is the greatest king who ever lived?"

"My what?"

"Dovid *HaMelech*. King David. He lived about three thousand years ago."

The boy swatted a mosquito on his neck. "Why was he the greatest?"

"Well, when he was just a shepherd boy he defeated a very bad giant with a single rock. Later, when he became King of Israel, he made Jerusalem the capital and brought together all the tribes of Jacob. He also wrote the book of Tehillim, or Psalms."

"I know the shepherd boy story," David said.

"I'm not surprised. It's a classic," Yossi Kugel said. He held his hand out to Marty. "And what's your name?"

Marty shook his hand and told him his name.

"You don't meet many Martys your age."

"Martin was his grandfather on his dad's side," Ida Mae said. "He was from New York, too, I think."

"What an honor to your grandfather that you carry his name," the rabbi said. "May you emulate his finest virtues, and may his spirit continue to shine through you."

Marty, having never been spoken to this way, didn't know how to respond. He just looked down at his Keds. Out of the corner of his eye, he saw a jackrabbit bound across the yard.

"Martin, look at people when they talk to you," Ida Mae said.

He looked up, cheeks burning. The rabbi chuckled good-naturedly. "I bet it's not every day that you find a rabbi at your door wearing a suit and hat on a hot summer day."

"No, sir."

"Although in the neighborhood I come from, most everybody dresses like me, summer, fall, winter, spring."

"Oh my," Ida Mae said invitingly. At thirty-seven she was still a looker, but her exhaustive beauty regimen couldn't quite conceal the lines etched around her eyes and the vertical worry marks between her brows. "You were telling me earlier," she said, "you and your wife are here on a kind of a . . . what? Mission trip?"

The rabbi's face pinched thoughtfully. "I wouldn't say we're missionaries; missionaries seek to convert those of other faiths. My wife and I aren't looking to convert anyone."

"Oh," Ida Mae said.

"What we do is provide for the spiritual needs of Jews who lack the tools and education to practice Judaism the right way."

David was getting shifty-eyed. He glanced past his mother into the living room.

"There aren't any Jews around here," Marty said.

"Sure there are," the rabbi said. "We've only just arrived in Moab and I've already gotten to know a few, and I'm due to meet several more."

"He found us by looking for Jewish-sounding names in the phone book," Ida Mae said.

"We're not Jewish," Marty said.

"What are you talking about? Both your father's parents were Jews, and my mother was born to Jewish parents."

A flare went off in the boy's head. "Hold it."

"How do you think I got your dad to marry me?" she said. "He was dead set on marrying only a Jew. I've told you this."

"No you haven't."

David, who could take it no more, darted into the house. A moment later the TV blared.

Marty was more than miffed that his mother had waited until now to drop this bombshell—as an aside, no less. But the dominant feeling was exaltation. A Jew! Marty Belkin. A *member*. He'd never been a member of anything, not even the Audubon Society.

"You were never curious why we never set foot in Ebenezer Baptist?" Ida Mae asked.

"No."

"'Cause we're not Christian, dummy."

"We celebrate Christmas."

"Christmas is a national holiday."

Marty turned to Rabbi Kugel. "The menorah in front of the yellow house. You put it there." *Menorah*. The word that had evaded him all afternoon slipped out of his mouth like a watermelon seed.

Rabbi Kugel's eyes lit up. "Yes I did. And the house is our *shul*—er, synagogue. It's also my wife Chana's and my home."

"What's *Chabad*?" Marty asked, mispronouncing it *tch'abad*.

The rabbi corrected him on the pronunciation. "Chabad means . . ." He glanced at his watch. "Well, because I'm a bit pressed for time, let's just say for now it's a type of synagogue."

"You live in your synagogue?" Ida Mae said.

"Any space can be a synagogue, as long as there's a congregation and a Torah."

"You have a Torah?" Marty asked, goggle-eyed. Once he'd watched a documentary on PBS about the Jews of Venice, which showed someone in a prayer shawl reading a Torah scroll in an old synagogue. He'd never imagined that a real Torah could find its way to a place like Moab.

"Sure," the rabbi said. "Handwritten with a quill on parchment." He eyed the boy contemplatively. "How old are you?"

"Twelve."

"Ah. When is your birthday?"

"November third."

"Well then. We'll have to get started on bar mitzvah lessons."

Marty felt a twitch inside him. "Bar mitzvah . . ."

"Absolutely. It's your rite of passage into manhood. Your brother's, too. I'll tell you what: take a few days to reflect on some of the things we've talked about, and I'll reach out to you boys again later in the week."

Marty nodded.

"Won't you come in for a glass of sweet tea?" Ida Mae asked. "You must be about ready to die."

"No thanks, Mrs. Belkin. I should be on my way. I've got lots more introductions to make." He took two steps back. "Why don't you and your boys come to shul this Saturday? Nine-thirty. We serve luncheon after services. Have you ever eaten cholent?"

"I've never heard of it."

"You're in for a treat."

"We'd be delighted."

"Marty knows where it is," he said, and winked. He walked across the yard to a wood-paneled Ford station wagon parked in the driveway. Old Mrs. McCoy across the street stopped watering her wilting magnolias to watch the gnome-bearded man in funeral garb get into his car.

"He wouldn't shake my hand," Ida Mae said in a faraway voice.

"What?"

"When he first got here I tried to shake his hand, and he said he isn't allowed to touch a woman who isn't his wife."

"Huh."

"He said something about how when a man and a woman touch, it's like a sacred moment, even if it's only a handshake. You ever heard anything like that in your life?"

She took a long pull from her cup. They watched the station wagon back a quarter turn onto Bragg Street, then on toward Dixieland Highway.

"Wouldn't even shake my hand," she said in wonder.

— CHAPTER 1 —

WHAT ARE THESE RITUALS TO YOU?

Mayer Belkin was so deep in study that when some schmuck came up from behind and whispered those incendiary words into his ear, he gave an embarrassing little yelp and whipped around. No one was there.

He got up and scanned the *beis medrash* for the wit who'd disrupted his holy labor—and with such an odd provocation to boot. Was he hiding in plain sight, chewing a fingernail over an open Gemara? Unlikely; as a top yeshiva in Brooklyn, Ohr Lev did not propagate bad apples. And even if there were a few bad apples, who among them had the gall to provoke the *rosh yeshiva's* son-in-law?

A dybbuk?

He laughed to himself. Such were the hazards of idleness; you risked hearing your own thoughts. Now, where was he? The prankster's taunt had flattened the house of cards he'd spent the better part of an hour building in his head. Well, he'd rebuild. But first he took a moment, as he often did before diving into the complex web of scholarly debate comprising the Talmud, to gaze around the cavernous space in which he'd spent most of the past quarter century.

How he loved the *beis medrash*, with its myriad bookshelves sagging with heavy Jewish legal texts, its checkerboard ceiling of missing panels crisscrossed with exposed pipes, its windowless walls evoking a bunker whose lights never went off. He loved the omnipresent odor of Nescafé and human musk, and the collective murmurings of five hundred young *talmidim* laboring over the Talmud.

Eighteen years ago the *rosh yeshiva*, *HaGaon HaRav* Yaakov Drezner, married his daughter off to Mayer, but with stipulations: he was never to train for the rabbinate or apply for a faculty position at Ohr Lev; he was to stay a full-time student for the rest of his life. In exchange, Rav Drezner would support the couple financially, even throwing in a house in Kensington within walking distance of the yeshiva.

Eighteen years later, Mayer still pinched himself from time to time to make sure he wasn't dreaming. Befitting a Drezner, he was privileged to a life of *ruchnius*—spiritual capital—without ever worrying about *gashmius*—material concerns. What a coup for a poor *frieh* from Georgia! Now he had his own housekeeper, who not only cooked and cleaned but kept the refrigerator so well stocked that Sarah was forever throwing out expired food—it being just the two of them in the house.

Revitalized by the sea of *talmidim* in study, he turned back to the Gemara. At issue was the atonement ritual for someone who had been cured of leprosy. According to the Talmud, the high priest needed four items for the ritual: a cedar branch a cubit long and a quarter the thickness of a bedpost, a hyssop plant no shorter than a handbreadth, a crimson strand weighing a shekel, and a sparrow. The priest would tie the branch to the hyssop with the strand, then press the bundle to the sparrow's wing tips and tail tips and submerge it all in a new earthenware container that held water mixed with the blood of another sparrow. He then sprinkled it on the back of the former leper's hand seven times.

What are these rituals to you?

Mayer clapped a palm to his ear as if a mosquito had flown in, and whipped his head around. No one was there. He banged a fist on his Gemara. What chutzpah!

"What are these rituals to you?"—*mah ha'avodah hazos lachem?*—was what the wicked son asked his father in the Passover Haggadah. By specifying "you" and not himself, he revoked his Jewish identity, and his father retorted

16

that had he been a slave at the time of the Exodus, God would have left him behind in Egypt.

Mayer wasn't superstitious, but in the unlikelihood that a dybbuk was the provocateur, it was a cunning one; if ever there was a time to plant skepticism in an unsuspecting mind, it was while said mind was grappling with *Maseches Kinim*, arguably the most esoteric tractate of the Talmud. Spiritual leprosy hadn't afflicted a Jew for two thousand years, so indeed what *were* these rituals to contemporary man? But any student worth his salt knew that practical applicability in Jewish law was peripheral to the act of learning itself; the Talmud was an extension of the Torah, and studying Torah was to the soul as food to the body. What's more, every moment of *bitul Torah*—not learning Torah—was a sin against God.

SARAH HAD REMINDED him of this very lesson last night. They'd sat on opposite ends of the cream-colored sectional in the living room. He read from a little book of Psalms. She, feet tucked under her, watched a TV drama on her phone—*Orange* something, about a women's prison. Though the show had ended several years ago, she still cycled through it regularly. Mayer would have preferred she watch no TV—barring that, TV without profanity—but he never said so.

He glanced sidelong at her. After eighteen years her face still enamored him—the high cheekbones, the almond-shaped eyes a shade above black, the long lashes, the enviably arched brows. She had a fine figure as well, but always secreted it in an oversized purple housecoat.

He cleared his throat. She didn't move. He spoke her name. She still didn't move. He spoke her name louder. She took out her AirPods.

"I forgot to ask," he said, "how was your day?"

"Fine, and yours?"

"*Baruch Hashem.*"

She started putting the AirPods back in her ears.

"I ran into Shuey Elbaum this morning," he said. "I think you know him?"

She thought for a moment. "His sister was in my class."

"Right." His eyes roamed the living room. It was pristine. The polished cherrywood floor reflected five recessed lights above, one at each corner and one in the center. There were no furnishings besides the couch, no artwork or photography on the antiseptic white walls. Sarah was ambitiously minimalistic.

"What about him?" she asked.

"Well, we were talking and, one way or another, he mentioned that one of his brothers-in-law and wife have been having difficulty."

"Having difficulty . . ."

"Getting pregnant."

She said nothing.

"Anyway, they started seeing this top fertility doctor in Manhattan by the name of Bodner. Jewish guy. And in just three months—"

"Mayer."

"Yes, *schefele*."

"How much money do we have?" Her face was implacable.

"What do you mean?"

"I'm curious if you know how much money we have. What our net worth is."

He deliberated for a few seconds. "I guess I don't."

"How about our credit score? Can you tell me that number?"

He looked at his hands.

"That's an easy one," she said. "We don't have a credit score. My father bought everything we own." She studied his face. "Do you know what a credit score is? Never mind. Do you know what credit is?"

He traced the lines on his left palm.

"Now, this Dr. Bodner. You say he's in Manhattan?"

He nodded.

"Which hospital is he affiliated with?"

"I don't know."

"What's his first name?"

"I don't know."

She rubbed her chin. "Shuey Elbaum said he's top of his field. Let's assume that's true. Specialists at his level are always pressed for time; they expect their patients to at least know the basics when they come in for a consultation. So tell me: what are your thoughts on IUI versus IVF?"

He said nothing.

"Any opinion on estrogen blockers versus injected hormones?"

"I'd have to look into it."

"What about costs? What kind of coverage would our insurance give us?"

He said nothing.

"What's the name of our insurance company?" she asked.

"Sarah."

"There's an insurance card in your wallet. Does it say United? Anthem? Aetna? Cigna?"

"Okay," he said. "Consider me dressed down. I'm sorry."

She tilted her head. "Why are you sorry?"

"For being ignorant and unprepared and for wasting your time."

She laughed, not unkindly. "But you have nothing to apologize for."

He frowned at her.

"Don't you see?" she said. "You're right not to fill your head with *gashmius*. Taxes, insurance, credit: those are my concerns, not yours. Why suddenly are you making doctors your business?"

"I was just talking to Shuey. He—"

She touched his fingertips, electrifying him. "I know how badly you want children—all the more so, me. But *Hashem* put the defect inside me. *Me*, not you. Let me worry about doctors and drugs and therapies. You keep davening that we should merit to conceive. Okay?"

"Okay."

"I'm counting on you."

He nodded. She withdrew her hand. "Now, no more about this. I feel a migraine coming on."

She got to her feet and started toward the stairs, stopping just before the first step. "Don't let me see you for a while, okay?"

He nodded with a single dip of his chin.

AFTER REVIEWING THE section of Gemara about atonement for the leper, he consulted with Rashi, the preeminent medieval commentator from France, whose notes filled the inner margin of the page. He then looked to the outer margin to see what Rashi's successors, the tosafists, had to say. Finally, he flipped to the back of the volume to consult with the sixteenth-century Polish Talmudist the Maharsha, the eleventh-century Algerian Talmudic master the Rif, and the Rif's fourteenth-century counterpart the Ran, of Catalonia.

"Rabbi Belkin?"

He looked up, half expecting to find himself peering into the yellow eyes of a malicious spirit. Instead, it was an acne-faced boy of fourteen named Kivi Klopfer.

"Yes?" He didn't correct Kivi on *Rabbi*; it was customary at Ohr Lev for *talmidim* to address their betters with the honorific.

"You have a phone call."

Mayer frowned. In all his years at the yeshiva, he'd gotten five phone calls, all from Sarah. His thoughts went back to their conversation last night and a ripple of unease traveled up his back.

"Are you sure?"

"They asked for you."

He thanked Kivi and started across the *beis medrash* toward the double doors at the opposite end of the room. Beyond them was a vestibule with a second set of doors opening to Ocean Parkway. On one wall hung two pay phones side by side. Cell phones weren't allowed in the building, so it was a minor miracle when one of the pay phones was vacant long enough to receive a call.

A boy with a unibrow spoke Israeli-accented Hebrew into one. The other dangled from the box by its metal cord. Mayer uttered a brief benediction that *Hashem* guide his tongue, and scooped up the phone. The mouthpiece smelled like apricots decomposing in the sun.

"Hello?"

"Marty!"

He pulled the phone away from his ear and looked at it.

"Marty? You there?"

He was about to tell the guy he had the wrong number. But then in his mind's eye a grainy profile came into focus. "David?"

"How are you, brother?"

He put a hand to his chest. It had to be eight years since he'd last heard that mash-up accent of Popcorn Sutton and Venice Beach stoner. "Surprised," he said. "But in a good way. How are you?"

"Okay. But you are one tough guy to get hold of. I'd keep a flip phone on you for emergencies."

"How did you get this number?"

"I called your house phone."

"You spoke to my wife?"

Mayer heard the flick of a cigarette-lighter wheel, the crackle of something burning. "I did."

"How long did you speak?"

"I don't know. A minute? Minute and a half? Why?"

"No reason. You caught me off guard is all."

This was an understatement. When he was thirteen, Mayer, then Marty, had bid his home state of Georgia goodbye to start a new life in Brooklyn—leaving David in the care of their hapless mother. The twins kept in touch at first, but over time their talks turned sporadic and formal, then seldom and fraught, and finally, nonexistent. So it went when two lives diverged in opposite directions.

"So, to what do I owe the call?" Mayer asked.

There was a long pause.

"David? Did I lose you?"

"You'd better sit down."

"What's wrong?"

"Are you sitting?"

"Yes," he lied.

"It's Mom."

Mayer's torso tightened. "Go ahead."

David didn't go ahead.

"Well, is she okay?" Mayer asked.

"No."

The younger Belkin glanced at the boy on the other phone, then lowered his voice to a near whisper. "Tell me she didn't get arrested."

"She didn't."

He heard the lighter wheel flick again, the burning crackle, the exhale. "I'm sorry to break this to you, Ese. Mom's dead."

IT WAS AS if someone had injected novocaine into the base of his spinal cord. Less than ten minutes ago he was researching ancient cures for leprosy.

"What?"

"I'm sorry."

"You're telling me she actually—" He lowered his voice again. "Passed away."

"She's not alive anymore."

"But how? Was she sick?"

"Not specifically."

"What does that mean?"

David sighed. "It means she was clinically obese and two teagaritas away from a liver transplant, but otherwise healthy as a pig in mud."

"Then how?"

A band of boisterous eleventh graders came into the vestibule from Ocean Parkway with shopping bags from the corner grocery. Their banter echoed about the high-ceilinged room, drowning out David's next words. When the *beis medrash* door closed behind the last boy, Mayer said, "Sorry, David, you were saying?"

"I was asking if you're still sitting."

"I never was."

"Well, this time you'd better."

"Please, just spit it out."

David did. Mayer wished he'd heeded his brother's suggestion.

Earlier that morning, Yossi Kugel, the rabbi of the only synagogue in Moab, Georgia, arrived at work to find the entryway locked. This was unusual, but not concerning. His longtime secretary, Ida Mae Belkin, typically got to work before him, but not always. He let himself in, walked past her vacant desk and went into his office. An hour later, he phoned her and got voicemail. He worked for another half hour and tried her again, getting the same result.

He paid some bills, then made an alms call to one of the shul's more reliable donors. After that, he met for forty-five minutes with a shul member who was having second thoughts about her fiancé. Then he tried Ida Mae a third time. Getting a premonition, he drove to her house. Her Mercury Sable was in the driveway. He rang the doorbell. When no one answered, he banged on the door. Then he called the police.

David paused. Mayer was starting to feel like he'd swallowed Drano, but urged his brother on.

"Well, it turned out that last night Mom fixed her usual sweet tea and Beefeater. She put on her favorite *Office* episode, the one where they play Yankee Swap at the Christmas party. You know that one?"

"No."

"Seriously?"

"David."

"Right. Okay. She got cozy on the couch, and . . ."

Mayer ground his jaws together. "And?"

"God, this is hard to say."

"Say it before I have an aneurysm."

"She killed herself."

Mayer's knees buckled. "No!"

"Sorry, bro."

"How?"

"Cops say she downed a whole bottle of Oxy."

Mayer felt as if a colony of wasps had staked a claim inside his head. "She committed suicide?" He put his hands on his knees. The phone slipped from between his ear and shoulder and jounced on its cord. He looked up. The uni-browed boy was eyeing him warily. He put the phone back to his ear.

"Marty?" David said.

"*Baruch dayan ha'emes.*"

"What's that mean?"

"Blessed is the true judge. It's what you say when somebody dies."

"I just spoke to her a few days ago," David said. "She was upbeat. We talked about *The Bachelorette*."

When had Marty last spoken to their mother? Two months ago? All he could recall from the conversation was her complaining about the Georgia heat.

"Anyway, Yossi's taking care of all the arrangements," David said. "The closest Jewish funeral home's in Atlanta. Apparently, per Jewish law, we've got to get her in the ground as soon as possible, so . . . I guess you've got a flight to catch."

Flight! The week's itinerary unfolded in his head, each step bleaker than the last. There was booking the airline ticket—how did one even do that?—and packing. There was the airport to worry about, the flight itself, the arrival airport, transportation to the funeral. There was a eulogy to be written, a body to bury, a shiva to sit with his estranged twin in their dank and dingy childhood home.

"Listen, let me cover your plane ticket," David said.

Mayer almost smiled. David, forever on the run from debt collectors, always had a generous heart. "I think I'll manage."

"You sure? It would be my pleasure. Really."

"Thanks anyway."

They said goodbye. Mayer hung the phone on the cradle and thought of the provocation whispered in his ear a short while ago. *What are these rituals to you?* How innocuous it now seemed in light of . . .

Suicide. He pinched the bridge of his nose, then hastened back to the *beis medrash* to ask Rabbi Moshe Feig, the ninety-year-old *Rosh Kollel*, for an urgent meeting.

— CHAPTER 2 —

AFTER THE FLOOD, GOD COMMANDED NOAH, "BUT THE BLOOD OF YOUR SOUL I WILL REQUIRE FROM THE HAND OF EVERY beast, and I will require it from the hand of man, from the hand of every man's brother, I will require the soul of man."

Rashi and his contemporaries interpreted "the blood of your soul" as a prohibition against suicide. Some five hundred years later, Rabbi Joseph Karo affirmed this in his seminal compilation of Jewish laws, the *Shulchan Aruch*: "One who commits suicide with a sound mind is not attended to in any way, and one does not mourn for him and one does not eulogize him."

Yet contemporary rabbis tended to strike with a softer gavel than their forebears. Most agreed that suicide was not a transgression unless it was committed *lada'as*—with a sound mind. As suicide was almost never a rational act, nearly every suicide victim was entitled to a Jewish burial.

Mayer knew all of this, but what concerned him was Ida Mae's method: swallowing pills in the comfort of one's living room was, he assumed, a peaceful and, he hoped, painless way to die. It certainly wasn't as terrifying as jumping off a roof, as painful as slitting one's wrists or as messy as a gun to the head. Could Ida Mae have committed suicide with a sound mind?

Rabbi Feig, a Holocaust survivor with a white beard that came to a yellow point, heard Mayer's dilemma with the staidness of a Supreme Court justice. He offered a single word of consolation—"*Nebach*"—before leaning back in his creaky old swivel chair. His office was no bigger than a walk-in closet. Books so jammed the floor-to-ceiling shelves that one couldn't tell the paint color on the wall. The old sage pointed to a shelf behind Mayer and asked for a particular volume, leather bound and a century out of print.

Macular degeneration necessitated Rabbi Feig to press his nose to the page to read the letters. But his mind was still nimble as a schoolboy's. After several minutes, he raised his head from the book and declared Ida Mae's death not *lada'as*—but in an abundance of caution, he'd double-check with a *posek*—legal scholar—in Jerusalem. He advised Mayer to book a flight on the presumption that he was correct, and in a few hours he'd call Mrs. Belkin with a definitive answer.

Mayer thanked him from the bottom of his heart. Then, haltingly, he said, "This *posek* you'll talk to—you won't mention my name, yes?"

"Why do you ask?"

"Discretion is of the utmost importance."

Deep pleats formed in the old man's wizened forehead. "Has anyone accused me of breaking confidentiality?"

"No, Rav. I'm sorry."

The nonagenarian's unseeing eyes peered at his protégé. "Let me tell you a story, Reb Mayer. Yesterday, someone asked me if he should trust the kosher certification on pre-peeled hard-boiled eggs he found at the supermarket. Hello?"

"I'm listening, Rav."

"Such a harmless question, yes? Yet he came to me in confidence—and so I will keep his identity under lock and key. Now you come to me in your darkest hour with this question about your mother, and ask if I'll be discreet?"

Mayer thanked him again, then went home to break the bad news to his wife.

THAT SHE WOULDN'T ask the cause of death was a long shot, but he prayed for it anyway.

On hearing the news, Sarah pressed her fingers to her mouth. "*Baruch dayan ha'emes!* How?"

So he told her. She gasped. Her eyes went wide. She led him into the house. After making him comfortable on the couch, she got out her laptop and booked him a flight to Atlanta. She found his old hardshell suitcase in the basement, dusted it off and packed it. Then she went to the drugstore for travel accoutrements, including an inflatable neck pillow.

It went unsaid that Mayer was traveling alone—Sarah was afraid to fly—but she insisted on accompanying him in the livery car to LaGuardia Airport. They sat on either end of the back seat, the suitcase between them. As the driver pulled onto Ocean Parkway, Mayer tried to remember the last time he'd left Kensington. The neighborhood, just a quarter of a square mile, had everything he needed—the yeshiva; his general practitioner, Dr. Mermelstein; his dentist, Dr. Wolfowitz; the dry cleaners; and the kosher supermarket built by Sarah's grandfather of blessed memory.

Four years. It had been four years since he'd set foot outside Kensington, to attend his sister-in-law's wedding in Monsey. How time flew.

Traffic moved well until the Prospect and Gowanus expressways merged and the air turned rank with chemical fumes rising from the Gowanus Canal. "By the way," he said, "you should be getting a phone call from Rabbi Feig in the next couple hours. I had a question about—"

"You told Feig?" Sarah asked, an edge in her voice.

"Should I not have?"

"You should have consulted with me first."

"Sorry."

"Did you remind him to keep his lips sealed?"

"I ... yes."

"Did you or didn't you?" she asked.

"Not in those words, but yes."

"What was his response?"

"That my secret is safe with him."

She looked unsatisfied, but didn't speak further on the subject. Traffic picked up on the Brooklyn Queens Expressway. She dug into her handbag and pulled out a black rectangular object.

"Don't argue," she said, placing it on the suitcase. "It has no internet. You can barely text on it. It's just so I can reach you while you're away."

He picked up the flip phone, unfolded it and slid his thumb over the dial pad. "It's not as if I'll be leaving my mother's house," he said. "Can't you reach me at her number?"

"She disconnected her landline years ago, remember?"

"That's right."

Even though he didn't want the phone, the gesture touched him. How would he survive a week without her? He looked across the East River at the iconic view of Lower Manhattan. It was the same panorama Sarah had picked as a backdrop for their engagement photos.

"Remember?" Mayer said, beckoning at the overlook over the expressway where the photo shoot occurred. Her mouth stayed flat but her eyes crinkled in a smile. He took a mental snapshot of her face. He'd need it in the days ahead.

FOUR HOURS AND four minutes after he got the terrible news, Mayer buckled into an aisle seat on a 193 Airbus bound for Atlanta.

He stared at a TV embedded in the back of the seat in front of him. It showed a cartoon he remembered from childhood: a mom with yellow skin and a blue beehive hairdo stood at a supermarket checkout. The cashier ran the mom's baby over the price scanner and put her in a grocery bag. Mayer pressed the off button and the screen went dark. He saw in its reflection a puffy face with a bread-dough complexion.

He looked away. His seatmate was a woman of nineteen or twenty wearing pink-striped pajama pants and a T-shirt, knees tucked under her chin. She was watching something on her iPhone. Sensing a stranger's gaze and not liking it, she twisted around until her back was to him. Embarrassed, he took out his little book of Psalms and opened it. It was hard to focus. Since learning of his mother's death, he'd been struggling to come up with a eulogy.

Ida Mae had bequeathed him scant material to work with.

What he knew of her early life couldn't fill a single page, double-spaced: she was born on November 22, 1963, to Eaton and Ingrid Abernathy in Port Gibson, Mississippi. Eaton was a hog farmer, Ingrid an undemonstrative house-wife of German-Jewish lineage. There was poverty and violence at home, and at fourteen Ida Mae ran away. At eighteen she married a merchant marine ten years older named Ike Belkin. They settled in New Moab, Georgia, where hous-es were affordable. At nineteen she birthed the twins. When they were in kin-dergarten, Ida Mae was informed that Ike drank a bottle of Henderson and fell overboard into the South China Sea. They never found his body.

Was Ida Mae a bad mother? She hugged like a bear and kissed like a lam-prey, called Marty "Monkey" and David "Doodle," and saved every art project they brought home from school. She also had a weakness for gin, amphet-amines and men who smelled like motor oil. On good days, she baked choco-late chip cookies and emceed dance-a-thons with the boys to *Club MTV*. On bad days, she locked herself in her bedroom with a quart of Beefeater and a pitcher of sweet tea and didn't come out for as many as thirty-six hours.

One Saturday morning she staggered out of her room in a nightshirt and a pearl necklace, her hair a rat's nest. She grabbed her handbag off the hook and walked out of the house without closing the door. The boys, watching *Pee-wee's Playhouse*, didn't hear her drive away. For three days they subsist-ed on Dorito–and–Miracle Whip sandwiches, fun-size Snickers and Ocean Spray. They never left the TV except for food and bathroom trips. They were seven. When Ida Mae returned in a brand-new jumpsuit, her hair permed and her face made up, she took one look at her sons sprawled on the floor like cadavers and said, "Where's that goddamn babysitter?"

THE *unfasten seat belt* ding jolted Mayer out of his thoughts. He looked out the window and saw clouds below. Two flight attendants were moving a cart up the aisle, handing out drinks and snacks.

He silently uttered *Tefilas Haderech*, the traveler's prayer. Now what? He'd happily study Talmud, but Jewish law prohibited mourners from Torah study because it was considered a joyful act. He made another attempt at a eulogy, but after a minute or so his thoughts scattered like feathers in a chicken coop. Eventually they came to rest on his long-lost brother, whose biography, unlike Ida Mae's, Mayer would have preferred to know less of.

When David was fourteen, he snorted his first line of cocaine the same night he lost his virginity to his twenty-nine-year-old supplier. By his eighteenth birthday, he'd tried twelve illegal drugs, stolen fourteen cars, spent eight months in juvenile detention, hitchhiked through forty-eight states, been in three bar fights, swallowed one live scorpion, smoked fifty-six thousand seven-hundred and forty-four cigarettes, slept with forty-four women and caught two venereal diseases.

At which point he decided to scale back on the debauchery and pool his efforts into getting rich. There were a few modest victories but mostly busts. His Achilles' heel was timing: he started a digital camera business just before the iPhone came out; he partnered in a Blockbuster franchise in 2009; he invested in an energy drink called Ride the Lightning the day before the Feds arrested the company's CEO for funneling profits to al-Shabaab.

Through it all he lived like a VIP, borrowing money at ludicrous interest rates from men who wore cheap cologne, and spending lavishly on women with whom he had an ironclad no-fourth-date policy. One of these birthed him a daughter named Kaitlin—or was it Caitlin?—whom he'd never met. He had a boyish sweetness and a "What, me worry?" worldview that people found infectious. His favorite party trick was pulling a pristine roll of hundreds out of his pocket and calling it his bail money. He drove a 1992 T-Top Corvette with two hundred thousand miles on it. He quit cigarettes, but smoked more weed than Willie Nelson.

David's antics wore Mayer's nerves raw. Things came to a head seven years ago when a guy named Sasha beat the elder twin with a tire iron over an unpaid debt, rupturing his spleen and putting him in a coma. David divulged the incident over the phone as if recounting a gut-busting *Curb Your Enthusiasm* bit. For the first time since they were kids, Mayer lost it: "Do you have a death wish?" he shouted. "Can you not get a real job?" To which David replied that his fortunes were about to change; he'd scraped together some money to buy into the emerging e-cigarette business.

"I'm telling you, Ese, this is gonna be the next big thing," he blustered. Mayer slammed the phone down and never spoke to him again until today.

THE PLANE LANDED at Hartsfield-Jackson Atlanta International an hour and a half before the funeral. Mayer still had no eulogy. He wanted to celebrate Ida Mae's life—but what life? Sure, he could doll her up with generic abstractions and half-truths, maybe accessorize with a homily equating her to King Solomon's *Aishes Chayil*, the proverbial Woman of Valor. But that was bottom-feeder stuff. No self-respecting man would ever pull that drek at his own mother's funeral.

To get to the baggage claim he had to traverse an M. C. Escheresque diorama of escalators and moving sidewalks. He felt the eyes of numerous passersby linger on his fedora and tzitzis. The weight of their gaze did not disconcert him but made him walk taller; a Jew *should* stand out among the goyim, as it was written in Leviticus, "And you shall not follow the practices of the nation."

He checked his phone and saw he had a voicemail. He typed in the password as Sarah had taught him, and her voice came on instructing him to meet David at the baggage claim. She also said Rabbi Feig called to tell her that Ida Mae had not killed herself with a sound mind; she could be buried in a Jewish cemetery, and her sons could sit shiva and say kaddish for her. This was the ruling Mayer had anticipated, but he was relieved all the same.

"By the way," she added, "I reminded Feig in no uncertain terms not to tell a soul about your mother."

The baggage carousel was tightly flanked by weary-faced travelers. He spotted among them his seatmate with the pink pajama pants, but did not see David. He found a sparsely populated space at the end of the carousel where it fed into a wall. A buzzer buzzed. Suitcases and duffels appeared. Shoulders extended, hands clasped, arms heaved. The crowd quickly thinned.

Five minutes passed with sightings of neither suitcase nor brother. Tardiness was one of the big schlemiel's many weaknesses, but today of all days he might have stepped on it. It dawned on Mayer to call David with his new phone, then realized he didn't have his number. Two more minutes passed. He chewed the inside of his cheek. Sarah had given him an emergency fifty-dollar bill, but was fifty enough to cover car fare to the funeral home? Where was the funeral home, anyway? He started rocking from foot to foot to ease his mounting irascibility. Should he call home for a lifeline? Doing so could irk Sarah, but he was running out of options. And where was his *farkakte* suitcase?

There were eleven people left at the carousel when his darting gaze stopped at a man in a robin's-egg-blue suit, thumbing his iPhone screen. His head was shaved and his skin golden brown; he looked like he'd just stepped off a yacht at Marina del Rey. Mayer's eyes had passed over the man at least a dozen times, but only now did he study his face. It was baby smooth around the forehead and eyes, taut against cheekbones and jaw, with a fashionable carpet of scruff.

Mayer moved toward him tentatively. Every step closer heightened the sensation of looking into a funhouse mirror. "David?"

The handsome man looked at him blankly, and Mayer—despite knowing for a fact now that it was his brother—wished he'd stayed put. Then David's lips pulled back in a wide smile, revealing capped teeth of dazzling whiteness.

"Ese!"

David rushed him, fell upon his neck and seized him in a bear hug. Mayer, feeling hard muscle beneath the fabric of his brother's suit, returned the embrace limply. He winced as David kissed his cheek.

"It's damned good to see you, brother."

"It's good to see you too," Mayer said. "How long have you been standing here?"

"Fifteen minutes at least."

"How did you not see me?"

"How did you not see *me*?"

Mayer knew he was being baited for a compliment. He gave his brother a quick up-and-down. The suit was custom tailored, the single button of its unstructured jacket straining teasingly against a jutting chest. The trousers, just snug enough to outline quad and calf muscles, cut an inch above a pair of oxblood brogues—no socks—polished to a mirror shine.

"I guess I didn't recognize you," he said.

David beamed. "It tickles me to hear you say that. Paleo diet. CrossFit. Pilates. Competed in a few triathlons. You're looking . . . great, too."

Twenty-five pounds heavier since their last reunion, Mayer still swam in an eighty-nine-dollar suit with shoulder pads befitting a defensive tackle, sleeves that touched his fingernails and untailored trousers that bunched at his ankles. His rubber-soled Florsheims were scuffed white at the toes. A casual observer would have to look twice to believe the men shared DNA, let alone were twins.

"So what happened?" the younger brother said, changing the subject. "Did you buy a winning scratch-off?"

"I told you, bro. E-cigarettes."

"Seriously?"

"It turns out smokers aren't social pariahs after all. All they needed was to update their tech."

"Well, congratulations."

"I'm living high, brother. I've got my own chauffeur, my own penthouse in Buckhead. I've got a pool table. I've got a wooden toilet with armrests that plays 'Le bon roi Dagobert' when you lift the seat. You have to come see it."

"That's wonderful. I'm so happy things worked out for you."

David smiled demurely, the way he once might have when someone hurrahed him for tying his shoelaces properly. "God, is it good to see you," he said, "despite, you know, the circumstances."

"Yeah."

"You and me, we're all we've got left. No aunts, uncles, cousins, grandparents—at least that we know of."

Mayer looked at the carousel, now vacant but for a lavender dress bag. The Belkins were the only people still here. David flicked a wrist to expose a Yacht-Master Rolex. "We'd better move. Rabbi Kugel said to meet him at Mom's house."

"He wants us to go to Mom's house before the funeral and then loop back to Atlanta?"

"Uh-huh."

"What for?"

"He didn't say."

"With traffic? We'll miss the funeral."

"We won't miss our own mother's funeral," David said. "They might just have to wait for us."

The carousel halted. Mayer felt for the first time like a man in mourning. "Why didn't I just bring a carry-on?"

"Seriously. I haven't checked a bag in years. I'd rather just buy new clothes to avoid the headache."

"Let's give it five more minutes. My tefillin are in that suitcase."

David squeezed his shoulder. "Don't worry, we'll get it back. I'm sure the rabbi has extra tefillin. Now let's get out of here before they really do bury Mom without us."

AS THE AUTOMATIC airport doors slid apart, the heat slapped Mayer in the face like a wet towel.

David chuckled. "Missed it?"

"Was it always this hot?"

"No, but you didn't used to dress blacker than Johnny Cash, either."

Indeed. The polyester-wool fabric of his suit clung to him like papier-mâché.

"As luck would have it," David said, "we're in day one of what they're calling a record heat wave. Triple digits for days."

Mayer, who'd consumed no food or water since breakfast, saw the horizon tilt. His brother took him by the arm and walked him to a black Lincoln Town Car parked at the curb. A heat shimmer rose from the hood. A driver in a navy uniform and cap bounced out of the car, came around the back and opened the rear passenger door.

"Ruben, this is my kid brother, Marty."

"Pleased to meet you," the chauffeur said.

The roomy car interior was miraculously chilly, the malevolent sun no match for the powerful AC and double-tinted windows. Mayer put his hat in his lap and stretched his legs out, the leather upholstery like a cold pack on the back of his neck.

"Military grade," David said, thumbing at one of the air vents, "same as they put in the Humvees in the Middle East."

"It's fantastic," Mayer murmured. As they pulled away from the curb, he eyed his brother's gleaming dome. "Maybe it wouldn't hurt to put on a yarmulke?"

"Oh yeah." David dug into a pocket, pulled out a white satin kippah and plunked it on his head.

As Ruben steered them toward the airport exit, Mayer asked, "How did he sound?"

"Who?"

"Yossi. Rabbi Kugel. When he called about meeting him at Mom's."

"He definitely didn't sound himself. Who can blame him, finding his longtime secretary dead on her couch?"

They got on the I-85 toward downtown Atlanta. Mayer looked at the maple, oak, magnolia and pine trees hemming the fourteen lanes of highway. "Wow."

"Wow what?" David said.

"When you live in Brooklyn for a long time, you forget that trees are a dime a dozen everywhere else."

"I bet. So what's your theory on Mom?"

"What do you mean?"

"Her motive for ending her life."

Mayer shrugged. "Whenever I talked to her, she seemed in pretty good spirits."

"Yeah, but you know she drank and drugged more than Janis Joplin."

"That was always the case."

"Exactly," David said. "She reached a point where she needed to escape from her own escapism. Her only gratification came from working for Rabbi Kugel, and in all that time she never embraced Judaism—which is ridiculous, when you think about it. What kind of person scarfs bacon every morning and spends the next eight hours in an Orthodox synagogue?"

"You don't think she found gratification outside of work?" Mayer asked.

"Not really."

"Not even bringing two Jewish boys into the world who, despite the odds, surpassed anyone's wildest expectations?" As soon as the question came out of his mouth, pistons in his head started whirring. Ever since boarding the plane in New York, he'd racked his brain for a kernel of something real that he could stretch into a ten-minute eulogy. Had it been in front of him all along?

David's success in business was ninety percent luck, ten percent indefatigability and zero percent Ida Mae. Mayer's achievements in Torah scholarship originated from an altogether different formula. Had it not been for his mother, he never would have gone to yeshiva and been accepted into the Drezner clan. Sure, his success story had a supporting cast—Rabbi Kugel, Mrs. Kugel, his early yeshiva mentors—but when Ida Mae revealed her Jewish identity to her sons that blistering summer day, she set everything in motion.

Mayer was her legacy, her gift to the world: a Jew in the image of God.

He had his eulogy.

— CHAPTER 3 —

WITH THE EULOGY ALL BUT WRITTEN IN HIS HEAD,
MAYER COULD AT LAST MOURN UNIMPAIRED. HE TOOK THE TEHILLIM
out of his jacket pocket, turned to Psalm 77 and soon lost himself in King
David's spare, raw supplications:

*My voice is to God and I will cry out, my voice is to God and listen to me. On
the day of my distress I sought the Lord . . . my soul refuses to be comforted.*

"Rabbi Kugel gave you that for your bar mitzvah?" David asked.

"Mm-hmm."

"I got one just like it. No idea where it is now."

"Mm-hmm."

Mayer was in his element now. The Torah and its vast catalog of subsid-
iaries spoke to him like no human ever could. He discovered this at Darchei
Yosef Yitzchak, a yeshiva in Crown Heights, Brooklyn, that had a special pro-
gram for secular Jewish kids. He was a quick study, compiling a basic Hebrew
vocabulary in a matter of months. By the end of his first year he'd already
started on the Mishnah, the six-part code of laws that is the foundation of
the Talmud.

He'd often look back on his old life and reflect that someone with a com-
parable upbringing might have described those years as abusive. He wouldn't
agree. Grungy, squalid and seedy, no doubt, but not abusive. When he thought
about his childhood, it wasn't to confront trauma but to suss out the perti-
nence of that time in the first place. God put him on one path, only to divert
him to another. What had been the point of the first path?

Midway through his second year, his rabbis encouraged him to enroll at one of the local yeshivas for seasoned *talmidim*. But he already had his sights four miles southward on Ohr Lev, one of the most prestigious yeshivas in the country. To a poor boy from small-town Georgia, an acceptance to this great institution would be his answer to the homeless-to-Harvard TV movie. It would also be a significant cultural shift; Darchei Yosef Yitzchak, a *Lubavitcher* yeshiva, prioritized spiritual growth, balancing Talmud study with abstract disciplines like philosophy and mysticism. Ohr Lev was proudly *litvish*, stressing Talmud over all other disciplines.

He was already braced for rejection before even mailing the application. To his surprise and delight, Ohr Lev called him a few days later to schedule an interview. The admissions chair, Rabbi Waldvogel, was taken by Mayer's origin story, his precociousness and resolve. He was doubly impressed when the boy recited an entire tractate of Mishnah by heart. Ohr Lev would acquire him, the rabbi said, but would have to hold him back a grade so he could catch up. The *frieh* from Georgia had but one question: "When can I start?"

Almost immediately, it turned out. His days started at five every morning. Emulating his hero Rabbi Akiva, the fabled Talmudist who, before the age of forty, had never read a word of Hebrew, Mayer crammed like it was his last day on Earth. He eschewed companionship from other *talmidim* for that of Rashi, the tosafists, the Rambam and the Mishnah Berurah. By eleven at night, when the *beis medrash* was empty but for a few students, Mayer reviewed what he'd covered that day with painstaking scrupulousness.

By the time he was fifteen, he'd settled on the perfect adjective to describe his childhood: insignificant. Truly, his personal history didn't even merit reminiscence. It was a dud, a waste, an utter mediocrity in comparison to the infinitely richer—and infinitely more tragic—history of *K'lal Yisroel*, the Jewish people, which began with God's covenant with Abraham four thousand years ago. As Mayer adopted the collective history of the Jews—or it adopted him—his own biography got reduced to a reference point for how far he'd come and how much further he had to go.

That year, he distinguished himself as an advanced *talmid*, matching, often surpassing, boys whose fathers were prominent yeshiva heads, judges and legal authorities. He came to embody a yeshiva archetype, supplanting his Southern twang with a Brooklyn yeshivish inflection: when he was being didactic, his sentences adopted a singsong intonation; he'd fill a pause between words with a hesitational *tsk*; he weaved Yiddish, Hebrew and Aramaic words into conversational English.

But for all his passion for, and fastidiousness in, all aspects of Jewish life, no one was more surprised than he when, at twenty-two, he was called into the office of the *rosh yeshiva*, the legendary Rav Yaakov Drezner, who asked if he'd like to meet his daughter.

"HEY, RUBEN, CRANK out some tunes."

"You got it, boss."

The driver tapped a button on the center console and a country crossover number blasted from the surround speakers, its male vocalist crooning in dreamy soprano:

> *When hope is gone and the night is endless*
> *I remember your eyes and I see us together*
> *Running hand in hand, making footprints in the sand*

Mayer clapped his hands to his ears. "Shut it off!"

"Jesus, what's wrong?"

"No music! No music!"

"Ruben, you heard the man!"

The driver punched the button and the car fell quiet. Mayer let his hands drop to his lap. "Sorry about that."

"Don't apologize," David said, "that song is crap. How about something more our speed?"

"No, we can't listen to music during the year of mourning. I can't, anyway."

The elder brother considered this. "Not even, like, Beethoven?"

"Not even."

"Jewish music? Klezmer?"

"No."

"Fuuuuck," David said. "You hear that, Ruben? No music for a whole year."

"Tough break, boss."

Mayer resumed reading Psalms. The *aninus* period of mourning, which started at the moment of death and would conclude with the burial, was a sacred time of prayer and reflection. He'd lost enough time fretting over Ida Mae's eulogy. But when he tried to focus on his Psalms, he found himself distracted by the repetitive flutter of David's thumb across his iPhone.

"What is it you do on that thing, anyway?" he asked.

"Nothing."

"You're going to get tendonitis with all that thumbing."

"Nah."

"Consider giving it a rest. It's a holy day."

A ringing phone interrupted the conversation. "I think that's yours," David said.

Mayer pulled the flip phone from his inner jacket pocket. "Hello?"

"How was your flight?" Sarah asked.

"*Baruch Hashem.*"

"You got my message about Feig?"

"I did, thank you."

"Your brother picked you up at the baggage claim?"

Mayer glanced at David, swiping again. "We're in his car now on the way to my mother's."

"Your mother's?"

Mayer filled her in on Rabbi Kugel's orders to meet him there. "Odd," she said. "Why not just meet at the funeral home?"

"I was wondering the same thing. But never mind that. Sarale . . . I had some tsuris at the airport." He briefed her on the airline's blunder that left him without clothing, toiletries, and his precious tefillin.

"Uch. Morons," she said. "Don't worry, as soon as we get off the phone, I'll make some calls and sort this out."

"Oh, would you?"

"Of course."

"*Shkoyach*," he said, thanking her.

"Let's talk after the funeral," she said.

"Wait, are you still there?"

"I'm here."

"Did you mention to your parents that my mother died?" Mayer asked.

A pause. "You don't really need me to answer that, do you?"

AS THEY MERGED onto State Route 43 bound for New Moab, Mayer put the finishing touches on Ida Mae's eulogy. And if he did say so himself, it was a fine one. It venerated her as a warrior matriarch who refused to be bested by a hellish childhood, premature widowhood and destitute adulthood. Intuiting that her imprint on the world would be through her sons, she raised them to be men of integrity and honor. Both boys surpassed everyone's wildest dreams—except her own, for she was nothing if not a hard taskmaster. In her merit, Mayer and David would strive to be a shining light for the Jewish people.

Hyperbolic? More than a little. But the basic idea was true enough, and besides, wasn't every eulogist a revisionist historian?

They drove through Moab to get to Ida Mae's, and it was here that Route 43 became the fabled Dixieland Highway, whose every rise and curve the brothers once knew like the backs of their hands. Mayer was enlivened seeing the antebellum estates, with their columns and gables, their sculpted flower beds and acres of pristine lawns, and the live oaks draped in Spanish moss that stood guard on either side of the road.

Downtown Moab had changed, but not really. The Bank of Moab was now Bank of America, Grandma Coralee's Biscuits was Starbucks, and Johnny Reb Records was an H&R Block. But CVS was still CVS, and would stay CVS until Armageddon; the Central Plaza movie theater still advertised Wacky Wednesday matinees at half price; McTaggart's Antiques still proudly displayed its Confederate collectibles in the window. Outdoor cafés bustled as always with an all-white crowd lunching on wedge salads and shrimp toast.

The public library, the sheriff's department and the municipal court stood three abreast in all their brutalist glory. On the lawn outside the courthouse was the old illuminated sign for the Elks, the Sons of Confederate Veterans, the Kiwanis, the Rotary Club and the Loyal Order of Moose. At the next block stood the Ebenezer Missionary Baptist Church, whose towering white steeple still gave it bragging rights as the tallest building in town.

It was here, at the intersection of Virginia and Dixieland, that Ruben braked at a red light. Had Mayer looked out his window he'd have seen the yellow house next door to the parsonage. Chabad of Moab now had a proper synagogue a few blocks away, but Rabbi Kugel and his family still lived in the yellow house. The menorah was still on the front lawn, gleaming like polished gold in the sun. But Mayer did not look, and when the light turned green they moved on.

At the town border, they came upon a startling sight—a brick wall some fourteen feet high and two feet thick that spanned east and west as far as they could see. It had crenellations on top, as on a medieval castle wall. The only apparent gap in the partition was an archway that let Dixieland traffic through. Two Moab sheriff squad cars were parked on either side of the arch facing oncoming traffic.

"When did this go up?" Mayer asked.

"I wanna say ten years ago," David said.

"Why?"

"Why do you think?"

If New Moab was in decline when the Belkins were boys, it was in its death throes now. Half the houses along Dixieland had boarded-up windows and lawns turned to dumping grounds. The road was in such disrepair that it forced Ruben to slow to twenty to prevent a flat tire. Glassy-eyed pedestrians trudged about like aimless windup toys. Teenage boys, wearing hoodies in the heat, stood at street corners fidgeting with their waistbands.

"*Ribono Shel Olam*," Mayer murmured, in supplication to the Master of the World.

"Pathetic, right?" David said. "The population's dropped by half since our day. The homicide rate's one of the highest in the country per capita. Hey Ruben, pull up to that dilapidated shitbox with the white siding, will you?"

Ruben steered the Lincoln up to a cookie-cutter colonial with aluminum siding that had been white once but was now dirty eggshell. The windows and door were clapboarded over. Someone had tagged the word "Bolo" on the facade in purple bubble letters. Eight treadless car tires were piled on the lawn.

As the car came to a stop, David gave his brother a wolfish grin.

"What?" Mayer said.

"You don't remember?"

"No."

"This is Whitney King's house—or was, anyway."

"Who?"

"Whitney King. She was a few years older than us. She had the really big . . ." With his cupped hands he filled in the blank. The outlines of a Polaroid image materialized in Mayer's mind. Color filled his cheeks.

"Remember how we used to climb that tree over there with your bird binocs?" David said.

"Can we go?"

"Oh, relax, it was all in good fun."

"It wasn't fun, it was terrible. I'm shocked you'd bring this up now—or ever."

David's grin melted away. "Sorry, Ese. I just thought you'd get a kick out of it."

"Well, you were wrong."

"Ruben, get us out of here."

As Whitney King's house fell behind them, David reached under the middle seat and slid out a refrigerated drawer that contained bottles of Fiji water. He offered one to his brother.

"No thanks."

"You look a little dry."

"I'm fasting."

"Even from water?"

"Even from water."

David unscrewed the bottle cap and took a long pull.

"No more stops on the sightseeing tour, okay?" Mayer said.

FOUR BLOCKS LATER, Ruben turned onto Bragg Street. Mayer became aware of a rising pulse in his neck. And suddenly there it was, the fifth house to the right. It had the same dismal brown siding, the same weedy yard, the same saggy roof. It was the sort of charmless house that, from the first day of construction to now, no passerby ever stopped to admire. The only new addition, as far as Mayer could tell, was the red Mercury Sable in the driveway. The last time he was here it was a silver Eldorado.

"Pull up behind that Kia," David said, indicating a black Sorento in front of the house. Ruben parked, then came around to Mayer's side and opened the door. When he got out, a furnace blast of heat made his knees buckle.

"You okay?" David asked.

"You spoiled me with that military-grade AC."

"Have some water."

"No."

Flanked by the two burlier men, he waded through a dozen species of weeds, all thriving in the subtropical humidity. He slapped his neck, and when he drew his palm away it held a dime-sized circle of blood.

The front door was unlocked. The house was so dim that Mayer needed a few seconds to adjust his eyes. Even with the window-unit AC running at full blast, the indoor temperature was a balmy eighty. Smells of cigarettes, frying oil and Secret antiperspirant emanated from the carpet and furniture. He hung his fedora on the door rack, next to a similar hat with a wider brim. David dismissed Ruben, who happily retreated to the car.

"Rabbi Kugel?" David called.

There was no answer.

Mayer wandered into the living room, the epicenter of Ida Mae's life and the locus of her death. Other than a flat-screen TV in place of the old Zenith, the room was unaltered: the green carpeting, the loud floral wallpaper, the faux-wood walls, the dusty window blinds and the plaid velour couch where she'd put up her swollen feet for the last time—all the same.

Suddenly, the thought of spending a week here without so much as a *blatt* of Talmud to distract him compelled him to unfasten a collar button. He glanced at the grandfather clock in the corner by the entryway, a purchase Ida Mae bought on an installment plan but only ever made one payment on. The funeral was in forty minutes. Ruben would have to make like a Grand Prix driver to get them there on time—and only if they left in the next five minutes.

"Hello?" David called out.

Still no answer.

"Rabbi?"

"Yossi?" Mayer shouted.

A grunt sounded from somewhere. The brothers glanced at each other and made their way to the kitchen. The room had once been carpeted white, inexplicably, but countless Heinz misfires and Ocean Spray spills had rendered it Autumn Rhythm. Oven smoke and grease vapors had drained the luster from the once-cheerful wallpaper.

Sitting at the breakfast table was a wisp of a man with a long graying beard. Though only thirteen years older than the boys, his sallow cheeks and rheumy gaze gave the impression of a much older man. He propped a fifth of Jack Daniels on the table by the bottle neck.

"Yossi?" Mayer said.

The rabbi stirred.

"Rabbi Kugel?" said David.

He let go of the bottle and his arm fell to his side. He turned his head creakily to face the Belkins and made a pathetic attempt to smile.

"Boychiks . . ."

"Did you just escape from the gulag?" the elder brother asked.

"It's good to see you both. How long has it been?"

"Never mind that," Mayer said, eyeing the stove clock. "What's so important that we had to meet you here? And when can we leave?"

At this, the rabbi seemed to retreat inside himself, a human tortoise. The twins nodded at one another. Each hooked the clergyman by an underarm and lifted. But he made the letter Y with his arms, denying them purchase.

"I don't need help," he said.

"You're toasted, man," David said. "Look, let's just get this funeral over with. In a couple hours I'll match you shot for shot."

Yossi put his elbows on the table and rubbed his face. David propped his hands on his hips and said, "He's in bad shape, Ese. Is there another rabbi we can get in a pinch?"

"None that I know of."

"How about you? Can't you do it?"

"Theoretically," Mayer said, "but I've never heard of anyone officiating his own mother's funeral."

He gave the rabbi's shoulder a little shake, but it was like trying to rouse a corpse. David went over to a cabinet above the laminate counter, where Ida Mae had kept her Solo cups. He plucked three from the stack and returned to the table, pulling out a chair across from the clergyman. He poured a finger into each cup. He offered one to his brother, who declined. He gulped his down, then chased it with the other.

"What are you doing?" Mayer said.

"Fighting fire with firewater, as Mom used to say. Come on, Yossi, say l'chaim."

The rabbi peered through his fingers at the cup in front of him, considered it for a moment, sighed, picked it up, clicked it against David's and said, "L'chaim." He winced as it went down.

"Have another."

Yossi shook his head. The drink was bringing clarity to his eyes and color to his cheeks, and it occurred to both brothers that it might have been his first of the day. David gave the man's hand a squeeze. "Alright, you summoned us here on the day of our mother's funeral without saying why—and that's cool, but the clock's ticking. So how about let's hop in my car and talk about it on the way?"

"I'm afraid that's not going to work."

Mayer was losing patience. "Yossi, shame on you. We know how much our mother meant to you, but we're her children. If anyone has a right to drag their feet, it's us."

"You don't understand," the clergyman said.

"That much is clear," David said.

"This isn't easy for me."

"Obviously, but you've got to pull yourself together, or we're just gonna have to do this thing without you."

The rabbi slammed his hand on the table, catching the boys off balance. "You don't understand. There's not going to be a funeral."

The room fell silent.

"Say that again," David said.

The rabbi did.

"Whatever happened, I'm sure we can sort it out," Mayer said. "Was there a scheduling snafu at the funeral home?"

The rabbi shook his head.

"Oh no. Did they misplace the body?"

The rabbi shook his head but said nothing. Mayer quieted an impulse to slap him.

"Did Mom donate her body to science without telling us?" David asked.

The rabbi shook his head, and this time Mayer did slap him—then clapped a hand to his own face, horrified. "What have I done?"

"No, I needed that," Yossi said. He twisted around and pulled his suit jacket from where it hung on the back of his chair. It snagged, and David helped free it. He lay it across his lap and felt around the inner pockets. One had only sugar packets, the other a sheaf of thrice-folded notebook paper with fringes on one side.

"This arrived at my house two hours ago. Priority mail."

"Who sent it?" David asked.

Yossi answered with his eyes.

"Mom had a letter delivered to your house, posthumously?"

"Yes."

"And she sent it to you and not us."

"I think she thought I should be with you when you read it. For support."

"Okay. Let's see it."

Instead of handing it over, the rabbi kept talking. "I guess she trusted me as a friend and a spiritual guide. The trouble is . . ." He gave a mirthless chuckle. "I don't think I'm qualified."

"Qualified for what?" Mayer asked.

"No offense, Rabbi, but you are one prize mindfuck," David said. He snatched at the letter, but Yossi held it to his chest and extended his other palm.

"In a second. But first, another *l'chaim*."

"You know I'm fasting," Mayer said.

"Well, I'd urge having one anyway."

"First sensible thing you've said all day," David said. He poured a double into the three cups, said "*l'chaim*," and tossed his back in two swallows. The rabbi downed his in one. Mayer didn't touch his.

"Now," Yossi said, "you might ask, once you've read this, why I didn't burn it. I almost did. I had the matchbook in my hand. But in the end I decided it wasn't my place."

He gave the letter to David.

Eyes never leaving Yossi, David took two steps back and unfolded it. He began to read. The only sounds were the refrigerator hum and the vibrato of the air conditioner. Mayer scrutinized his brother's eyes for clues as they ping-ponged through the first page, then the second.

Somewhere on page three, his body went rigid. He brought the letter two inches closer to his eyes and squinted. "Hang on."

He read some more. "Oh my God."

Yossi grunted an affirmation.

"What does it say?" Mayer said.

"No, no, no." David dropped the hand with the letter to his side and looked fixedly at Yossi. "Am I reading this right?"

The rabbi's nonresponse was answer enough. David brought the letter back to his face and read a few more lines. "This is unreal, Rabbi. Un-*fucking*-real!"

"I couldn't have said it better myself."

"What?" Mayer demanded. "What's unreal?"

David read on. Mayer lunged for the letter but David sidestepped him, his pendulating eyeballs not breaking stride.

"Give it to me!"

"You should have gone with your first instinct, Rabbi."

Mayer lunged again, too far, his forehead butting David's so that they bounced apart like same-pole magnets. Mayer managed to get the corner of the sheaf between two fingers, but his brother ripped it free and jammed it under an armpit, then shoved him in the solar plexus. Mayer recovered and charged shoulder-first, and David dodged him with a neat pirouette. Momentum carried the younger twin to the kitchen counter. He cracked his hip.

"Ow!"

"Ese, you've got to trust me," David said.

Lips crimped white and face splotched red, Mayer grabbed his brother's shoulder and tried to pry his fingers into his underarm. David broke free with an abdominal swivel.

"Boys," Yossi said.

"Give me that letter!"

"Just let me summarize it for you," David said.

Mayer flailed again for the pages, but his brother was too nimble. He sidestepped, did a little spin and thrust it at the rabbi. "Burn it!"

Yossi didn't move. Mayer came at his brother again and was rebutted with another shove to the chest.

"Then I'll do it," David said.

He started toward the stove. Mayer, jacked with fury, leapt on his back. David raised the letter high above his head. Mayer reached, his fingertips only grazing the pages. He grabbed his brother's wrist and pulled, but David managed to pass the letter to his other hand.

A shrill whistle sounded. The men froze, tangled up in one another. Yossi removed his pinkie fingers from the corners of his mouth and gave them a reprimanding look. They separated themselves.

"Sorry," David said. Mayer snatched away the letter and marched to a sliver of countertop between the refrigerator and stove. He shot his brother an acid look before smoothing out the pages. He whispered a prayer for strength. But really, he thought, how bad could it be?

— CHAPTER 4 —

Dear Yossi,

I know what you're gonna say.

You're gonna say, but what about all the money Ida Mae borrowed from me for credit card bills and car payments and that $1000 ER visit when she thought her appendix burst but it was only heartburn from eating one of those chicken & donut gut bombs from KFC?

Well, I'm sorry. You're not ever gonna see that money. Not from me, anyway. But you knew that all along, didn't you, you sweet man? You really are the best friend I ever had, and God's got a seat beside him with your name on it when you die.

Talk to David. Maybe he can write you a check. I hear he's loaded from all those e-cigarettes he gets kids hooked on.

I guess I owe you and the boys an explanation for why I've punched out early. Am I depressed? Do I hate myself? Do I feel guilty about something bad I've done? Yes, yes, and yes. On top of it all, I'm bored!!! Bored with the world and bored with myself, and too fat to do anything about it.

You and the missus have been kind to disagree, but please: I'm 284 pounds and counting, and Lord knows I haven't got it in me to diet or exercise. If I could afford a gastric band, you probably wouldn't be reading this letter. But when your chin starts looking like a third tit, it's either shape up or ship out.

You know what else I'm so done with? The weather. Georgia's like six shades of Hades, and I'll be glad to be out of it (hopefully not to somewhere hotter though!!!). Even in the winter I'm sweating like a hog in a sauna. All my life I've thumbed my nose at the global warming kooks, but in my old age I'm thinking they might be onto something.

The decision to end my life didn't come lightly. I even tried to talk myself out of it by making a list of all the stuff I'll miss: scratch-off lottery cards, sweet tea with lemon, Virginia Slims, biscuits with milk gravy, fried chicken, bacon, pimento cheese with Duke's mayonnaise, deviled eggs, buttermilk in a glass with a drop of Tabasco, vinegar pie, chocolate turtles, Beefeater gin, Old Grandad bourbon, Bailey's Irish Cream, Judge Mathis, Pat Sajak, Chris Hemsworth, Jimmy Fallon (Lord have mercy, that man), Patsy Cline, Conway Twitty, Merle Haggard, Dolly Parton, Taylor Swift, Adam Levine. And oh God, that dream machine Dominic Day who even though he's in a wheelchair, that song of his makes me feel like I'm 17 and in love for the first time.

The list goes on and on. But then I look in my vanity mirror and remember that that song ain't about me. Which brings me back to why I'm writing this letter. Yossi, my love, I'm calling on you to serve as the executor of my estate. There's not much to execute. The only thing I've got of value is a deep dark secret I've been hanging on to for more than 20 years, and you're gonna need to pass it on to the boys, 'cause I just haven't got the balls to do it myself.

Wait—and Ryan Seacrest! Not to take anything away from Dick Clark, but Ryan made New Year's Rockin' Eve an art form.

Okay, the secret. Deep breath.

Remember all those years ago when you showed up at my house dressed like a kid in his dad's suit, and you wouldn't even shake my hand? You were so sweet and pure. You turned our lives around. You gave me my first and only steady job. Marty went off to yeshiva because of you and that paid dividends—what with his becoming a Torah scholar and marrying into money. And David, well . . . maybe things didn't work out so well for him for a long time, but he made it in the end.

The thing is this: remember how I said I was Jewish? Don't get me wrong, I'm Jew-ish in the sense that my husband was Jewish, all of my friends are Jews, my boss and best friend is a rabbi. I consider myself an honorary member of the tribe. But I know your mother's got to be a Jew in order for you to be a Jew, and my mother? Not a Jew, Lord no. She hated Jews more than my dad. In fact her dad, Grampa Karl, was a Nazi of some kind. SS I think. Or Gestapo? Anyway, he and his family escaped to Argentina after "Der Krieg" before coming to the USA. Frau Abernathy would've flipped a biscuit if she ever found out I'd married a "Judensau."

For years and years I wanted to come clean. But whenever I came close, I thought of all the good things Judaism brought to our lives. And who likes being a party pooper? But now as I stand at the edge of eternity, I ask myself, Ida Mae, are you really the sort of woman who'd let your own children go the rest of their lives thinking they're something they're not? Is that what love is?

Now, this news is gonna hit Marty harder than David, and I'm hoping you can be there for him. He ought to tell his wife, and that'll take real finesse 'cause she's a fragile woman. Counsel him. Can you convert him or find someone who can? I don't know how these things work, so I leave it in your capable hands.

One more thing: when I was a little girl I found one of our pigs dead in a pasture, half eaten by maggots. I decided then and there I wanted to get cremated when I died. I worked it all out in advance with an old ex who runs Thornton Mortuary. By the time you read this he'll have picked me up from the morgue and flame-broiled me like an all-beef patty. He's throwing in an urn at no extra charge. David's gonna need to cough up the $1499.99 because he's the guarantor (I faked his signature—sorry, Doodle!!). Just do me a favor and don't keep my ashes on some closet shelf or on a fireplace mantel. Set me free. Sprinkle me somewhere that will make me smile from on yonder.

Lots of love,

Ida Mae

P.S.: Tell the boys there's lasagna in the fridge. Microwave medium for 1½ min.

Mayer closed his eyes. There were no thoughts, just granules of thoughts drifting about as though his head were a snow globe. That was good. He'd be content to stay thoughtless, aware of only the dark behind his shuttered eyelids and the *lub-dub lub-dub* of his heart in his ears, for the rest of his life.

Regrettably, it wasn't to be. He opened his eyes. He saw his hands drag the sheets of paper across a countertop. They cleared the edge and stuck to his palms for a second, then seesawed lazily to the floor. One page landed face up across the toe of his Florsheim. He stared at his mother's loopy Hollywood signature.

The first physical sensation was of ice water seeping between his vertebrae. It pooled in his chest. It circulated through arteries and veins and into capillaries. It numbed fingers, toes, lips and even teeth. If this was what dying felt like, he thought, it wasn't bad. Not bad at all.

"Marty?"

He turned and saw David as if through the wrong end of a pair of binoculars.

"You alright? You look kinda . . ."

Black roses bloomed about David's face, then blotted it out entirely. A pinhole of light appeared. It widened into a circle. Mayer saw the kitchen ceiling. It widened further, unveiling David on one side and Yossi on the other.

"Should we call an ambulance?" the rabbi said.

"Nah, he'll be alright," David said.

"I'll get some water. Why don't you get something for his head?"

The men disappeared but soon came back, David with a plaid sofa cushion. He propped it under Mayer's head. Yossi lowered a Solo cup to Mayer's mouth. Mayer pinched his lips so that the water ran down his cheeks and into his ears.

"Fasting," he rasped.

David and the rabbi looked at each other. The former stepped away. The latter squeezed the supine man's hand. "Mayer, it was a shock to me, and I can't even imagine how much more so to you. But now more than ever, you've got to have *emunah*."

"*Emunah*," Mayer repeated. Faith.

"It's not the end of the world."

"Not the end of the world."

"You've got to remember that the Almighty is the grand orchestrator of all things. Remember what the Talmud says."

"What does the Talmud say?"

"Whatever the merciful one does is for the good. Have *emunah*. See the positive."

"What's the positive?"

The clergyman wavered. "Well, we don't always see it right away. But at the very least there's a straightforward solution to the most pressing problem. I can help arrange an appointment for you with a *beis din* for your conversion."

Mayer pinched the skin on his forearm in the unlikelihood he was dreaming. He did it again. "My life is over."

"You don't mean that."

Mayer draped an arm over his eyes. He lay quiet for a moment. Then, from deep in his chest came an Edvard Munch scream that made the two men recoil. He caught his breath and screamed again. Then came a succession of softer cries resembling those of an animal whose leg had been caught in a steel-jaw trap for hours. He writhed and blubbered, choked and sputtered, a display of emotion so primitive that David and Yossi couldn't help but stare in morbid fascination.

TWENTY MINUTES LATER, he was sprawled on the couch Ida Mae had died on, suit jacket blanketing him from chin to waist. Yossi and David sat on chairs they'd carried in from the kitchen. The latter had his bare feet propped on the TV stand. He was swiping his iPhone with one hand and sipping from a Solo cup with the other.

"She always did have trouble with fact and fiction," Yossi said. "But I never imagined—"

"Don't overthink it," David rejoined.

Mayer wasn't listening. He wasn't ready to contemplate the staggering cost of Ida Mae's deception, not least his lost *schar*, the spiritual currency he'd earned clocking some hundred thousand hours of Torah study. Or thought he'd earned. His heavenly portfolio was only ever Monopoly money.

For now, all he could think about was Sarah—Sarah who was not his wife, who had never been his wife, and who, he'd wager, never would be.

Oh, there'd been a wedding, a no-holds-barred affair with over a thousand guests, and a *gadol hador*—a rabbi whose greatness was once-in-a-generation—flown in from Israel to officiate. The dancing had gone on until two in the morning and was so high-spirited it left a sheen of perspiration on the walls. The *simcha* concluded under the new linen of the couple's marriage bed, where Sarah cried for the duration. *Baruch Hashem*, she only cried that first night; in the ensuing years she received him with silent resolve, and now he understood why: her *neshama*, her soul, was taking a stand against the unholy union between Jewess and gentile—a granddaughter of Auschwitz and a great-grandson of, well, Auschwitz.

Now he knew why God hadn't answered his prayers for children: God simply hadn't been listening. This realization filled him with such despair that he whipped his head from side to side to eject it, and in doing so noticed that Yossi's chair had become vacant. David was asleep, one shirttail untucked, iPhone rising and falling on his belly. A turquoise weed pipe lay on the carpet below his dangling hand.

"David?"

His brother stirred. "Hmm?"

"Where's Yossi?"

David licked his chops. "Dunno."

"How long have I been lying here?"

David looked at his Rolex. "Two hours?"

"Two hours!" Mayer sat bolt upright and got out his phone. He turned the screen on to check for missed calls. There were none, thank God. He breathed a sigh of relief and sank back against the couch. "I must have drifted off."

"How are you holding up?" David asked.

Mayer didn't answer.

"You gonna tell Sarah?"

"I don't see how I can avoid it."

"Can't you just convert on the down-low and then go back to her like nothing happened?"

Mayer gave his brother a contemptuous look.

"What?" David said.

"You don't think that would be hypocritical?"

"I guess so, but—"

"More relevantly, Sarah and I aren't married. We were never married. If I were lucky enough to win her back after telling her she's been living with a . . ."

"A one-eighth Nazi."

"A gentile all these years, I'd have to not only convert but have another wedding ceremony."

David scratched his upper lip. "You really don't think she'll want you back? She *is* your wife—maybe not technically, but you know what I mean."

"She'll be completely destroyed. It's as if she'd been eating *treif* meat for eighteen years because the butcher claimed it was kosher when it wasn't."

"Exactly—unknowingly. It's not her fault any more than yours."

"I'd contest your second point," Mayer said, "since I never took the trouble to authenticate our lineage. Mom declared us Jewish one day and I went with it."

"Yeah, but come on. Who would lie about something like that?" David asked.

"Anyway, Sarah won't care whose fault it is. All she'll care about is that the man she thought was her husband was . . ." The word took its time coming to Mayer. "Counterfeit."

"Okay but . . . she's your wife."

"She's not my wife."

"I know, but there's history. A partnership. That's got to be worth something."

The front door opened and Rabbi Kugel strode in looking ten years younger than he'd looked at the kitchen table with his hand wrapped around a Jack Daniels bottle. Ridding himself of Ida Mae's letter was apparently the equivalent of Superman breaking free of Kryptonite chains.

"I just got off the phone with Itzik Slomowitz, an old friend who now sits on the *beis din* of Flatbush," he said. "We've traded favors over the years, and he says he can squeeze you in a week from today for a *giyur*."

"What's a *giyur*?" David asked.

"A conversion."

"Awesome!" David said. "I knew you'd bail us out."

Yossi's jaw shifted. "Well, by *you* I mean Mayer—but only because he requires no training. Normally you need to study a year or two first."

"What about our dad being Jewish? Doesn't that at least get me halfway there?"

"There's no such thing as half Jewish. If your mother is a Jew, you're a Jew. If she's not, you're not. But look, why not accompany your brother when he goes in next week? Get a feel for the process. Ask questions."

"Wait a minute," Mayer said. "I can't wait a week. I need this to happen today. Yesterday."

"Consider yourself lucky. They work a full schedule up there, and conversions are just a part of their operation."

Mayer let this information seep in. Then a notion struck him. "Tell me you didn't tell him who my father-in-law is."

The rabbi sat heavily. "I needed all the leverage I had. Itzik is an old friend, but not the most sympathetic guy I know, especially since he became a judge. But not to worry. Discretion is part and parcel with his line of work."

Mayer folded his arms. "I still say we got shortchanged. If you dropped the name Drezner, he should have put me at the top of the pile."

"He did."

"What am I supposed to do for an entire week, twiddle my thumbs?"

"Whatever you would normally do."

"Like what—learn Talmud?"

Yossi raised a finger to counterpoint, then let it drop.

"What's the problem?" David asked.

Yossi said, "According to Maimonides, non-Jews aren't supposed to study the Torah, or its various elucidations and legal coda, such as the Talmud, even if they're Noahides."

Mayer squeezed his eyes shut. "Don't say 'Noahides.'"

"What are Noahides?" David asked.

"The righteous gentiles. The so-called Sons of Noah. After the flood, Noah became the new father of all mankind. He was the original righteous gentile."

"Interesting."

"The Noahides observe seven commandments known as the *sheva mitzvos bnei Noach* in order to be in compliance with God."

"What are they?"

"Let's see," the rabbi said. "Don't worship idols, don't curse God, don't kill, don't steal, don't cheat on your spouse, don't eat the flesh of an animal while it's still alive, and one more . . . ah yes: follow a court system."

"Eat an animal while it's still alive," David said. "Who would ever want to do that?"

"They say it was a pretty common practice in biblical times."

Mayer's phone rang. He lifted his jacket by the quarters and the device slid out of an inner pocket. He picked it up and looked at the screen, then hurried out of the room and into the foyer.

"Hello?"

"Good news," Sarah said. "I just got off the phone with the airline."

Mayer plunked himself on the second step of the staircase. "Oh yeah?"

"It took two hours, but I got them to track down your suitcase."

"*Gevaldik*, Sarale. You're the best."

"It should arrive tomorrow morning, by courier."

"Amazing."

"It took a lot of hair pulling. At first they insisted you drive to the airport and pick it up yourself. I said, 'My husband's sitting shiva and can't leave the house.' Even then, they gave me a headache. They were like, 'Then he'll have to pick it up before his return flight.'"

"Unreal. How did you turn them around?"

"I said there are religious articles in the suitcase that my husband needs for daily prayer. Withholding them is a violation of his civil rights."

Mayer seized a pleat of excess carpet on a stair edge and dug his fingernails into it. "You should have been a lawyer," he said.

"They'd better be there first thing in the morning."

"What would I do without you, *schefele?*"

"By the way, how did it go?"

"How did what go?"

A pause. "The funeral."

He pulled at the pleat of carpet so hard the stitching started to tear. "It went, it went."

"Who showed up?"

"A few friends. Very small crowd."

And just like that, Mayer told Sarah his first lie.

"Did you speak?"

"I did." The second lie.

"What did you say?"

"What did I say?"

"My God, it's like pulling teeth. What did you say in the eulogy?"

He flung the phone against the wall and threw open the front door. He ran up the block to Dixieland Highway. He ran into Moab. He kept going. He ran to Atlanta. He ran clear through the state of Georgia, across the Florida panhandle to the Gulf of Mexico. He swam across the gulf, the Caribbean Sea and halfway across the Atlantic Ocean. He stopped at the Mid-Atlantic Ridge, where he floated on his back and became one with the big blue yonder.

"I'm not sure I want to repeat it," he said.

"Give it to me in summary."

He licked his dry lips and lumbered through an abridged version of the eulogy he would never give, wondering all the while how to tally the lies—by the word?

"Well," she said, "I suppose it was the best you could do with the time you were given."

WHEN HE RETURNED to the living room David and Yossi were huddled on the couch, conversing in hushed tones.

"How'd it go?" David asked.

"I don't want to talk about it."

"Did you tell her?

"No."

"Good."

"Why good?"

"I think you'd better keep the bad news on the back burner for now," David said. "Wait until after you've converted."

"Why?"

"Imagine you broke Sarah's favorite coffee mug. What would get better results: telling her about it right away, or buying her a replacement first and then telling her?"

Mayer sank into Yossi's chair. "First of all, I'm no coffee mug. Second, I'd have to lie to her repeatedly for a whole week to keep her in the dark. That's a lot of lies to confess to."

David gnawed on a cuticle. "Okay, but eventually you'd explain that those lies were all for her protection."

"What do you mean?"

"You tell her you made a judgment call that she'd handle the news better if you were a Jew when you told her."

"You've done this sort of thing before, haven't you?"

"Dovid's got real *yiddishe kop*," said Rabbi Kugel, tapping his temple.

"Speaking of," David said, "Yossi and I were doing some brainstorming while you were gone."

"That sounds hazardous."

"You and I are no longer housebound right? I mean, shivabound."

"Go on."

"Matter of fact, we're not bound by anything anymore, except for the seven Noahide laws. Right, Yossi?"

"Right."

"And due to an unprecedented turn of events, we find ourselves facing an entire week with empty schedules."

"You're talking about a vacation," Mayer said.

"A rehabilitation period to wrap our heads around the existential vortex we've fallen into."

"A vacation."

"A pilgrimage."

"I don't need a vacation. I don't want to wrap my head around this. If it were up to me, I'd spend the week in a medically induced coma."

"Listen, Ese, if there's one thing I've learned, it's when the going gets tough, the tough get in a car and drive."

"A road trip. Even worse."

"This would be a very special road trip. You ever read *On the Road?*"

Mayer looked at him blankly.

"*Travels with Charley?*"

"No."

"'*The Road Not Taken?*'" David asked in a rising tone.

Mayer shook his head.

"You've read the Torah, right? Book of Exodus?"

"No, is it any good?"

"Don't be an ass. According to Scripture, after the Israelites fled Egypt they set out for the land of Canaan, which would have been a two-week journey for anyone with a decent pair of legs."

"Very good," Mayer said in a deliberately patronizing tone.

"Ass. Anyway, God, instead of getting the Israelites to the Promised Land in two weeks, put them on a wildly circuitous route that took forty years. Do you know why?"

"Enlighten me."

David spread his arms. "Because of the *journey*. The wayward passage to the Promised Land is literature's original road odyssey."

Mayer stared at him with a wooden expression.

"To hell with flying to New York. Let's get in a car and take the scenic route. Let's see things, do things. Let's climb a water tower. Let's cannonball naked into a plunge pool. Let's set off fireworks in a scrapyard."

"What happened to wrapping our heads around our existential vortex?" Mayer asked. "Doesn't that kind of thinking require four walls?"

"The opposite: knocking down walls."

"Distracting ourselves."

"Exactly."

"Taking a vacation."

"No," David said. "Freeing our minds so we can get reacquainted with our souls."

Mayer sighed. "Your heart's in the right place, but the last thing I need is a spiritual awakening."

"I'm not sure I agree with that," the rabbi piped in. "Your situation presents a unique opportunity to see *hashgacha pratis* at work."

"What's *hashgacha pratis*?" David asked.

"Divine providence," the rabbi said. "The Talmud teaches that all of God's actions, even ones that seem bad, are for the good."

"I see," Mayer said. "So this nightmare is only a perceived nightmare. It's really just God's way of saying 'You're not having enough fun.'"

"I can't speak for God," Yossi said. "I just think it's no coincidence that two hours after you get the worst news of your life, you find yourself with a whole week to do pretty much whatever you want."

"Ah-ha. So what do you suggest? I hear Epcot's nice."

"I suggest that you take advantage of the opportunity. Roll the windows down. Let your mind roam. Maybe, if you're up to it, open a line of communication with the Almighty."

"And communicate what, exactly?"

Rabbi Kugel smiled. "Your thanks."

Mayer's brow furrowed as though he were just given the word *insouciant* at a spelling bee. "My thanks? Are you serious?"

"Set a goal that by the end of the week you at least see the *possibility* that your mother's deception was, in the long run, something to be thankful for."

Mayer shot to his feet. "What total *narishkeit*. There's nothing to be thankful for. And I'm not spending a week letting my brother drive me to whatever *farkakte* places he dreams up."

"Harsh," David said.

"Well, sorry, but who knows what kind of schmutz you'll rub my face in."

"What schmutz?"

"You know what I mean."

"No. Tell me."

"I want to be pure when I go before the *beis din*, okay?"

"Pure by what standards?" David said. "Jewish?"

"Yes."

"Jewish standards set by God?"

"Yes!"

"The same God who made you a counterfeit Jew?"

Hearing his own turn of phrase used against him pushed Mayer over the edge. He tackled his brother. They wrestled on the couch like kids in a school-yard, the younger dominating only briefly before the elder, easily the fitter of the two, got on top. He fought to pin him, but Mayer buckled and thrashed with surprising vigor.

For the second time that afternoon, a shrill whistle ended the fight. As they lay panting on the floor, Yossi sang a hymn from Psalms. "*Hineh matov umanaim sheves achim gam yachad.*" Behold, how good and how pleasant it is for brothers to also dwell together.

— CHAPTER 5 —

AS ALWAYS, THE MAN WITH THE BILLFOLD WON THE DAY.
Mayer had but fifty dollars to his name, and David refused to front him the cash to fly back to New York on his own—today or a week from today. Yossi, asserting tough love, backed the measure.

"This is blackmail," Mayer said.

"You will *not* regret this, Ese," David said. "And I promise, no schmutz."

With that settled, the group dispersed—Yossi to Thornton's to pick up Ida Mae's remains, David to the kitchen to eat something and reserve a rental car, and Mayer upstairs to take a shower.

The carpet was only slightly less bedraggled on the second floor than on the first. Halfway to the bathroom at the end of the hall, he stopped at a closed door from which hung a plastic "Beware of Dog" sign. He grasped the doorknob, let it go and shuffled on. He paused, exhaled and turned back. He opened the door.

The room was a narrow rectangle with a vaulted ceiling and a single window at the far end. A startling amount of sunlight streamed through compared to the rest of the dingy house. The furnishings were spartan—a metal-framed bunk bed and a writing desk made of particleboard. On the desk were an off-brand boom box, a coffee mug with *Marty* written on the side in bubble paint, and a plastic globe. He spun the globe and let his fingertip drag across land and sea until it came to rest at an enormous beige landmass comprising much of Europe and Asia.

The globe was propped on a book whose spine said *Field Guide to the Birds of North America*. He freed the book and smiled at it with affection.

The cover, spiderwebbed with white creases, featured a bald eagle with spread wings. The disintegrating spine had been reinforced several times with packing tape. If Mayer tallied the hours he'd spent reading this guide—in the pine barrens, in bed, in the bathroom—it would be enough to complete two tractates of Talmud and start a third.

He placed it on the bottom bunk—David's—and took off his shirt, tinted eggshell yellow from the day's many sweat washes. It smelled of ammonia and sharp cheddar. He removed his sodden four-cornered woolen undershirt, which peeled off like a wet dressing. From each corner hung tzitzis, the ritual tassels that Jewish males were instructed to wear every day from age three. He folded it lengthwise and rolled it up, kissed each tassel and put it next to the bird guide.

He took a shower as hot as he could stand, scrubbing himself pink with Ivory soap. He then re-donned his malodorous clothes, sans tzitzis, maligning the airline's negligence under his breath. He stuck the bird guide beneath an underarm and stuffed the tzitzis in a trouser pocket. In the kitchen he found his brother at the table, thumbing his iPhone and eating lasagna off a paper plate. He'd changed into a crisp pair of chinos, blue suede penny loafers—again, no socks—and a white polo. He took one look at Mayer and coiled his face.

"I thought you were getting cleaned up."

"I did."

"Freakin' airline really screwed you."

"Uh-huh."

"Well, no big deal. We'll get you a new wardrobe."

Mayer scrutinized his brother's fresh attire. "When did you find time to go shopping?"

"I keep an overnight bag in my car," David said.

"What for?"

"Emergencies." He stuffed his cheek with lasagna, and as he chewed, observed the crown of Mayer's head. "I guess you're not gonna part with your yarmy."

Mayer touched his black velvet yarmulke, practically an extension of his hair. Unlike tzitzis, the yarmulke was a custom, not a Torah commandment. In theory, anyone could wear one.

"I've got to ask you something," he said.

"Go ahead."

"Gun to your head, hand on the Bible: Did you know about this? About Mom's secret?"

David looked at him disbelievingly. "Are you seriously asking?"

"Yes."

David raised his palm. "Hand on the Bible, I had no idea."

They heard the front door open. Mayer's Adam's apple lurched. In walked Yossi with an oblong cardboard box under his arm, looking like he'd rather be carrying a human head. He set it upright on the kitchen table, gave David his credit card, and needlessly dusted off his hands.

"Take your time," he said, backing away. "I'll be in the living room."

For a good while, the brothers just stared at the box. The Torah forbade Jews to desecrate their bodies with so much as a tattoo, in life or death. Ida Mae, true to form, had bequeathed her boys the perfect memento.

"I'll do the honors," David said. He picked up the box, shook it, put it down again. He pulled back one cardboard flap, then the other, and took out a pewter cylinder the volume of a youth-size football. He held it at a distance like Hamlet pondering Yorick's skull, then set it on the table.

"Well?" he said.

"Well, what?"

"She said she wants to be sprinkled somewhere that'll make her smile from the afterlife."

Mayer hadn't given thought to Ida Mae's final request. The whole business was as alien to him as ritual cannibalism.

"I want no part of it."

IT WAS JUST after four o'clock when the three men walked out of the house. Across the street, old Mrs. McCoy's impeccably pruned magnolias had long ago been choked out by hogweed, which now grew as tall as the rain gutters. From the crumbling concrete stoop, a barefoot boy of nine observed the odd-looking trio. He squinted at David; was that the *Fast & Furious* guy? He almost got up and ran over for a better look, but common sense—and laziness—prevailed.

The Lincoln was gone, David having told Ruben to take the rest of the week off. He called shotgun on Yossi's Kia, consigning his brother to the back between two booster seats.

"Sorry about the matzo crumbs," the rabbi said. "It's all my grandkids eat."

On the way to the car rental place, Mayer instructed Yossi to be at his mother's house bright and early tomorrow to sign for the delivery of his suitcase. If by some miracle Sarah wanted to remarry him after he broke the news to her, he'd ask Yossi to ship it to their house in Brooklyn. If not, well, the suitcase would be the least of his problems.

"Don't think about that now," David said. "Focus on the positives."

"Name one positive."

"How 'bout Mom getting rid of her landline? If not for that, you'd be tethered to the damned phone all week in case Sarah called."

"That's true."

At the car rental office, Yossi told the boys he'd wait outside until they were all set. The rep behind the counter had platinum hair and wore blue eyeshadow. Pinned to her company shirt was a name tag that said "Tami."

"Will it be just the two of you?" she asked.

"And our mother," David said. "She's waiting outside."

Tami scrutinized the Belkins. "You're brothers?"

"Twins," the elder said proudly.

Tami looked skeptical. "Uh-huh. So will this be a pleasure trip, or . . . ?"

"We're celebrating Marty's newly won bachelorhood."

Mayer cringed.

"With your mother," Tami deadpanned.

"That's right."

She handed over their paperwork and directed them to a two-level car lot behind the office. There, David beelined briskly past the economy and SUV bays.

"Where are you going?" Mayer asked.

Grinning wickedly, the elder Belkin beckoned him to keep up. They weaved between the premium and luxury bays and on to a far corner of the lot bearing a small but impressive selection of midlife-crisis sports cars. David checked the assigned number on his rental agreement, then the parking spot numbers. "Two-nineteen, two-twenty, two-twenty-one . . ."

At two-twenty-two he came to a stop. Like a director behind a camera, Mayer panned his gaze from the ground up to reveal a sixties-style muscle car with twenty-first-century hardware. It was octane red with an intimidating grille and two heat extractors on the hood. Its contours made him think of a cat getting ready to pounce.

"Well?" David said.

"It's a little extravagant."

"A little? It's the most powerful Charger on the market, a goddamn edifice on wheels."

The word "Charger" brought back memories of a syndicated TV show from their early childhoods starring two hooligan brothers, a sister who always wore short-shorts—and a red Charger named after a Confederate general.

"Ah," he said.

"I'd have found us an actual '69 if I'd had time—but then I'd have to learn stick. Can you drive stick?"

"I can't drive," Mayer said.

"Stick?"

"Period."

David's head cocked. "Do you have a driver's license?"

"No."

"Why the hell not?"

"Nobody in New York drives."

"No. You need a license. It's called being a grown-up."

Mayer looked at his toes, abashed. David clapped him on the back. "Hey, forget about it. I wasn't gonna let you drive her anyway."

"Her?"

"And as captain, I'll bestow myself the honor of naming her." He ogled her rounded fenders, her ample hood. He snapped his fingers. "Daisy."

"Ah."

They climbed into the spacious interior, which smelled like a new wallet. Mayer, sinking into his quilted leather bucket seat, had to hand it to his brother: this might well have been the most comfortable chair he'd ever sat in.

"Ese," David said, "can you feel it?"

"Feel what?"

"How right this is?"

Mayer didn't answer. His brother unzipped a side pocket of his overnight bag, pulled something out and stuffed it into his trouser pocket. He tossed the bag into the back seat and hit the ignition. Daisy emitted a wet, hungry growl that triggered not unpleasant vibrations up and down Mayer's thighs.

David rounded the car out of its spot, straightened the wheel and leaned on the gas. Daisy lurched. He stomped the brake and she screeched to a stop. He caressed the dashboard, and in a voice just above a whisper said, "Papa's gonna take good care of you."

THEY FOUND RABBI Kugel waiting in the shade of a Chinese maple, playing phone solitaire in his shirtsleeves. He gave the Charger a passing glance when it pulled up beside him, then did a double take. A thousand-watt smile broke out on his face. "This is what I'm talking about."

David answered with a rev of the engine. The rabbi came to the passenger's side and squatted by the open window. He gave the passenger's shoulder a squeeze. "*Nu*, Mayer?" Well?

"*Nu?*"

"What's gonna be between here and Brooklyn?"

Mayer punted the question to the guy behind the steering wheel. David took a philosophical air. "Abraham never wrote a handbook for this, did he?"

"I'm afraid you're in uncharted territory," Yossi said.

"I guess we are."

Suddenly, a sparkle came to the elder Belkin's eyes. He retrieved his overnight bag, unzipped it and pulled out three torpedo cigars. He handed out two and produced a camo-colored Zippo that Mayer recognized as the one he'd had as a kid. David lit the rabbi's, then offered the flame to his brother, who declined. He lit his own, rolling it for an even burn that infused the car with a sweet, earthy smell.

Yossi took a few puffs. "Can we get serious for a moment, Mayer?"

"I guess."

"I get that you and I differ on the age-old question of why bad things happen to good people."

"On second thought, let's not get serious," Mayer said.

"None of this happened randomly, my friend. God did this to you for a reason. I've never been more certain of anything in my life."

"Okay."

Yossi searched his one-time protégé's face. Then he straightened up and went back to the maple tree, where he'd left Ida Mae's urn. The younger son wouldn't accept it, so the elder took it instead. He got out of the car and nestled it in a crook in the back seat. After a moment of consideration, he buckled it in with a seat belt.

The rabbi shook each brother's hand.

"Keep me posted on your travels."

"Will do," David said. "And Rabbi?

"Yes?"

"You're all right."

Yossi smiled. "Now, *lech lecha*." Go forth.

"GODDAMNIT!"

Less than ten minutes after bidding Yossi goodbye, David brought Daisy to a dead stop behind an exhaust-spewing tractor trailer on the I-75. He slammed his palm on the top of the steering wheel.

"Full stop!" he bugled. "Bumper to fuckin' bumper."

He'd been jonesing to test Daisy out, but after only half a mile on the interstate they'd come to a glacier of red brake lights. He snatched his iPhone off the dash mount and zoomed in on the map. "Oh Jesus, miles of this. Miles. And no exits."

"What's causing it?" Mayer asked.

"Car wreck." He pounded the steering wheel again.

"Relax," Mayer said. "It'll clear up eventually."

They moved forward in fits and starts—mostly fits. Exhaust fumes rippled all around them like the spirits of massacred eels.

"I hope whoever crashed is okay," Mayer said.

"I don't." David rolled down his window a crack to ash his cigar, then veered Daisy into the middle lane to get a better view of the shimmering land bridge of automobiles. He cursed again.

Mayer dug into his jacket for his trusty Psalms, then remembered—a thorn in the heart—that they were not his to read. He reached instead into the door compartment where he'd stashed *Field Guide to the Birds of North America*. Flipping to a random page, he saw a checkmark next to *Picoides borealis*, the red-cockaded woodpecker. In tiny but readable penmanship he'd written in the margin, "Pine barrens, 09/04/91."

As a kid, his infatuation for birds bordered on the obsessive. He loved them for their beauty and mystery, their vast diversity in size, behavior and habitat, and their inviolability; like the crown jewels in London, you could look but not touch.

He quit birding when he started yeshiva. He didn't have time, and Brooklyn's avian catalog was comparatively slim pickings anyway. But mainly he gave it up for fear his *rebbeim* and fellow *talmidim* would think him eccentric. But he never stopped loving birds. Early in their marriage, he and Sarah would walk the pedestrian path on Ocean Parkway, the tree-lined thoroughfare modeled after Avenue de L'Impératrice, and Mayer would name the different species—blue jays, sparrows, wrens and the like. Sarah, for whom all birds were pigeons, got a kick out of her husband's uncommon knowledge. For the first few months, anyway.

Needing Sarah out of his head, he closed the book and looked out the window. A garbage sack lay torn open at the bottom of the grassy median. Varmints had eaten what they could and left behind a heap of Styrofoam clamshell containers, Big Gulp cups, and chicken bones. He looked at David, who swiped his iPhone back and forth like a windshield wiper. The screen was, as always, tilted out of view.

"You should try Windex," he said.

"Hmm?"

"Every time I look at you, you're rubbing that screen like there's a smudge on it."

David grunted.

"Seriously, what is it you're always doing on that thing?"

"Just the commerce of everyday life."

He put the phone back on its mount, the screen showing a map with a burgundy line delineating the highway. Mayer looked to his right at a hornet-yellow Volkswagen steered by a thirtyish woman with a floppy straw hat and tortoiseshell sunglasses. Behind her sat a young boy watching something on a tablet. Alerted by a sixth sense, the boy looked out the window at his next-lane neighbor, who offered a tentative wave. This caught the mother's eye. She bared her teeth at him.

David cracked up. "Busted!"

"Shut up."

"ALRIGHT IF I smoke a jay?"

"A what?" Mayer said.

David pinched his thumb and index finger and put them to his lips.

"Absolutely not."

"C'mon man, we've been sitting like this for almost an hour. I need an at-titude adjuster."

"It's drug use."

"It was drug use thirty years ago. It was recreation twenty years ago. Now it's just oxygen with a little kick in the ass."

"What if the police see?"

David looked through windows on all sides. He dug into his pocket and pulled out the camo lighter and a sandwich bag containing a half-smoked blunt. Ignoring his brother's objections, he stuck it in his mouth and lit up. Mayer rolled his window all the way down. The humidity and exhaust fumes coated his windpipe and made him cough.

"David," he pleaded.

"One more." David sucked in another mouthful from the blunt and pinched it out.

Mayer rolled his window back up. "The car rental's gonna charge you for the smell," he said.

"Don't care." Sighing with contentment, David eased his grip on the wheel. After a minute or so, he started to laugh.

"What's so funny?"

"I was just thinking of Reynolds for some reason. You remember Reynolds?"

"No."

"Yes you do. The neighbor's dog. That old hound they kept hooked up to a clothesline all year long."

"Oh yeah."

"Remember what we used to do?"

"No." Then, after a beat, "Oh, you mean with the firecrackers."

David dissolved into laughter.

"Why must you keep bringing these things up?" Mayer asked.

"He'd be like, *rrrawwww!*" David said, "and jump ten feet high."

"It was cruel."

"Please. We were that dog's best friends, and vice versa."

"It was still cruel."

"Give me a break. *We* were the victims."

"How do you figure that?"

"Two kids left to their own devices all summer long? It's a wonder we didn't get ourselves killed."

"Killed how?" Mayer asked. "From boredom?"

"We had good times."

"Did we?"

The elder twin eased up on the brake and Daisy rolled another six or seven feet. He started fidgeting with the radio knob. Pretty soon, out of the speakers blasted the country pop tune they'd heard earlier in the Lincoln.

When hope is gone and the night is endless
I remember your eyes and I see us together
Running hand in hand, making footprints in the sand,
I walk—

Mayer pushed the knob and the car went quiet.

"What the hell, Ese?"

"You said earlier it's a bad song."

"I said it's a crap song, but it's the good kind of crap song. More relevantly, Mom loved it."

"What are you talking about?" Mayer asked.

"In her letter, remember? She devoted a whole paragraph to Dominic Day."

"I don't know who that is."

"He's the kid in the wheelchair who sings 'Walk with You.' Mom said every time she heard it, it made her feel like she was in high school and in love for the first time."

They heard the *potato-potato-potato* of a motor and looked to their left as a Harley passed them at an enviable seven miles an hour. Its operator wore a helmet that looked like a souvenir from the Wehrmacht.

"I don't recall, sorry," Mayer said. "I got hung up on the part about her grandfather being in the SS."

"Well, hell, I need music," David said. He unmounted the phone and tapped at it. Then he pressed the volume knob. What came on was a no-chord guitar shuffle that bloomed into a bright, electric boogie. Though Mayer hadn't heard it in more than twenty-five years, he still remembered the lyrics. It had been a staple on Z93, played every three hours along with "Sweet Home Alabama," "Sweet Emotion" and "Carry on Wayward Son."

As John Fogerty crooned about all the happy creatures he saw out his back door, Mayer got strangely sentimental. David hadn't been wrong about those endless summer days: they'd had good times, even sublime ones—especially when Chris LaPree and the other boys from the block came over to play.

Chris LaPree, he thought. *Man.*

He thought about those summers for the whole two minutes and thirty-five seconds of "Lookin' out My Back Door"—about two minutes more thought than he'd given them in the past decade. When Fogerty strummed that final C chord, Mayer almost asked his brother to play it again.

AT LAST THEY rolled up to the culprit, an eighteen-wheeler whose operator had miscalculated the height of an overpass.

"Holy shit," David said.

"Thank God no one was hurt," Mayer said.

The Freightliner had been going so fast its nose made it into the sun on the other side. Most of the trailer's roof had peeled back like a sardine can lid. In an overabundance of caution, its operator laid out a parabola of emergency flares so outspread that anything wider than a Honda Fit had to slow to a snail's pace to get by.

The driver—pink-faced and beady-eyed, with strands of thinning hair sweat-plastered to his forehead—sat mournfully on the guardrail in the shade. David rolled down his window.

"Hey friend, how 'bout an ice-cold Coca-Cola?"

The man's eyes lit up. "Say, that'd be—"

"Fuck your mother, dickhole!"

The teamster recoiled as if slapped. David slammed the gas pedal and Daisy shot out of the bottleneck like a champagne cork. He tapped his phone and the anti-Vietnam anthem "Fortunate Son" came on. Mayer felt his back go flush with the backrest as they went from zero to sixty in five seconds flat. As all four windows came down at once, he clamped his yarmulke to his scalp lest it get sucked into the vortex.

"Halle-fucking-lujah!" David hollered. "Free at last, free at last!"

Mayer said something, but his voice got swallowed by the helter-skelter of Daisy's shifting gears, the roaring wind and "Fortunate Son" cranked to eleven. In no time they caught up to the speed limit stalwarts, and David started threading between them. When he came up behind a black Mustang doing a paltry eighty in the passing lane, he swerved to the right, gunned it and swung back in place with mere inches to spare.

Mayer saw one hundred on the speedometer and tried again to get his brother's attention. To his horror, David's eyes were squeezed shut and he was belting out Fogerty's angry lyrics with maniacal fervor.

Mayer punched his brother's shoulder. The tires screeched and Daisy almost skidded into the embankment. David lifted his foot off the pedal and cranked down the volume. "Jesus Christ, Ese, you trying to kill us?"

"I left my hat at the house."

The windows came back up. "You what?"

"My black hat. I left it at Mom's."

"Okay."

"We need to turn around."

"No. We didn't sit through that highway to hell for two hours just to turn back and do it all over again."

Mayer's voice shrank. "But I need it."

"I'll buy you a new one."

"It's a specific style. Most hat stores don't carry them."

"I know, dummy. We'll find you a Jewish hat store somewhere on the way—Baltimore, or wherever. Just don't go to pieces on me, okay?"

At College Park they got on the I-85 and David flicked on the headlights. They passed back-to-back billboards for, respectively, First Southern Baptist Church, Covenant Baptist Church, Centennial Baptist Church, and Strokers—the last showcasing a shapely female silhouette gripping a pole with two hands, head tossed back and hair tickling hindquarters.

Mayer looked out his window at the sun, which hung like a ripe orange over the western hills. Something about it was amiss, but in an inscrutable way he couldn't puzzle out. It was like an optical illusion in which the image looks normal, but it can't be normal because otherwise it wouldn't be an optical illusion. Then a gap opened in a row of red oaks, revealing a brightly lit sign, and his thoughts moved to the pragmatic.

"Hey," he said, "Maybe we could—"

"Already on it, Ese," David said, getting in the exit lane.

— CHAPTER 6 —

MAYER PULLED THREE WHITE DRESS SHIRTS OFF A
RACK AT THE TJ MAXX MEN'S DEPARTMENT AND PUT THEM IN HIS
shopping cart. He was about to start off in search of underwear when his
brother returned from wherever he'd wandered off to. He looked at Mayer's
selection.

"I don't think so," David said, and put the shirts back on the rack.

"What are you doing?"

"These aren't gonna work."

"Work for what?"

"If you have to ask, then I can't help you."

Mayer looked at him with bewilderment. "It's what I wear."

"It's what you *wore*, and maybe what you'll wear again someday. But not
today."

"Why?"

"Because I'm not having Willy Loman be my wingman."

"*Wingman*," Mayer echoed. "First honest word you've spoken all day." He
reached for the shirts again and heard the commanding snap of fingers. He
halted and turned. His brother was rubbing his thumb and forefinger together.

"So that's how it is."

"Let's check out True Religion," David said, and steered the cart toward
chinos and denim.

IN MAYER'S PREVIOUS life, shopping meant a biennial trip to Silber-
stein Men's and Boy's for a duplicate of the outfit he'd walked in with. He left

TJ Maxx laden with bags of jeans, chinos, Henley T's and short-sleeve button shirts, plus suede moccasins, tennis shoes, undergarments, toiletries and a fine leather duffel to hold the loot. It all went in the trunk, along with a swappable wardrobe David had picked out for himself.

By the time they got out of there, the sky had turned geranium and the temperature was a relatively nippy eighty-six. David stopped at a Shell station near the interstate on-ramp. He set the pump on automatic and went into the snack mart to use the bathroom. He came out with a party size bag of Doritos and two bottles of Yoo-hoo.

Mayer accepted a Yoo-hoo without a thank-you. He checked the label for a kosher certification and, finding it, swilled half the bottle—his first calories since the bygone morning. The Doritos, which he knew without checking weren't kosher, he didn't touch.

"Ese?"

"What."

"Remember the time we stuck a bottle rocket in Mr. Bixby's exhaust pipe 'cause he flunked me in history?"

The memory took its time rising to the surface—and detonated. "Oy, the poor guy went into cardiac arrest," Mayer said.

"Oh yeah." David started the car. "Didn't he retire after that year?"

"He was eighty. Why do you get pleasure out of reminding me of horrible things we did?"

"For some reason I remember this stuff fondly. I guess it's all about perspective."

"There's no good perspective on sending teachers to the ER or torturing dogs or—*ugh*—spying on underage girls."

"Who, Whitney? She was older than we were. And it wasn't really spying, because she knew what we were up to."

Mayer said nothing.

"I still say we taught Old Man Bixby a lesson."

"Which was what—to not grade kids fairly?"

"That you don't fuck with the Belkin boys."

"Well, that's idiotic, since no one ever found out who did it."

They passed a slash pine tree at the I-85 ramp just as a bird flew off a branch toward the setting sun. It had a long, slender beak, white spots scattered about its head, and shiny black plumage reflecting green and purple iridescence.

European starling, Mayer thought. *Sturnus vulgaris*.

He checked the bird guide for confirmation, but only as a formality. David was still on Mr. Bixby. "Easy for you to take the high road," he said. "You aced everything without studying and I got stuck wearing the dunce cap."

"*Vayigdalu hani'arim, vayehi Esav ish yodea tza'id ish sadeh v'Yaakov ish tam yoshev ohalim*," Mayer said. *And the boys grew up, and it was that Esau was a man who knew hunting, a man of the field, and Jacob was a man of integrity, living in tents.*

"Huh?" David said.

"Just quoting Scripture."

THEY PASSED ABANDONED barns and rusting silos that resembled copper obelisks in the dying light. They passed peanut fields and soybean fields and orchards of apples, nectarines, peaches and plums. They passed roadside fruit stands—shuttered for the night, or forever—with clapboard signs for watermelons, rock melons, honeydews, crenshaws, blackberries, dewberries, strawberries and sweet corn.

David cracked the windows, letting in aromas of hay bales, manure, primroses and sugarcane. Fireflies put on their light show above the grass beside the shoulder. David tapped his phone and on came Dusty Springfield's cover of "Willie and Laura Mae Jones," a song about a bygone time when neighbors worked the fields together by day and played music on the porch by night, and nobody cared whose skin was what color.

As Mayer watched the last of the sun disappear behind the western hills—the end of the worst day of his life—he realized why it had struck him as amiss earlier. "We're going south."

"Hmm?"

He looked needlessly out his window again. "We're going south."

"Yep."

"Away from New York."

"Yep." David relit the blunt and took a long drag. "I told you the route would be circuitous. And since you've never been to New Orleans—wait, *have* you been to New Orleans?"

Mayer crossed his arms. "When were you going to tell me?"

David plucked a scoobie off the tip of his tongue and flicked it away. "Did you not read any of the big green signs? We passed like thirty."

"Where are we now?"

"Alabama."

"Fantastic."

"Are you mad?"

"I'm not happy," Mayer said.

"Why?"

"Because I don't want to go to New Orleans."

"Why the hell not?" David asked.

"It's not Orlando, let's put it that way."

"Thank God."

"It's an American Sodom."

"For frat boys, maybe—and let them throw their money away on street bud and lap dances. The real New Orleans is an ethos. It reveals itself in food and architecture and music, and people who march to the beat of their own drum."

"Ethos," Mayer snorted. "Is that off your word-of-the-day calendar?"

THEY HAD JUST passed a sign for Montgomery when Mayer's phone rang. He plucked it out of the cupholder and checked the caller ID.

"Uh-oh."

"Sarah?" David asked.

"Who else?"

It rang again. And again.

"Are you gonna answer?" David asked.

"I don't think it's a good idea."

"How come?"

"She's intuitive," Mayer said. "She'll hear something in my voice and ask what's wrong. I can't lie to her."

"Tell her your mother just died."

"Very funny."

"I'm serious. Tell her you need some space."

After the fifth ring, Mayer put it back in the cupholder. David shook his head in disgust. "She's your wife, dude."

"She's not my wife."

"No, I get that, but—Jesus, that ring's annoying. When's it going to voice-mail?"

"I don't know."

It rang again. And again. And again, until David said "Fuck this" and snatched it up. Mayer tried to grab it back, but only succeeded in knocking it out of his brother's hands.

"Good going," David said.

"*Hello?*" came a tinny voice from the floor.

The brothers froze.

"*Hello?*"

Shit, David mouthed. He patted the floor between his feet while periscoping his neck to see above the dash. He found the phone and thrust it at his brother, who wouldn't take it. David gave him a dirty look and brought it to his ear.

"Hello?"

A pause.

"Sarah! Sorry about that, I dropped the phone. How've you been?"

Mayer tapped his shoulder with a frantic entreaty. *What?* David mouthed.

"Pull over," Mayer whispered. "She can hear the car noise."

David nodded. "Just a minute, Sarah." He put his thumb over the mouthpiece and swerved across two empty lanes and the rumble strip before braking on the shoulder. He looked at his brother. "Now watch and learn how to handle a woman."

He brought the phone back to his ear. "Sorry again. You caught me while I was in the bathroom." A pause.

"Well, I appreciate that. Yes, she was too young, far too young." Pause.

"Well, you know what they say, the Lord giveth—" Pause.

"Your husband? He's taking a nap. Poor guy's had a long day, and—" The corner of his eyebrow twitched.

"Well, I don't know if that's a good idea. He's super tired from all the—" An extended pause. "Okay, okay, hold please."

He put his thumb over the mouthpiece. "She wants me to wake you up. Says she's got a surprise for you."

"Don't wake me up."

"She's pretty insistent."

"Don't wake me up."

"I think I'd better."

"You said you could handle her. Handle her."

"Right." David brought the phone back to his ear. "I just checked on him, Sarah, and I tell you, a stampede of elephants couldn't wake him up. But I'll take a message and be sure to give it to him as soon as he—" Pause.

"I totally understand, but you're putting me in a tough spot. I really hate to—" He wiped his forehead with the back of his hand.

"No, I get that you're his wife, but—" He raised a hand, let it fall helplessly in his lap. Mayer, divining imminent collapse, grabbed the door handle to flee. Then he looked at the radio console and an idea sprang into his head.

"Alright, alright," David bleated in surrender. "You're the boss."

Mayer punched the radio volume knob and set it to one click above zero. He switched from FM to AM and rotated the tuning dial until he found the right frequency. He cranked the volume and a burst of radio static clamored from the speakers.

At first David looked puzzled. Then the corners of his mouth curved upward. "Sarah?" he said. "Sarah, can you hear me?" A pause.

"Hello? Sarah, you're cutting out. I can barely . . . hello?" Mayer swung the knob left and right, left and right. It sounded like a Martian dust storm.

"I think one of us caught some interference," David shouted. "A plane, maybe. Call back later, will ya? . . . K, bye-bye."

He ended the call and turned off the radio, then shut the phone in the glove compartment for good measure. "That was old-school, Ese! Outstanding."

Mayer massaged his temples, his gaze fixed on a billboard up the road that said "It's your choice . . . Heaven or Hell."

David found the blunt by the gear selector and lit up. "Man, I feel like I just got worked over by the KGB. May I recommend texting her from now on?"

"This phone apparently isn't designed for easy texting."

"That's okay, you can use mine."

"I don't know how to type."

"Of course you don't."

A barrage of flashing blue and red lights lit up the night. David looked at the rearview mirror. "Ah, fuck me."

Mayer turned his head around. The police cruiser was right behind them, beacons spinning in the rooftop light bar, more lights flickering from push bumpers and headlights.

David jammed the blunt in his pocket and rolled down the windows all the way. He batted the air.

"Are we in trouble?" Mayer asked.

"Not necessarily."

"What's that supposed to mean?"

"It means," David said, still swatting the air, "that we need to stay absolutely cool. Let me do the talking. Don't make any sudden movements. Look him in the eye if he looks you in the eye. Don't be shifty."

"David, what's wrong?"

"Nothing yet. But if he finds probable cause to search the car, he might find more pot where this came from. And some other stuff."

"How much more?"

"I dunno, four ounces."

"Is that a lot?"

"It's not a little." He glanced at the crown of Mayer's head. "Lose the yarmulke."

Mayer touched the skullcap. "Why?"

"It's bad enough I'm dressed like I just came from Augusta National. But you know who these Alabama brownshirts hate more than anyone? More than Blacks, even?"

"You're starting to worry me."

"Well, don't let him see that," said David, watching the mirror. "Listen, my business partners are evangelicals. They've got me on a short leash as it is. If they find out I got busted with enough dope to bake a hippopotamus, they'll boot me out of the company."

"Uh-huh."

"Not to mention we'll spend the night in jail and Daisy will get impounded. Our adventure will be royally fucked."

"Along with my chances of getting Sarah back," Mayer said.

"It won't improve them. So just stay cool and follow my lead."

They heard the door of the cruiser open, then bang shut. Mayer glanced back and saw a broad silhouette haloed by the colors of Old Glory, the heel of a palm rested on the butt of a service Glock. David hooked both hands on the steering wheel, puffed his cheeks and blew out slowly.

A slab of granite sheathed in navy oxford filled the window frame, a steel pin on the left breast inscribed with the words "Alabama Highway Patrol."

Mayer took off his yarmulke and jammed it between his thighs.

"Evening, officer," David said.

"Evening," the slab said in a bass-baritone drawl. "I passed you earlier and came around again and y'all are still here. Everything okay?"

"Yes, sir," David said. "I got a phone call and I decided I'd better pull over before answering."

"Just making sure you're not in need of aid."

"No sir, much obliged."

The officer stooped so that his face appeared about a foot from the window. He was Black, in his late forties, wearing a gray straw hat banded by a gold campaign cord, with a gold Alabama pin on the crown. His name tag said "Wilson."

"Evening," he said to the passenger.

"Evening."

Trooper Wilson looked back and forth between the brothers. "Y'all relation?"

"Pardon?" Mayer said.

"Are you fellas related?"

"We're brothers. Most people say we look nothing alike."

"You've got the same eyes."

Mayer pointed out that his eyes were brown and David's were blue.

"Different color, same caught-in-the-headlights look," Wilson said, and both Belkins felt their stomachs drop. Wilson broke into hearty laughter, revealing a gap between his upper incisors. "I'm only kidding. Where y'all headed?"

"New Orleans," David said.

"Paris of the South," the trooper said.

"It'll be my brother's first time."

"Well, that's pretty special. You guys from out of town? I see your license plate says Georgia."

"Born and raised," David said.

"Oh yeah? Whereabouts?"

"New Moab."

The officer's eyes scanned the stars. "About forty miles outside Atlanta."

"You know Georgia."

"My home state too." He took a step back to admire Daisy. "This is some ride."

"I wish I could say she's mine," David said.

"Horsepower?"

"Monster. Seven ninety-seven."

"Eight cylinder?"

"Do you even have to ask?"

"How fast?"

"Two oh three," David said. "Think we could outrun you if we put her to it?"

Wilson wagged his index finger gamely. With the same finger he pointed to David's car seat. "Napa leather?"

"Laguna."

"I do so love the smell of an all-leather car interior."

David pointed his nose roofward and took a deep drag. "If Heaven has a smell, right?"

The trooper moved closer. "May I?"

"May you . . ."

"Get a noseful of that fine leather?"

"Um."

"I won't be but a second." The officer moved closer still.

"I mean . . ." David said. He glanced at Mayer, who gave a slight but vigorous shake of the head. "I guess."

Trooper Wilson took off his hat, revealing an epic dome which he snaked through the window as far as his wide shoulders would allow. David pushed the seat back to get out of kissing range. Closing his eyes, the cop dilated his nostrils and took a long inhalation. Holding it in, he withdrew, tilted his face starward and exhaled.

"Mmm. If that isn't a treat."

"The man knows his leather," David said, voice as taut as a violin string.

For a pregnant moment the trooper drummed the window ledge. He put his hat back on. "Well, you fellas have a long way to go, and I hate to keep you."

"We'd be much obliged," David said.

"But there is the matter of the cannabis."

Mayer felt his heart sink to his ankles as the trooper unclasped a flashlight from his belt. He shined it into the car, momentarily blinding him. He lit up the back seat, spotlighting David's overnight bag and Ida Mae's urn, then brought it to the side of the driver's face. "Your license, sir."

Sir.

Pinching his lips, David dug into his pocket and pulled out an ostrich-skin wallet. The blunt popped out with it, arcing acrobatically before landing on the center console. No one saw it but Mayer, who picked it up and concealed it between two fingers. Wilson took David's license and shined his flashlight on it.

"Mr. Belkin," he said, his voice official, "the smell of marijuana in the car leads me to believe there *is* marijuana in the car. Is there anything you'd like to tell me?"

David stared disconsolately through the front window.

"I always advise people, come clean before I have to find out for myself."

David folded his arms.

"Okey doke," Trooper Wilson said. "Kindly step out of the car."

David reached for the door handle, but before he got around to pulling it, Mayer said, "It's mine."

Trooper Wilson shined the light in the younger twin's face. "I surrender," Mayer said, holding the roach to the light. "It's mine. My brother doesn't touch the stuff."

Blinded by the light beam, he couldn't make out the trooper's expression. "For your consideration," Mayer said, "my brother and I have suffered a trauma today that maybe justifies the transgression."

He counted four heartbeats before Trooper Wilson lowered the light and said, "Go ahead."

"This morning we found out our mother died. It was unexpected."

It might have been wishful thinking, but he thought he saw something soften around the edges of the lawman's eyes.

"From suicide," he added.

Wilson took a long breath. "I'm sorry for your loss. Are those her remains strapped in the back seat?"

"Yes. And that's not even the whole story, I'm afraid."

The officer said nothing, which Mayer took as a prompt. And so he narrated the day's events, starting with the fateful phone call to the yeshiva payphone. Trooper Wilson maintained an unreadable expression throughout. As concise as Mayer kept it, the monologue was an endurance run, each new act adding a degree to the incline. By the end he wanted a nap.

Trooper Wilson straightened and looked across Daisy's roof at the latticework of tree trunks and branches beyond the highway shoulder, invisible in the dark but for the flashing reds and blues of his patrol car. Time passed for the boys. It could have been ten seconds or sixty.

"In all my years on highway patrol, I've heard them all," he said. "'My husband must've cut my brakes;' 'But Waze told me I was going southbound;' 'This white powder? It's only flour from a busted stress ball.' One time I pulled over a guy going sixty over the speed limit. He said his girlfriend was in labor. I said, 'I believe you, partner, but where's the mom-to-be?' He'd run out of the house in such a panic that he left her there."

David pursed his lips to stifle a snicker.

"But this—this is new. And you know what else? I don't doubt that every word of it is true."

He looked at the toes of his boots for a beat, mulling something. He said, "Since we're sharing, mind if I tell you about my day? It won't take but a minute."

"Of course," David said.

"I responded to a motorcycle crash not five miles south of here. The guy was swerving across lanes like a tennis ball until he bounced off the side of a tractor trailer. He might have been okay, but he overcompensated and crashed into the traffic barrier and flew over his handlebars."

He stroked his chin, mulling some more.

"Now, I'm a lapsed Baptist, but God had to be watching out for this guy. He landed in a tall patch of onion grass, the only vegetation in a rock field. A few feet off the bullseye and he'd have been a smashburger. Came out of it with nothing but a broken arm."

"Damn," David said.

"His three-year-old son, on the other hand . . ."

Mayer pressed his fingers to his lips.

"The kid wasn't wearing a helmet—not that it would have saved him on account of the way he . . . Well, anyway, I stuck around while FD and EMS and road crews cleaned it all up. If you drive past the scene now, you'd never know anything was ever amiss. This was two hours ago."

Mayer suddenly became aware of the synchronized chirping of fifty thousand crickets.

"And I'm back on the beat." The cop looked at each brother in turn. "You wonder how I'm able to do that? Just go about my evening like it's all gravy?"

They nodded.

"Because the worst thing I saw back there wasn't the boy. It was the dad. When I searched him I found an eight ball of meth, and I looked in his eyes and . . ." A storm cloud scuttled across his face, and he forced a smile to clear it away. "It just gives me a skip in my step to know I'm not him."

Trooper Wilson handed David his license. "I was already gonna let you boys off with a warning on account of your mother. As for all that stuff about losing your religion?" He whooshed his hand over his head from front to back. "Have a safe and pleasant evening."

He marched back to the cruiser. The brothers, blind as bats in the sudden darkness, heard his door close. As the car pulled onto the highway, the whirling beacons on the roof went out and it became just another set of shrinking taillights.

— CHAPTER 7 —

THEY FUELED UP AT MONTGOMERY BEFORE GETTING
ON THE I-65 TOWARD MOBILE. DAVID WAS RARING TO ARMCHAIR-
quarterback their encounter with Trooper Wilson, but Mayer was fuming—
not least over "Alabama brownshirts." After a while the elder Belkin fell silent
and the younger drifted into an uneasy sleep.

When his phone woke him three hours later, they were parked somewhere. David was sprawled on the hood with his back against the windshield,
drinking a beer and staring into an inky black expanse. He had Ida Mae
against one hip, a six-pack against the other. The temperature had dropped to
pleasant thanks to a salty breeze wafting through the windows. Mayer found
the phone in the glove compartment and answered it.

"Did I wake you?" Yossi asked.

"No."

"How's the exodus working out?"

"We haven't killed each other yet."

"*Baruch Hashem.* Anyway, I spoke to Itzik Slomowitz."

"Who?"

"My friend on the *beis din* of Flatbush. I told him in no uncertain terms
that your marriage is on the line. If he must move mountains to get your *giyur*
to the top of the pile, then mountains he should move."

"And?"

"He bumped you to Sunday morning. That's the best he can do."

Mayer did the math. The bump expedited his conversion to four and a half
days from now—not great, but better than a week. "Yossi, you're a tzadik."

"Nah, just good at being a pest," the rabbi said. "By the way, where are you?"

Mayer looked outside. There was a wooden dock with a few dozen pleasure craft moored nearby, some with orange and gold lights strung along their hulls. A mile eastward was a waterfront amusement park, the rides powered down for the night.

"The ocean."

"The ocean! You boys don't waste time."

Mayer said goodnight and got out of the car. He gave his brother the update on his conversion. David drained his bottle and lobbed it. It shattered in the dark. He got a fresh one and twisted off the cap.

"Where are we?" the younger brother asked.

"Biloxi. Want a beer?"

"No. What time is it?"

David checked his Rolex. "Twelve thirty."

"Good."

"Why good?"

"The worst day of my life is officially over."

David took a long pull from the bottle and stared at the moon. It was the color of a new penny. Then something at his three o'clock caught his eye and he sat bolt upright. "Holy Toledo!"

"What?" Mayer peered into the dark, but all he saw was a tire by an unlit light pole about fifty yards away. David shimmied off the trunk and cantered toward the pole.

"What is it?" Mayer asked.

When David neared the tire, he halted. He dropped to a squat and duck-walked. Nearer yet, he extended his arm. The tire, which was no tire, scuttled on four legs to the far side of the light pole.

Unnerved, Mayer climbed on Daisy's hood.

Still squatting, David followed the thing. Round and round the pole they went, the thing orbiting inward until it hugged the base. David reached for it again. It flattened itself to the ground and made a noise like a squeaky hinge.

"Get away from that thing!" Mayer shouted.

His brother chanted an anodyne hymn of nonsense words. He reached out again. The thing whimpered louder, almost cried, and he withdrew his hand. He tried again and got the same reaction. He tried again and again, chanting persistently and lowering his hand in minute increments until he was almost touching the mangy fur. He made contact. The thing shook like a leaf but didn't cry out. Still chanting, David stroked the length of it. He applied gentle pressure. He introduced a second hand and rubbed circles on either flank.

After several minutes of this, he called his brother over.

"No."

"It's tied up. It's not gonna hurt you."

"No."

"God, when did you get to be such a weakling?"

The barb stung more than it ought to have—possibly because he knew David hadn't said it to goad him. He slid off the car and came over.

"*Ribono Shel Olam.*"

The dog was compact and squat-legged, with cropped ears and a tail docked to a nub. Its short gray coat was blackened with oily dirt, rib cage protruding from flanks trellised with sores. A long white scar cut diagonally from right ear to left jaw. The right eye, caught in the scar's path, was milky white and shuttered three-quarters by a nerveless lid. Somebody had tethered the animal to the pole with a length of parachute cord.

David traced the scar with his finger.

"Careful," Mayer said.

"Oh, please. He"—David peeked between the dog's hind legs to corroborate the pronoun—"wouldn't hurt a fly." The dog sniffed his ear. David nosed him back. They butted heads and nipped at each other, carrying on like two puppies. After a while, the elder Belkin said, "What should we do with him?"

"What do you mean?"

"He needs help."

"So cut him loose."

"That goes without saying, dummy. I mean after that."

"Call animal control?"

David looked appalled. "Seriously? They'll just put him in a shelter, and you know what happens to shelter dogs."

He brushed his fingers over the dog's xylophone rib cage, clicking his tongue pityingly. A notion came to him. He got up and ran to the car. After rummaging around, he returned with a bottle of water and a half-depleted bag of Doritos. He trickled the water into his cupped hand. The dog lapped it up until the bottle was empty. He poured the chips on the ground and the animal hoovered them, tonguing the orange dust until no trace remained, then looking up at his benefactor with an expression evoking Oliver Twist wanting more porridge.

"Over there," Mayer said, pointing to a snack machine by a public toilet at the parking lot entrance. David ran off for more provisions. The dog sniffed the ground, licking microscopic Dorito granules. Mayer had an unhappy notion of Sarah witnessing this bizarre scene, her stricken eyes ticking between husband and dog like a Kit-Cat Klock.

His brother came back with an armload of Cheez-Its, SunChips, pretzels, trail mix and granola bars. He got to work on the wrappers. The dog devoured the snacks as soon as they hit the ground.

"Popeye needs a real meal," David said.

"Who?"

"I named him Popeye. Because of his squinty eye."

Mayer put his hands on his hips. "David."

"Don't look at me like that."

"It's not happening."

"He'll die out here."

"He's a dog," Mayer said. "He has survival instincts."

"He's a stray. Eventually someone will call animal control. They'll euthanize him."

"I'm sure someone'll adopt him."

"Yeah right. He looks like he escaped from a leper colony." David took Popeye by the jowls and cooed, "You're an ugly sonofabitch, aren't you?"

"We're not taking him," Mayer said.

"But why?"

"If you have to ask, then you're beyond explaining to."

David argued, pleaded, even threatened—but Mayer stood his ground. Finally, the elder Belkin took a jackknife out of his pocket and cut Popeye's cord. The dog returned the favor by lapping at his liberator's cheek until it looked like a shellacked chicken cutlet.

"Say goodbye," Mayer said. "I'll be in the car."

He started toward Daisy. A pattering of paws followed him. He stopped, and so did the pattering. He broke into a jog, then a sprint. When he got in the car, he slammed the door behind him. The dog put his paws on the window ledge and wagged his stump. David came up behind him, grinning like an idiot. "He likes you for some reason."

"I like him too. But I'm compassionate enough not to reciprocate."

"You're a real St. Francis of Assisi."

"Hey, I know," Mayer said, "why don't you just rub your money fingers together? See where it gets you."

David glared at him. He knelt by the dog and pulled him to his chest. He whispered something in his ear.

Mayer rolled his eyes. "Oh come on, you don't even know him."

"Yes I do." He gave Popeye a last scratch behind the ears. "Life is cruel, pal. But you knew that already."

Popeye sat on his rump, legs splayed comically to the side.

"Beat it."

The dog stayed put. A line of slobber yo-yoed from his jouncing tongue.

"I said beat it, stupid!" David shouted and swatted the animal on the snout. The blow was hardly more than a tap, but Popeye cowered, lowering his ears and giving his assailant a look that asked *but why?*

"Sorry," David said, lowering his head.

Popeye aped the gesture, turned and sauntered off. He gave his would-be friends one last beseeching look before disappearing into the shadows. Neither brother moved until the rhythmic clicking of claws ebbed to silence. Then David grabbed Ida Mae and the six-pack off the hood. He tossed his mother in the back seat. He hurled the beer bottles, one at a time, into the dark. He got into the captain's chair, started the engine, threw the car into reverse and flicked on the headlights.

"Shit."

Popeye stood by the front bumper, his shadow so long it almost touched Biloxi Bay. His left eye, the good one, was as translucent blue as the waters of Isla Perro. David pulled out of the spot, shifted into drive, spun the wheel and stomped the gas.

He slammed the brakes. Popeye was in front of them again, looking for all the world like an orphan at a refugee camp. He came to the driver's side and got on his hind legs, his tail stump fluttering. David was powerless not to give the fool mongrel another scratch behind the ears. He turned to his brother.

"No," Mayer said.

"Ese."

"I said no."

"I'm not gonna do money fingers."

"The answer's still no."

"Ese, listen to me. We need this dog. Don't ask me why, but we need him more than he needs us. I've never been as sure of anything in my life."

"Confidence was never your weakness."

"Ese . . ."

"No."

"Marty . . ."

Mayer rubbed his temples.

"Just look at his ugly mug," David pleaded.

Against his better judgment, Mayer looked. It might have been the angle of the dog's head or the interplay of shadow and light on his muzzle, but Mayer would have testified in court that he was smiling.

"Ese?"

"Yeah?"

"Are you really gonna leave Popeye behind the way you left me in New Moab?"

Mayer's eyes flared. "That is a bold card to play, my friend."

"Bold but true."

"Here's the deal: he sits in the back. Only the back. If he bares his teeth at me, licks me, or even looks at me in a way I don't like, he's out the window. And I don't care if we're going ninety on the highway when it happens."

David's face lit up like a Christmas display. He grabbed his brother and kissed his forehead so hard that it left a red mark. He got out of the car and let Popeye in the back. The animal sprawled out on the seat like it was the Great Bed of Ware.

"You did the right thing, my man," David said. "You are a king!"

Pretty soon the car smelled like a plate of foie gras left in the sun. Mayer looked behind him. Popeye was curled up, scabby flanks rising and falling in an even rhythm. By the time they left Biloxi he was fast asleep.

AN HOUR LATER they were on the I-10, closing in on Lake Pontchartrain. Mayer had joined Popeye in dreamland, and neither woke up when David stopped at an all-night Walmart in St. Tammany Parish for pet supplies. Just before two thirty, he took the Twin Span Bridge over the lake.

Once on the other side, they were officially in New Orleans—but with miles to go before the city proper. First came the Bayou Sauvage National Wildlife Refuge, which, all but invisible at night, declared its presence aromatically via sulfur, brine and decomposing vegetation. They traversed the eastern suburbs and over the brackish waters of the Inner Harbor Navigation Canal. When the downtown towers came into view, David punched the ceiling and yeehawed. Bleary-eyed and sticky-mouthed, Mayer stared apathetically at his third and—God willing—final city center in twenty-four hours.

They got off the interstate at the Seventh Ward, taking St. Bernard Avenue past an array of ramshackle wooden houses, bars and saloons, and then onto North Rampart Street. Here was a more archetypal New Orleans of shabby-chic bars, and cafés with cast iron balconies. The majority of foot traffic moved southbound.

"Where are you taking us?"

David turned onto Conti Street, a narrow road lined with more bars, restaurants and witching-hour carousers—so many carousers, Mayer thought, and on a weeknight no less; what an incredible waste of human capital. Then David swung onto Bourbon Street, and all of Mayer's indignation fell away.

"*Ribono Shel Olam.*"

The street was like an Old West movie set with a Liberace makeover— every light pole and fire hydrant adorned, every denizen a street performer, merrymaker or lothario. There was a pear-shaped guy in a skin-tight bodysuit and ringmaster top hat gyrating before an open lockbox of loose change; a zaftig gal with braids and rouged cheeks, squeezed into a shiny gold Viking costume; a woman with facial scruff wearing a microskirt, thigh-high nylons, go-go boots and a bikini top.

All varieties of music blasted from every nook one could jam a speaker— the wailing guitars and cymbal-centric drums of hard rock, the trombones and trumpets of big band jazz, the synthesized drumbeats of hip-hop, the fiddles and banjos of bluegrass. From restaurants wafted aromas of battered *treif* fried golden brown, flame-broiled *treif* slicked with hot sauce, and *treif* jambalaya bubbling in pots the size of bourbon casks.

The tableau wouldn't have been quite so disquieting had Mayer ever visited Hollywood Boulevard, the Las Vegas Strip or even his own Times Square. But he'd never laid eyes on any of these meccas of excess, and so was powerless not to stare out the window in unblinking horror. And he'd have done so until his eyeballs started peeling had it not been for the breasts.

It was a low-slung pair, whey-colored and capped with tan nipples the size of silver dollars. Their owner, a florid-faced woman of perhaps forty-eight, was hooting like a college girl on spring break as she held the hem of her "Mardi Gras Mambo" T-shirt up with her chin, a beer in each hand. Mayer felt his head fill with hot oil. Hitherto, he'd only ever had one nude portrait in his memory vault—not counting that of Whitney King, who'd had a cruel habit of dropping the window blinds just as the going got good.

Now, just like that, there were two portraits.

Forgive me, Sarah.

A raucous fraternity of young men in cargo shorts dropped beaded necklaces on her from balconies. She gathered up the loot, strung it all around her neck and drank to her benefactors. The frat pack then set their snouts on tenderer prey, a passing sextet of young women in matching tees embossed with Greek letters.

"Show your tits! Show your tits!"

The girls held silent court, some tentatively nodding, others shaking their heads imploringly. The chant fanned out to street level. The girls were surrounded. Seeing only one way out, they made a telepathic sorority pact, clinked their beers—and in unison lifted hems, yanked down bras and war-whooped. Beads rained on their heads like manna.

Mayer turned to David, who, incredibly, wasn't looking out the window, but at his phone, the screen for once in open view. On it was a queue of photos of women that David shepherded ever rightward with his thumb. *This* was what he earmarked every spare moment for, even in the scorched-earth aftermath of Ida Mae's revelation? Mayer coughed out a chortle. The chortle graduated to a chuckle, and the chuckle to a laugh, and in no time he was doubled over, laughing so hard that tears ran down his cheeks and his lungs bleated for air.

HE OPENED HIS eyes to sunlight splintering through the window blinds. The TV was on, muted with closed captions. A local newsman was detailing a Dominic Day concert last night at Caesars Superdome. The broadcast cut to a wholesome-looking white kid in a wheelchair crooning to a delirious crowd of mostly teen girls.

The clock on the corner of the screen said eleven twenty-nine. Mayer blinked and read the number again.

Not twenty-four hours a goy and he was doing an outstanding job, waking at noon in a New Orleans hotel that smelled of beer and reefer and . . . lemongrass? How tempting it was to hold liable the mountain of comforter rising and falling beside him on the bed. But it wasn't as if David had ever put a gun to his head.

After Mayer's meltdown on Bourbon Street, his brother had called it a night and taken them to the Hotel Monte Cristo just outside the French Quarter. He argued with the desk clerk about the lone bed and was advised vacant rooms were a scarce commodity right now, but if he wished he could try his luck elsewhere. Neither Belkin wished that. Once they were in the room, Mayer collapsed onto the bed, too woebegone to pull back the comforter or even take his clothes off. Darkness was already seeping around the edge of his vision when he saw David grab Ida Mae and open the door.

"Where are you going?" he murmured.

"I'm taking Mom out for gumbo and beer. Wanna come?"

He was asleep before he could say no.

Now, keyed up by thoughts of yesterday, he got out of bed. Somehow, he was only wearing briefs. He looked on the nightstand where his yarmulke ought to be, but it wasn't there. The room temperature was Siberian, raising goosebumps on his arms and legs. Hugging himself, he unzipped his duffel, grabbed his toothbrush and opened the bathroom door.

The bathroom smelled like a kennel. Popeye, whom he'd forgotten all about, rose from a blanket on the floor and leapt at him. Before he could stop himself, Mayer boxed the dog's ear so hard the animal went down like a sack of potatoes. "I'm sorry, I'm sorry," he whispered. Popeye shook it off and skulked out.

Finally alone, Mayer brushed his teeth and cranked the shower to scalding. Inspired by a verse from Isaiah—"Wash, clean yourselves, remove the evil of your deeds from my eyes"—he scrubbed his skin as if the bar of soap were sandpaper, sloughing off the outermost layer of himself. Afterwards, he wiped the fogged mirror with a hand towel. Because the Torah discouraged male vanity, it had been years since he'd given his reflection more than a passing glance. Even while shaving, he never looked. But now, he felt compelled to size himself up.

He regretted it instantly. All that padding on his cheek, jaws and neck was to be expected. But what accounted for the broadening of his forehead, chin and nose? His figure was worse—a frozen turkey on stilts, the skin white as a fish belly and pebbled with freckles, moles, skin tags and the odd red dot. Threadbare *shtreimels* garlanded each nipple.

It had never dawned on him that his unsightly body might have something to do with Sarah's lights-out mandate in the bedroom. Surely women were drawn to beauty as much as men, and just as repelled by atrophy. If, God willing, he merited Sarah's hand in marriage when this was all over, a top priority would be joining a gym.

The cold air in the bedroom iced his damp skin. Chattering his teeth, he hurried to his duffel and grabbed the first outfit he found, blue jeans and a gray tee. The coarse denim felt at once alien and familiar. He slid his feet into the suede moccasins, which, he had to admit, were quite comfortable.

Popeye was sniffing at his empty food bowl, so Mayer refilled it from the kibble bag. His eyes breezed past the lopsided mountain of bedcovers to the window facing the French Quarter. Daylight had transformed the quarter into a family-friendly precinct where people ate po' boy sandwiches at outdoor cafés, perused T-shirts and postcards at souvenir stores and posed for photos in front of those ever-enchanting Spanish balconies.

He heard the rustle of fabric and looked once more at the tent of bedding. Part of him wanted to strangle David for dragging him to this American Mos Eisley. Another part was fairly desperate for breakfast and needed to stay in his benefactor's good graces to get some.

He was about to rouse his twin when he discerned something peculiar about the comforter. It was less mountain than mountain range, dappled with hills and valleys. David must have burrowed himself in there with all six bed pillows plus the two bolster pillows, Mayer theorized. But both bolsters were on the floor, and three bed pillows were visible outside the coverlet. So what accounted for all that extra mass?

As he puzzled the matter—and he'd keep puzzling until he devised an explanation alternative to the nightmarish one lurking in the back of his brain—the mound underwent a seismic shift. Mountains inverted to valleys and valleys to mountains, and something poked out the bottom. He tried to convince himself otherwise but dropped the feeble pretense, for any idiot could see it was a toe, and not just any toe but one lacquered fire-engine red.

Mayer stumbled back, tripping over himself and falling on his ass. Popeye pushed his snout into the man's face and got a shove in the skull for his trouble.

He thought, *No.*

He thought, *Anything but this.*

He mouthed the first words of the Rosh Hashanah *Hineni* prayer: *Here I am . . . poor in deeds, rattled and afraid.*

The toe went back under the comforter like a snapping turtle's head. Mayer got up and snatched his wallet and phone off the dresser. He grabbed the door handle and threw the door open. He ran down the hallway, turned a corner and collided with a housekeeper's cart. She raised holy hell as toilet paper rolls, towels and shampoo bottles fell everywhere.

He slammed the elevator's down button. When it didn't come immediately, he took the stairs. At ground level he bolted for the exit, heads turning as he half ran, half skated across the just-waxed lobby tiles. He burst out the door into another mercury-popping day, the sun a white disk in the immutable blue, and took his first breath of air since discovering that hell had no bottom.

— CHAPTER 8 —

HE AMBLED BLINDLY BY THE DAYSIDE DENIZENS OF THE FRENCH QUARTER—THE BRUNCHERS AND BUSKERS, panhandlers and streetscape painters, mail carriers, beat cops and stray cats. He drifted past palm and magnolia trees, sycamores, myrtles, hollies and pines, past shops hawking Mardi Gras costumes, voodoo supplies, used books, oil paintings and brass musical instruments. He ambled on until his inner Geiger counter advised him he was outside the invisible fallout radius of the Hotel Monte Cristo.

A night's sleep had done him one solid: he could now see how doomed this enterprise was from the second they pulled out of the car rental lot. It had been a ticking time bomb and, *Baruch Hashem*, it detonated today, and not a week from today when there'd be no time to regroup. Now he could throw himself into what had plainly been the mission all along: get to Brooklyn now and tell Sarah everything.

All he needed was money. The solitary Ulysses Grant in his wallet wouldn't get him to Lafayette, let alone New York. Well, he'd figure out money. But first, food. He was running on fumes; if he didn't get something in him soon—a slice of bread, some orange juice—he'd plotz.

He turned on his phone and set off in search of breakfast. The phone rang instantly—a number with an Atlanta area code. He stared at the number and waited. A breeze from the east carried an ammonia odor that mingled with the smell of lemon soap from a morning street cleaning. A *ding-ding* sounded and a little girl in a sailor dress rode by on a tandem bicycle with her father. When the phone went silent, he pressed the off button—but before it could power down, it rang again.

It was Sarah this time.

He'd answer it and tell her everything, he decided—just disgorge the whole toxic truth without giving her a word in edgewise. It was a reckless and impulsive move, but what a relief it would be to get it all out of him.

Or . . . should he wait until he got to Brooklyn? Apologies were always better in person; this was more confession than apology, but same principle. Also, how effective would he be off the cuff, delirious with stress and grief and malnutrition? With Sarah, one couldn't be careless with words. But now more than ever he ached for the familiarity of her voice. He pressed the green button.

"*Schefele!*" he said.

"Why was your phone off?"

He cawed out a laugh so dry it hurt his throat. "Would you believe I slept in this morning? I only just now realized it was off."

"Who turned it off?" Sarah asked.

"My brother must have."

"Why is your brother touching your phone?"

He could feel his scalp tightening. "I don't know."

"Keep it on you at all times," she said. "I didn't buy it for other people to play with."

"Okay."

A Heineken truck rounded the corner, its big-bore engine roaring.

"What's that noise?" Sarah asked. "Is that a truck?"

"Hmm?"

"Are you outside?"

"I'm home. I mean, by my mother's. By an open window. In my old bedroom." He winced with each lie.

A black Maserati drove by, blasting—what else?—Dominic Day's infernal summer jam that had America shackled by the eardrums. "That is loud,"

Sarah said. "What's going on, Mayer?"

He pressed at his eyelids, causing two ghostly blue circles to appear in his vision. "What can I tell you? The neighborhood's changed."

"All the *schvartzes*," Sarah commiserated, and Mayer, who had always hated that term, cringed. "Well, close the window. I can hardly hear you with all that racket."

"The air conditioner's broken. It's like an oven in here."

"Close it anyway."

"Okay," he said with a sigh, "just a minute." He thumbed the speaker again and broke into a jog, scanning storefronts for asylum. He turned up a narrow side street and spotted a saloon called Le Sous Bock. He ran inside. Chanson française played softly on the stereo.

"Bathroom?" Mayer said.

The bartender had a Teddy Roosevelt mustache and a center part in his pomaded hair. He gave the customer a quick up-and-down. "In the back."

Darting past a pump organ and down a short hallway, Mayer found the door that said *Hommes* on it. He shoehorned himself into a lavatory the size of a janitor's closet, latched the door behind him and freed up his phone's mouthpiece.

"Sorry, that window was a b—" To his horror, he almost said *bitch*. "A beast."

"Something is different about you," Sarah said.

"What's that?"

"Good example: you saying 'What's that.'"

"What's wrong with 'What's that'?"

"Nothing. Normally you just say 'what.'"

"I haven't been myself," Mayer said, rattling his own nerves with the unintended double entendre. "My mother, *zichronah livracha*." Of blessed memory.

"Your mother," Sarah said dubiously.

"Yes."

"Did your suitcase arrive?"

"My suitcase."

She exhaled with a chuff. "Yes! The one the airline misplaced with your tefillin and all your clothes inside. The one I spent two hours on the phone recovering for you."

"Of course, *schefele*, of course. It came this morning, *Baruch Hashem*."

She said nothing.

"Is something wrong?" he asked.

"The airline said they'd call me with a confirmation once they delivered it."

Mayer looked at the stamped tin ceiling. "You expected different from these nudniks? All that matters is it's back with me, *Baruch Hashem*."

"Well, I'm not happy they didn't confirm. I'm going to issue a complaint."

"Don't trouble yourself."

"I'll trouble myself. I bet they'll reimburse me half my plane ticket."

Fingers strummed an atonal chord in Mayer's chest. "Your plane ticket?"

He heard her smile. "Didn't your brother tell you I had a surprise for you?"

"Come to think of it, he did."

"Well," she said, "I booked a flight to Atlanta this Friday."

She got no response.

"Hello? I'm coming for Shabbos."

Silence.

"Hello?"

With great effort, he ejected a few words. "That's wonderful—*geshmak*! I can't believe it. Only . . ."

"Only . . . ?"

"You hate to fly."

"I'll live. And don't worry about food, I'll pack us beautiful Shabbos meals."

"*Schefele*, no."

"No," she echoed, as though unsure of the meaning of the word.

"You're so thoughtful, but please, save the money. I won't be much company for you, and my brother—well, the less you see of him, the better. Anyway, Mrs. Kugel has been cooking for us."

"You're not pleased," she said.

"What a thing to say. Pleased? I'm overjoyed."

"Then why are you telling me not to come?"

"Am I?" he said. "I'm just thinking out loud. Maybe the best thing for me right now is solitude. I'm grieving, you know? Processing."

Now it was she who left him hanging.

"Sarah?" He looked at his screen. "Are you there?"

"The house felt so empty last night."

He took a short breath. "It did?"

"You know how sometimes you don't appreciate the constants in your life until they're not there?"

"Yes . . ."

"I could stand to show you a little appreciation."

Mayer could have torn his hair out. How many years had he davened for Sarah to make this admission? The cruelty of the timing awakened something vindictive in him. Before he could stop himself he said, "Why not stay with your parents?"

Stunned silence. Then: "Are you mocking me?"

"No. Sorry. I was trying to . . ."

She released a world-weary sigh. "To be helpful, as usual. So? Do I have to beg to spend Shabbos with my husband?"

"Of course not, *schefele*," he said. "I should be begging you."

THE MYRIAD LIES he'd told Sarah—seventeen by his count—were like the links of an iron chain hanging from his neck. He dialed Yossi right away.

"*Shalom aleichem!*" the rabbi said. "How's the journey to the Promised Land?"

"Never mind that. I need you to wire me some money. Just enough to get me back to New Moab. I'll pay you back."

A pause. "Where are you?"

"New Orleans."

"You had a falling out with Dovid?"

Mayer's mind's eye caught that flash of toe again, more obscene than a hundred bare breasts on Bourbon Street.

"I don't want to talk about it. Can you front me the money? Please."

"I can Western Union whatever you need. But why come back to New Moab?"

"Sarah's flying down to spend Shabbos with me."

A pause. "But I thought we decided you'd tell her everything after your *giyur*. This way you could break the news to her as a Jew."

"*Mann tracht un Gott lacht*," Mayer said. Man plans and God laughs.

"I don't think this is a good idea, tzadik."

"Join the club."

The rabbi was quiet for a moment. "So you're going to tell her on Friday."

"Apparently."

"That could be awkward."

The understatement drew a dark chuckle out of Mayer. It was like laughing underwater.

Yossi said, "Do you think you'll still make your *giyur* Sunday? You're cutting it a little close."

Mayer tried to think, but his blood sugar was so low he could hardly recall his own surname. "I don't know."

"Alright, one hurdle at a time. We'll see where you stand after Shabbos. Meanwhile, let me deal with Western Union. I'll call you back with a location."

"One more thing," Mayer said. "Did my suitcase arrive?"

"Your suitcase?"

Mayer clenched his teeth so hard his molars squeaked.

"Oy! Forgive me," the rabbi said. "My memory. Chana was supposed to remind me, but lately she's been having senior moments as well. What airline was it again? Let me call them."

"No, just—please—drive over to the house right away and see if by some miracle they left the suitcase on the porch."

"Grabbing my keys as we speak."

Mayer was about to end the call when Yossi said, "Oh, by the way?"

"Yes?"

"You sound different."

"What?"

"I hear an accent," the rabbi said. "A twang. Very slight, but—"

"I've got to go," Mayer said, and hung up.

HE FOUND HIMSELF back on Bourbon Street, wandering without a rudder. He drifted past hole-in-the-wall cigar stores, absinthe bars, record shops, voodoo houses and restaurants boasting the best gumbo in New Orleans. He passed a mule-drawn buggy, the passengers cooling themselves with battery-powered fans. He passed an eight-piece brass band seated on overturned buckets, the vocalist doing a strikingly good Billie Holiday.

Sure, the French Quarter had charm. But for Mayer, real charm was exposed pipes and faux wood paneling, fold-out tables and plastic chairs, floor-to-ceiling shelves buckling from the weight of sacred books. His crowd was Rabbis Akiva, Eliezer, and Elazar ben Azaria, Rashi, the Rambam, the Ramban, the Rashba, the Maharsha, the Mishnah Berurah—all dead, but always referred to in the present tense.

"Excuse me, are you Jewish?"

He spun around. A boy of about fifteen in a black suit and a black fedora stood in the shade of some palm fronds. Before him was a table with a stack of glossy pamphlets, boxes of candles and two velvet bags with Hebrew writing on them.

"What did you say?" Mayer said.

"Are you Jewish?"

Mayer reached for his yarmulke but touched only hair.

The boy picked up one of the bags. "Do you want to put on tefillin?"

"Do I . . ."

"Do you know what tefillin are?"

"No. Yes."

The teen blinked. "Would you like to put on a pair?"

When no reply came, the kid got shifty-eyed. Mayer commiserated. "No thank you."

"It's a quick mitzvah."

"No, I mean—I'm not Jewish."

"Oh." He put the tefillin down.

"But, you know—keep up the good work."

The boy nodded, eyes scanning foot traffic again.

"May you continue to be an *ohr lagoyim*."

The teen snapped his head back in the oddball's direction, but Mayer had already turned his back to him. After a few paces, though, he stopped and turned around. "But if I were Jewish, for argument's sake, where could I go for a kosher breakfast?"

HE ARRIVED A few minutes later at an open-air coffee shop with a green-and-white awning. It was obviously a tourist destination: the line to order was at least thirty people long, and it wasn't even breakfast time. He got behind a young family of four speaking in Mandarin. The dad took family snaps using a selfie stick, the café behind them in every frame. Across the street, a white-haired trumpeter leaned against a wrought iron fence and played Dixieland standards.

The belligerent sun was at its apex by the time Mayer stepped into the shade of the outdoor pavilion. It was packed, and everyone ate the same thing—golden pillows of fried dough dusted with powdered sugar. The aroma taunted his barren stomach. He gave his order to a skinny guy in a starched white shirt, black bow tie and soda jerk hat: two plates of beignets—as the pastries were called—a café au lait and two glasses of ice water. He chugged one water at the counter, then carried the tray into the crowd in search of an empty seat.

Eighteen seconds into his search, he heard someone joyously shout out, "Ese!"

The word blitzed the back of his neck like bird poop. Reflexively he turned to its source. David waved exuberantly from a table twenty feet away, a powdered-sugar mustache on his lip. He looked tan and pristine in a new white polo and crisp linen trousers. Ida Mae was on the table, and in the chair next to David, a woman. She was in her early thirties, slender and long-limbed, wearing denim shorts and a sleeveless blouse. She also wore a knotted head wrap and gold hoop earrings that touched her jawbones. Her skin was Baltic amber, her teeth brilliant white against crimson lips. David said something into her ear and her eyes lit up.

Rival impulses to flee and save face fettered Mayer to the ground. It was perhaps the awkwardest moment of his life. *Goyhood*, he thought—*the state of rebounding from one travesty to the next.* Mercifully, his legs relieved his brain of duty and carried him to the table. He set down his tray and sat without making eye contact with anyone.

Popeye, leashed to a table leg, put his face in Mayer's lap, his docked tail wagging like it got snagged by a fishhook. Powdered sugar dusted the tip of his nose. He'd had a bath since their last encounter and looked worlds better, his coat gleaming, his angry sores pacified by soapy water and clean towels. Mayer pushed him away and locked his knees.

"What did I tell you?" David asked the woman.

"That all roads lead to Café Du Monde," she said.

"Marty, this is Charlayne," David said. "Charlayne, Marty."

She offered her hand. He ignored it. "I've heard so much about you," she said.

Mayer gave a limp nod. His appetite was gone. Why hadn't he just walked away?

"Dave and I met at a silent retreat in El Paso about a year ago," Charlayne said. "We never did get much talking done, but our spiritual bond was instantaneous."

"And unbreakable," David said. "Anyway, I saw on Instagram that she was in New Orleans and figured I'd say hello in person, so we met up last night at Preservation Hall."

"That turned out to be some hello," Mayer muttered. His phone rang and he flipped it open so belligerently that it almost snapped in two. "Tell me you have good news."

"There's three hundred dollars waiting for you at a Western Union at Decatur and Wilkinson," Rabbi Kugel said.

"You're a lifesaver. What about the suitcase?"

"That news, not so good. They left a note saying they'd try again tomorrow."

Mayer blew air through puckered lips. "Did it say what time?"

"No. How about I track it down and pick it up? It's the least I can do."

"You've done more than enough. But please, *please* be there in the morning."

"You can count on me."

Mayer hung up and looked up at his tablemates. David was snapping pictures of Charlayne holding a beignet in her teeth. She did several kittenish poses—head tilted skyward, big smile, medium smile, profile with medium smile.

"Try one," David urged his brother.

"I'm not hungry."

The elder Belkin made a "your loss" face. Charlayne said, "David tells me this is your first time in New Orleans."

Mayer grunted in the affirmative.

"And?"

He shrugged.

"I hear you, it can be a lot. Also—sorry to hear about your mother."

He said nothing.

"Apologies on my brother's behalf," David said. "He's not used to being around women."

"No worries," Charlayne said. "Maybe I'm the one who should apologize. I had to check out of my pensione, and I was gonna just stay out all night and sleep on my ride out of town. But by four in the morning I was the walking dead, and Dave offered me a bed. He said you'd be okay with it."

Mayer shot his brother a look that could curdle milk.

"So," she said, changing the subject, "do you live in Atlanta as well, Marty?"

"Mayer. And no, New York."

"Cool! Whereabouts?"

"Brooklyn."

"Ooh, which part?"

"Kensington."

"Mmmm, don't know Kensington. Is that near Williamsburg? Bed Stuy?"

"I don't know."

Two prolonged seconds passed. The deep-fried smell was making his stomach roil.

She said, "You've got an apartment there, or . . . ?"

"We own a house."

She glanced at his unadorned ring finger. "You and . . . ?"

Mayer tasted something bilious in the back of his throat. "I don't mean to be rude," he said, "but who are you?"

"Hey, lighten up, Ese," David said. "That's no way to talk to a celebrity."

"Oh please," Charlayne said.

"Influencer."

"Better."

"Charlayne's a brand ambassador," David explained unhelpfully. Then, to Charlayne: "Marty's been living in a router-free hobbit hole for thirty years.

It's a long story."

"So you've never heard of Instagram?" Charlayne asked.

"No," Mayer said.

"TikTok, X, YouTube, Facebook?"

"Maybe one or two of those."

"Well," she said—and gave him a sixty-second crash course on social media platforms, branding and influence. "I've been at it for three years. I've been to three continents and thirty-three states, courtesy of my sponsors."

"Fascinating," Mayer said. He scooted his chair back. "Well, Ms. . . . ."

"Valentine. But you can just call me—"

"I ought to be going."

"Going?" said David. "Where?"

"Wait, if you don't mind," Charlayne said. "I want to hear about this hobbit life of yours. It sounds so liberating."

"Like my brother said, it's a long story." As Mayer turned to leave, he felt feminine fingers touch his wrist. He yanked his hand away like a snake had bitten it.

"Jesus, what's gotten into you?" David said.

Mayer couldn't help it: his whole body stiffened. He bared his teeth and clenched his fists. Charlayne looked uneasily from one Belkin to the other, then stood. "Back in a minute."

She threaded her way between tables to the ladies' room. David watched her go. He picked up a beignet from his brother's plate. "Ain't she something?"

Fast as lightning, Mayer slapped the pastry out of David's hand. It sailed over diners' heads and outside the café enclosure, where a flock of rock pigeons set upon it.

"What the royal fuck?" David said.

Through teeth gritted so hard they ached, Mayer said, "One more word and your head's next."

"What did I do?"

Mayer wound up his arm, and David raised his own in self-defense. Half a dozen concerned faces swiveled their way.

"You could have been a good guy," Mayer said, leaning into him. "You had the choice of good and evil, and you went evil."

"What are you talking about?"

"You brought a woman to my bed. *To my bed.*"

A patron rose from his seat and moved swiftly toward the indoor area. David raised two hands in surrender. "Okay, okay, put it into neutral."

"You pig."

David's mouth fell open.

"You planned this all from the very beginning, didn't you? This idiotic New Orleans detour was never about showing me the ethos of a city that marches to the beat of its own drum. It was about rendezvousing with some strange woman you once spent a weekend with, and luring her back to our hotel to have—I'm going to be sick—relations in the same bed as me."

"Wait a minute, Charlayne is no stranger."

The front door to the establishment opened and a manager came out, followed by the patron who'd fetched him. Surmising the probable outcome if he didn't cool it, Mayer sat.

"And we didn't have relations," David said. "She just slept over. We've only ever been friends."

Mayer snorted.

"And even if we did have relations—I mean sex—I'd never do it in the same bed as my own brother. I mean, I've done some kinky shit, but—"

"Yes, I'm sure a bathroom stall or alleyway would've sufficed."

"I might have overstepped my boundaries," David admitted, "but my intentions were pure. It was either she slept with us or on a park bench. Maybe you have no problem leaving people out in the cold, but I do."

David had played the guilt card in Biloxi and it had won him a stray dog. Mayer wouldn't let him play it twice.

"With all your money, you couldn't get her another room?"

"It was four in the morning," David whined. "God, how many times do I have to apologize?"

"How about once?"

The manager, evidently presuming that the worst was over, went back inside.

"And what about our safety?" Mayer said. "What if she'd made off with our wallets while we were sleeping?"

David flapped his hand. "Horseflop."

"You don't know her, not really."

The elder brother was about to counter when his eyes flickered with a notion. "It's because she's Black, isn't it?"

"What?"

David crossed his arms. "You think because she's Black, she'd steal from us."

"I absolutely do not, and I'm appalled you'd say such a thing."

"Maybe I'd better go," said Charlayne. She'd reappeared without either brother realizing it. Her arms were folded across her chest, hands cupping her elbows. "You guys look like you've got some things to work out."

"Oh, no, Marty and I were just having a little brotherly spat."

"Feels like more than a spat."

"Please. You should see the scars we gave each other in the nineties."

"I should really go. I have a bunch of packing to do."

David patted her seat. "Please stay."

"I really don't think I ought to."

"Please?"

Popeye put his chin on the seat and gave her a look that tipped the scales. "Alright, for a few more minutes."

IT WAS ONLY a matter of time before the conversation circled back to the younger twin's twenty-five years a hobbit, at which point David—Mayer too dispirited to object—told Charlayne the whole story.

To his credit, David was a surprisingly skilled narrator—artful and economical, with the good tact to omit Sarah from the narrative. Charlayne sat through it without so much as gesturing or even shifting her weight. She offered her first observation after the tale was done.

"It's like mourning an empty casket."

"Literally," David said.

"But Mayer, my God—how do you come to terms with such a thing?"

"If it's all the same to you, I'd rather not talk about it."

"Of course."

The trumpeter across the street finished "I've Got the World on a String" and moved on to "Potato Head Blues." Mayer asked himself why he was still here.

"So, this journey you're on," Charlayne said, "it's a kind of *Rumspringa*?"

David chuckled. "Kinda."

"What's *Rumspringa*?" Mayer asked.

"You've heard of the Amish, right?" David said.

"Of course."

"So when Amish kids become teens, they set out to experience Western civilization for a while. They dress like us and eat like us, and sometimes surrender to vice like us."

"Why?"

"To figure out while they're young that the pleasures of the world are fleeting, and God and community are permanent."

"I didn't need Rumspringer to figure that out," Mayer said.

"*Rumspringa*," Charlayne corrected him. "Well, it's an important lesson either way. I've been on my own variation for three years, and I can say unequivocally that chasing adventure full time has its perks, but after a while you feel like a dog chasing its tail."

Hearing his cue, Popeye rested his muzzle on her lap. She gave his face a generous rub. "Plus it gets lonely."

Mayer took his first sip of coffee. It was cold. Beyond the enclosure, he saw four birds with orange and black plumage take flight from a banana plant.

Icterus galbulae. Baltimore orioles. Males.

"How about you let us take you to the airport?" David said.

"Oh, I'm not flying."

"Then let us take you to whatever transportation hub you're leaving from. Where are you headed, by the way?"

"Georgia."

"Oh yeah? Whereabouts?"

"It's called Springer Mountain."

Mayer looked Charlayne square in the face for the first time. "You're hiking the Appalachian Trail?"

She nodded.

He couldn't help staring. As a kid he'd dreamed of hiking the epic mountain trail from Georgia to Maine, keeping a log of the birds he saw along the way. He'd thought maybe he'd publish a book about it someday.

"It's kind of late in the season to get started, isn't it?" he said.

"Why's that?" David asked.

"Well," she said, "the trail is 2,190 miles, most of it up and down mountains. Thru-hikers—the ones who hike the whole thing in one shot—usually give themselves six months, and they start out in the spring so that they'll finish before the cold comes."

"I see."

"It's my fault. I spent way too much time planning the trip and buying all this hiking gear. I probably don't even need half of it. And then some sponsorship opportunities came up and the next thing I knew, it was the middle of June."

"What made you want to turn Jim Bridger for six months?" David asked.

Charlayne didn't answer. Her eyes were locked on a pair of twenty-some-things getting up from a nearby table and leaving hand in hand. Mayer noticed she was fingering a gold charm bracelet on her wrist. Then he noticed a scrawl of white lines on the underside of her wrist.

"How will you get to Springer Mountain?" he asked.

She looked at him. "I was going to take the Greyhound from here to Atlanta and then figure it out from there. The trail starts about eighty miles north of the city, so I figured—"

"Greyhound?" David shook his head. "No, no, no. Marty and I'll take you."

"What?" Mayer and Charlayne said in one voice.

"Absolutely."

"Don't be ridiculous," she said. "You just got to New Orleans."

David waved away her objection. "We've done the tourist's terzetto—Bourbon Street, Preservation Hall, Café Du Monde. Besides, I've been here a hundred times, and Marty's hated the place ever since he got here."

"Even so," Charlayne said, "Springer Mountain is hours out of your way."

"That's just it—we don't have a way."

"I'd be a third wheel."

"Perfect. You'll keep us from tipping over."

Charlayne chortled a note of disbelief. "I don't know what to say. You guys are reckoning with the Everest of spiritual crises. What you need is each other, not me."

"What we need," David said, putting a hand on her forearm, "is a break from each other."

"Uh-huh. Who's to say you and your brother won't go *Deliverance* on my ass?"

"God as my witness, Charlayne Valentine, we will deliver you to Springer Mountain unharmed."

Just then a red Mazda convertible came skidding around the corner, blasting music that scattered any pigeons within twenty feet. Charlayne's eyes lit up. She raised her arms and gyrated in her seat. David mirrored her performance. There was a rustle as turning heads put their table in the limelight again, and with shocking speed the table tango sparked a flash mob; diners raised their arms and sang along to the mellifluous chorus.

When hope is gone and the night is endless
I remember your eyes and I see us together
Running hand in hand, making footprints in the sand,
I walk with you, I walk with you

Dancing past last call, making up our own songs
Climbing up rooftops, howling at the moon
Two fools breaking rules, skinny-dipping in the pool
I walk with you, I walk with you

Soon, the whole place was up in arms. Phones came out to document the spectacle—a testament to the unifying powers of a song that was impossible to get out of your head.

— CHAPTER 9 —

MAYER TOOK ONE LOOK AT THE CHEST-HIGH MOUND
COMPRISING CHARLAYNE'S POSSESSIONS AND ASKED HIMSELF WHAT
he'd been asking himself over and over for an hour.

Why am I still here?

His money was at Western Union. His bus was at Union Passenger Terminal. And he was in the lobby of a Beaux Arts pensione waiting to aid a drifter who'd helped herself to his bed this morning. Her mountain of crap included a rucksack big enough to hold a cadaver, sleeping bag, tent, trekker poles, Nalgene bottles, gas stove, cooking fuel, mess kit, a portmanteau's worth of clothing, folding knife, climber's rope, candle lantern, water filter, headlamp, maps, bug spray, GPS, baggies of lentils, boxes of macaroni and cheese, pouches of beef jerky, first-aid kit, tampons, toilet paper, MacBook, and a dog-eared paperback titled *A Grief Observed*.

By a stroke of luck, the pensione's millennial desk clerk was one of Charlayne's more ardent Instagram followers. He'd relinquished her the lobby for storage, cordoning her stuff with stanchions for good measure. He even granted her a post-checkout shower, which was what had the Belkins twiddling their thumbs downstairs. Popeye had to wait outside, leashed to a fire hydrant.

"How's she supposed to lug all this crap for two thousand miles?" David asked.

Mayer didn't answer.

"Ese?"

Silence.

"You're really mad about Charlayne sleeping over?"

Mayer exhaled a long breath. "I'm not going with you to Georgia."

"What?"

"Yossi's wiring me some cash to get me back to New Moab."

David's eyes narrowed. "What's going on?"

"What's going on is you betrayed me and I'll never forgive you."

"Right, but why are you going back to Mom's?"

Mayer mumbled something.

"What?"

He sighed. "Sarah's coming down for the weekend, okay?"

"Bullshit."

"She told me this morning."

"And you didn't tell her no?"

The younger fixed the elder with a stony stare. David shut up. Half a minute later, Mayer sighed again. "She already bought the ticket. There's nothing I can do."

"But she can't see you like this, especially not at that condemned hell house."

Mayer's shoulders rounded slightly.

"Can I at least take you back to Mom's?" David asked. "It's on the way to Springer."

"No."

"It'd be a lot more comfortable than a Greyhound."

"No."

"Well, at least let me drive you to the bus station. We can stop at Western Union on the way."

"Fine. Fine. Let's be quiet now."

Soon came a clatter of metal, and the doors of an ironwork cage elevator parted. Out walked Charlayne in shorts and a Missy Elliott cutoff tee. Her hair, no longer concealed by a headscarf, framed her lovely face in tight, buoyant curls that hung to her neck. She smiled—then looked at the heap and turned contrite.

"Lend a girl a hand?"

IT TOOK FOUR rounds of trunk Tetris to load everything, the back seat bearing the overflow. Charlayne volunteered to squeeze in the back with Popeye.

"Don't be silly," David said. "You take shotgun. Marty's getting off at the bus terminal."

She looked disappointed. "Really?"

"I have to get back to our mother's house," Mayer said, "to tie up some loose ends."

"But isn't that on our way? Let's all drive up together."

"No," he said in a tone that put a lid on the matter. She got in front while Mayer crammed in with Popeye on the lumpy bed of camping supplies in the back. His hair brushed the ceiling and he couldn't see his feet. What he could see was the urn between Charlayne's thighs, and for a fraught moment he wondered what it would feel like to trade places with Ida Mae for a few minutes.

They drove to the Hotel Monte Cristo to pack up and check out, then Western Union to pick up Mayer's three hundred dollars. From there they went to Union Passenger Terminal, a 1950s modernist building downtown.

"We'll wait here till you're all set," David said.

"No need." Mayer grabbed his duffel, and with a curt "Bye" walked inside without looking back. Ignoring the splendid wall murals depicting scenes of the history of the Big Easy, he approached a ticket window staffed by a bespectacled woman and requested a one-way bus ticket to Atlanta.

She punched a few keys into her computer, then craned her neck to see down her bifocals. "Next bus at nine-ten."

He looked at the clock. It said two thirty-two.

"There's nothing sooner?"

"Next bus at nine-ten."

"When does it get to Atlanta?"

"Seven twenty-five tomorrow morning."

Purgatory, he thought. Was there anything worse than a bus that made stops? Then again, by the time he boarded he'd probably be so tired he'd sleep most of the ride.

"One ticket, please."

"Seventy-eight dollars."

He counted out four twenties.

"Hang on," the woman said, staring at her screen. "Bus sold out."

Mayer's heart sank. "When's the next bus?"

"Nine-fifteen in the morning."

"How about the train?"

"There's one train per day to Atlanta and that also leaves nine-fifteen in the morning."

He pictured how his life would play out over the next eighteen hours— the food, the lodging, the transportation to and from the station, the endless pacing back and forth. And then the trip itself.

"Well?" she said.

TO DEPART THE Crescent City, David opted for the Lake Pontchartrain Causeway, the twenty-four-mile span linking suburban New Orleans to St. Tammany Parish. The thermometer hit one hundred and one just as they merged onto the I-10.

"So what about you, Char?" he said.

"What about me?"

"Well, in the short time we've known each other—and that's counting our silent weekend in El Paso—you've had no problem teasing out the perti-nent details of our lives."

Charlayne half smiled. "But."

"But."

She watched Caesars Superdome drift past her window. "I'm not great at talking about myself. Call me your standard-issue Insta extrovert slash real-life introvert."

"Why introvert?" David said.

"Oh, you know. Part nature, part nurture."

"I'm listening."

"Well, my hometown wasn't exactly the touchstone of diversity. We were the only Black family on my street."

"Where's this?"

"Duluth, Minnesota. Don't get me wrong, it wasn't bad, comparatively speaking. It was a lot of white folks with good intentions. But sometimes you wanted to ride your bike to the corner store without seeing your otherness in their eyes. The teacher always knew my name, know what I mean?"

They crossed the Seventeenth Street Canal, where the interstate joined the Pontchartrain Expressway. "It's funny," David said. "Marty's and my childhood was the film negative of yours."

"You were the only whites on the block?"

"Yeah."

"So you know what it's like."

"Not really. Everybody treated us like we were one of them."

Ahead, the causeway narrowed to a needlepoint on the horizon. A string of brown pelicans flew close to the brackish water to the east, prowling for speckled trout, sheepshead and redfish.

"So what else?" David asked.

"What else do you want?" Charlayne asked. "My CV?"

"Why not?"

She gave it. An only child of two doting parents, she graduated from high school with honors. She went to Stanford, then Columbia for her MBA, and got a job at Goldman Sachs as a financial analyst. After two years, she left New York and moved back to Duluth.

"How come you moved back?"

"So I could marry my high school sweetheart."

"Awww."

"It ended."

"Ah. When?"

"Three years ago. Hey, look at that." She pointed to their ten o'clock, where an angler on a charter boat a half mile away was reeling in something huge, his rod bent to the shape of a question mark.

"You boys know all about that, I'm sure," Charlayne said.

"Fishing?" said David.

"Someone you love derailing your life."

"Depends who you ask," David said, glancing in the rearview at Mayer. "My brother blames God, not our mother."

Mayer, in that instant, had a crushing epiphany: he could have simply flown to Atlanta. "I do not blame God," he said.

"Oh yeah, I keep forgetting—according to you, gentiles are God's belly button lint. Who could blame the Lord for flicking us in the wind?"

Charlayne turned around. "You really think that?" she said.

"David oversimplifies," Mayer said.

Forty feet ahead of them, a flock of purple martins traced lines across the sky. David tapped his phone, and on came a gentle acoustic lick, soon accompanied by the quavering tenor of John Denver extolling his favorite state in the union.

"I don't know," Charlayne said, "I wasn't religious growing up but I did go to Sunday school for a minute, and I remember how they'd speak of God in fatherly terms. That's how I always pictured him: a loving father who gets surly sometimes, but there's always that underlying love."

She looked at Mayer, who did not look back. "It's okay to be angry at

God, you know."

"Okay," he said.

"You're not mad?"

"No."

"You devoted your life to God only to get the rug pulled out from under you, and you're not mad."

"That's correct."

Her mouth an inverted U, she faced forward again. John Denver finished his ode to West Virginia, then rhapsodized about being a country boy. A pencil line appeared far ahead where water met sky. Over the next few miles, the line thickened to green crayon.

Charlayne saw a book wedged spine-down in the passenger door compartment and took it out. "No way! I had one of these when I was a kid. Whose is this?"

David arced his thumb over his shoulder. She turned around again. "You're a birder?"

"It was a childhood hobby," Mayer said.

"Me too. I was the youngest member of the Duluth chapter of the Audubon Society."

He sat up a little straighter. "Oh yeah?"

"Don't laugh, but I actually thought I wanted to be an ornithologist one day. In fact . . . why are you looking at me like that?"

"No reason."

"Anyway, I used to ride my bike every Sunday to Hawk Ridge, this nature reserve a few miles from my house."

"Hawk Ridge?" Mayer said, altogether forgetting to be aloof. "That's one of the best raptor sites in the country."

"That's right," Charlayne said. "You've been?"

"No, but—wow. What a gift to live so close."

"Oh, I was spoiled. I saw more eagles than blackbirds. I saw hawks, falcons, owls. I saw some Cooper's hawks. I saw a few gyrfalcons."

"I never saw a gyrfalcon. What was that like?"

"Everything you'd hope for. And bald eagles."

"I never saw a bald eagle either," Mayer said. "They were still on the endangered list when I was a kid."

"I've seen quite a few. They're the best."

"I bet."

David emitted a loud snoring noise. Charlayne ignored him. "How about you? What was your favorite birding spot?"

"We didn't have anything like Hawk Ridge," Mayer said. "I'd sometimes go to Moose Hill, which was pretty good for warblers, tanagers, grosbeaks."

"Nice," Charlayne said.

"But mostly I liked to hang around this pine forest near us. One time I was out there by myself and saw a red-tailed hawk up close."

"Oh wow!"

"I'm sure you've seen a million red-tailed hawks," he said.

"Not that far south," Charlayne said. "That's very special."

"God, get a room," David said.

She swatted him on the arm. Then she flipped through the book some more, stopping here and there to read the pen notes in the margins.

"Do you still bird?" Mayer asked.

"Not as much as I'd like to, though I'll definitely keep my eyes to the skies on the AT. Do you?"

The green line in the distance was now a vibrant landscape of oaks and cypress trees dappled with stately lakeside homes. Many had docks jutting into the water with fishing boats moored beside them.

"Brooklyn's no place for a birder," he said. "Not my neighborhood, anyway."

"No trees?"

"There's trees, just no birders."

"How come?"

"It's hard to explain."

"Is it a Jewish thou-shalt-not?"

"No."

"Do Jews dislike birds?"

"No, it's just that people in my community tend to have common interests."

"And birding isn't one of them."

"Right."

"And you don't want to be the only Jew in Kensington carrying around binocs and a field guide."

"Right."

IT WAS CLOSE to three o'clock when they rolled off the causeway into the affluent suburbs of St. Tammany Parish. Condensation rose from sun-boiled wetlands, bringing to mind the old Hollywood tactic of putting cheesecloth over the camera lens to soften the focus for love scenes.

"I'll tell you something, Char," David said. "My brother was the only guy I knew who made bird-watching look cool."

"Oh?"

"He was a pint-sized Brando: moody, mysterious, kind to children and animals. Smart as a whip too. Taught me everything I know—how to ride a bike, how to blow smoke rings, how to shoplift."

Charlayne cast a playful glance behind her. "I bet the girls were all over you, Hawkeye."

Hawkeye? Mayer thought.

"You should've seen them swoon when he rode around on his beat-up bike with a cigarette tucked above his ear." David looked in the rearview. "Bro, if you'd hung around New Moab another year or two, you'd've been chin-deep in poon."

"Dave!" shrieked Charlayne—but Mayer, who'd seen it coming, had already cut the wire linking ears to brain. Popeye took that moment to tentatively rest his muzzle on his seatmate's thigh. Receiving no objection, he closed his eyes.

At Slidell, David merged north onto the I-59. They crossed Old Pearl River, then blazed a trail through the northwest tip of Honey Island Swamp, a mossy wilderness of cypress and tupelo trees in which lurked alligators, wild boars and, if the stories were to be believed, a seven-foot-tall Sasquatch known as the Honey Island Swamp Monster. Two minutes later they were in Mississippi.

The miles passed quickly as David entertained Charlayne with tales of the Belkins' boyhood. There was the frigid February night they got stuck high in the branches of an old oak and kept each other awake until dawn telling dirty jokes and ghost stories; the time they were crawling through a marsh looking for ducks' eggs when a water moccasin bit David's forearm, swelling it to the girth of a young tree trunk; the time Marty hit a line drive that struck Ida Mae's boyfriend Lee in the solar plexus, stopping his heart for a minute.

"I'm confused," Charlayne said. "Are these the good memories or the bad ones?"

"The good!"

"In that case, your mother deserves a medal for putting up with you two reprobates."

Mayer would have preferred they drive nonstop through the Magnolia State, but the others wanted to stop in Hattiesburg for an early dinner. Mayer wouldn't eat nonkosher food, so they made a quick stop at a Piggly Wiggly for a box of snack crackers and a mini jar of mayonnaise.

"That's the opposite of food," Charlayne said.

"I practically lived off this stuff in yeshiva," Mayer said.

The others decided on a Yelp-recommended soul food spot called Grigg's Diner. David, Charlayne, Popeye and Ida Mae went in while Mayer sat in the car and ate his first solid food since Tuesday morning. Then he went into the restaurant, where he found his company at a corner table.

"Perfect timing," David said. "I was just about to tell Char my favorite Marty story of all time."

Mayer sat. The place had a rustic vibe, with unvarnished pine floors, exposed brick walls on which hung paintings by local artists, and furniture built from repurposed barnwood.

"The thing about my brother," David said, "is he hated to fight. But when he had to, there were none better."

"You're kidding," Charlayne said.

"Don't get me wrong, I could hold my own too. The difference was, I was your garden-variety bruiser. I went home with bloody knuckles. His knuckles were always dry."

"How'd he pull that off?"

David pointed to his mouth. "Words. Did you ever get in a confrontation with somebody and you couldn't think of the right thing to say, and only after it was long over did you come up with the perfect dig?"

"Of course."

"Marty always had the perfect line when he needed it. Like he was reading off a movie script."

"My brother's good with lines too," Mayer said, "especially hyperbolic ones."

David raised a palm. "Everything I'm about to tell you is true, so help me God. There was a kid named Beau Pruitt."

"David, don't," Mayer said.

"Who's Beau Pruitt?" asked Charlayne.

"Beau was this inbred miscreant, a genuine bad seed. He used to shoot at kids with—I kid you not—a hopped-up paintball gun loaded with ball bearings."

Charlayne clapped a hand over her mouth.

A waiter came with their drinks: a Yuengling for Charlayne, a milk stout for David, and for Mayer, a Dr Pepper with a lemon slice on the rim of the glass.

"Beau was twisted," David said. "I could tell you more about him but you'd lose your appetite."

"How was this kid allowed to run rampant?" Charlayne asked.

"His dad was sheriff of Moab. That's the town over from ours, very chichi. Moms and dads in New Moab were afraid to call the cops on Beau because of what his dad might do. Think Sheriff J. C. Connors in *White Lightning*."

"Never saw it."

"Well, you ought to. Anyway, one day Beau and a couple of other guys decided to go hunting for some easy prey who'd crossed the border from New Moab. You remember his two bootlickers, Ese?"

Mayer stabbed the ice in his glass with a straw. "Denny Riggs and Ryan McMurty."

The waiter arrived with their food: hot tamales and corn on the cob for David, fried catfish and okra for Charlayne and a chicken-fried steak for Popeye. David took a few bites before picking up where he left off.

"Beau and Denny and Ryan never gave Marty and me problems because they knew we could hold our own. We'd go to Moab all the time; they've got the big old plantation houses and live oak trees and flowers everywhere, and the best nature spots, too, like the pine woods Marty was telling you about. Well, one Saturday we took a ride out to the pines, which were way out on the outskirts of Moab. Along the way, we heard something."

"Heard what?"

"The most godawful screams coming from just over a rise. It sounded like a coyote that got itself run over and was still alive. Marty and I looked at each other thinking the same thing: should we turn around and go home? 'Cause even though nobody from Moab ever gave us trouble, nobody was rolling out the red carpet for us, either, if you know what I mean."

He picked up a cob of corn and glazed it with a pat of butter.

"Well, we went ahead to see what it was. Denny and Ryan were holding a kid by his arms, and Beau was using him for target practice from about thirty feet away. He kept nailing him in the ribs and chest, not hard enough to maim, but enough to break skin."

The whites of Charlayne's eyes appeared to turn pink. She dropped her fork on her plate and pushed it away. "I suppose no one walking by could find it in themselves to put a stop to it."

"In fairness," David said, "there's hardly any foot traffic in Moab beyond downtown. Most of the houses are too far back from the road to make it worth anyone's while. But no doubt in my mind, folks were watching from their windows."

"So what happened?"

"Well, Marty and I happened to be good friends with the kid on the ground. He lived two doors down from us, in fact."

"Chris LaPree," Mayer murmured. He was staring at the bubbles rising to the top of his glass.

"That's right," David said. "We used to go to his house all the time to play Legend of Zelda. His mother'd feed us dinner because she knew all we had to eat at home was Spam on toast."

"What ever happened to Chris?" Mayer asked.

"He went to Georgia Tech on full scholarship. Lives in California now, works for Google."

"Good for him."

"So what happened next?" Charlayne asked.

David smiled. "Marty did his thing."

He pantomimed shaking a cigarette out of a box and sticking it into the corner of his mouth, then flicking up the lid of a Zippo, lighting the stick, snapping shut the lid, taking a deep drag and blowing the imaginary smoke out his nostrils.

"He just stood there with his cig like Tommy Lee Jones, waiting for someone to say something. It was enough to rattle Denny and Ryan, who were really just pussies anyway. They let go of Chris and sort of faded away. But Beau held his ground. He looked at Marty and me and said, 'I'm looking for a couple of deputies.'

"'Say that again,' Marty said. Beau did.

"'I just wanted to know for sure,' Marty said.

"'Know what?'

"'If you're really as stupid as you look.'"

Charlayne sucked in air through her teeth.

"Now mind you, Black or white, rich or poor, nobody talked to Beau Pruitt that way. So he just blinked his eyes a few times, like he wasn't sure he'd heard right. I was tending to Chris, and he and I looked at each other like we'd pinned the wrong guy for crazy."

Mayer sipped his soda, a funny little grin on his face.

"Before Beau could find his words, Marty said, 'You ever heard of Rodney King?' At the time, Rodney King was still a household name. Beau looked at Marty like he'd just asked him to name all the signatures on the Declaration of Independence."

"Unreal," Charlayne said.

"So Marty told Beau who Rodney King was, and you could tell by the look on Beau's face that he didn't get the relevance. See, Beau was an equal opportunity sadist, but Chris happened to be Black. So Marty said, 'What if word gets out that the son of the Moab sheriff drove a Black kid out of town with a paint gun loaded with ball bearings? He'll be out of a job faster than a fat kid chasing an ice cream truck.'"

"Daaamn."

"Wait, it gets better," David said. "Beau's face contorted and turned all colors. See, his only takeaway was that someone just talked shit about his old man. He cocked the rifle and aimed point-blank at my brother's face. He said, 'You take that back or I'll shoot your eye out.'"

"No," Charlayne said.

"Yes. Everything went quiet. The breeze died. Even Chris stopped squirming. All I could think was, 'Take it back, Marty. Just take it back.'"

"Tell me he didn't take it back."

"Would I be telling you this story if he did? He took a half step forward and pressed his eye socket flush against the barrel. And he said, 'Your dad wouldn't get hired as a shopping mall rent-a-cop.'"

Charlayne picked up her napkin and waved it in surrender. "No bullshit, Hawkeye—did you really do that?"

"Have him tell the legend of Paul Bunyan next," Mayer said.

David slapped the table so hard the fork and knife rattled on his plate. "God as my witness, I'm telling it like it happened. The quotes, everything, verbatim."

Charlayne sat back and folded her arms. "Go on."

"So again, there was this absolute stillness in the air, like the whole world had stopped to watch how this was going to play out. Beau's finger was white against the trigger, and you could see the sweat running down his face in little rivers. And Marty went, 'You'd better pull that trigger or they'll brand you the biggest pussy in Moab.'"

Charlayne made a show of looking at the clock.

"Beau's face got so red that even his eyes turned red. And then . . ." David looked at the ceiling like it was a projector screen playing the movie adaptation. "He started to cry. He lowered the gun until the barrel touched the sidewalk, and he just bawled his eyes out. It was the most beautiful thing I ever saw."

Charlayne slow clapped three times.

David held a hand up. "Wait for the kicker."

"Love a good kicker," she said, dry as stale bread.

David leaned into the table. "Marty still had the cigarette in his mouth. He took it out and flicked it against Beau's chest. Then he grabbed the gun out of his hands and axed it on the ground—just Pete Townshended the shit out of it until all he was left holding was the metal rod, which he handed back to Beau."

"That's great," she said.

"I tell you, it happened just the way I said."

"Uh-huh."

"Back me up, Ese."

"I was on the edge of my seat," Mayer said. "Should we get the check?"

"Yep," Charlayne said.

David raised a finger to counter, let it drop. He sagged in his chair, lowering his chin to his chest until he resembled a deflated beach ball.

BACK IN THE car, David offered his passengers a joint. Mayer wouldn't even look at it. Charlayne said, "Why not?" On the exhale she started coughing until tears ran down her face.

"Goddamn. You play hardball."

They conversed in fits and starts through stage two of their Mississippi tour, leaving most of the orating to Bob Dylan. As the Bard lamented about the luckless, the abandoned and forsaken, Charlayne fingered her charm bracelet and watched slash pines whiz past her window. Mayer rehearsed and re-rehearsed his two-pronged pitch to Sarah the day after tomorrow—the bomb drop, the white flag. Popeye took it easy, his head on Mayer's thigh. David just drove.

Around seven o'clock, with plenty of sunlight to go, David spotted a hand-painted wood sign by the exit for Pachuta and got off there. He turned onto the state highway, passing an A&I and a Dollar General before pulling onto the grassy shoulder behind a pickup whose bed was full of watermelons. A Hispanic man with thick forearms got out of the truck holding a machete. He and David exchanged a nod. The man grabbed a watermelon and placed it on a table made of plywood and sawhorses. He chopped it in two with one stroke, and with admirable speed carved it up. In the evening sun the flesh looked aggressively red, like it had leached the saturation out of the countryside to get that way.

When he was done carving, he beckoned the travelers out of the car. Popeye bounded off to pee. The others sat on plastic lawn chairs lined abreast under the shade of a dogwood tree, where a tomcat lay sprawled out on the grass. The man handed out slices on paper plates and set a tray with the rest on the ground. Forgetting himself for a moment, Mayer said the blessing of *Borei Pri HaEtz*—thanking the Almighty for creating fruits—and dug in. It was luscious and sweet and had a pleasing snap. They all ate leaning forward so that the juice bled on the grass instead of their laps.

Popeye trotted back from his pee and sniffed the cat, who didn't move. David offered him a wedge of melon and was rebuffed, so he got the water bowl from the car and put it on the ground by his chair. Popeye lapped water while the others ate as though they could never stop. Charlayne broke stride only to take selfies with juice dripping down her chin. When only rinds remained, their benefactor appeared with another melon. They accepted it with alacrity, but only managed half before throwing in the towel. David leaned back and basketed his fingers over his distended belly.

"You look like a boa constrictor that just ate a hippo," Charlayne said.

Mayer leaned back too, so he could more easily watch two turkey vultures— big and dark with dihedral wings and gloriously ugly heads—circle above. He listened to the buzzing of insects and the river-like rush of the interstate, and, from somewhere just out of view, the languid ringing of cowbells.

"Do you miss her?"

He looked at Charlayne. "Who?"

"Your wife."

He gave a tentative smile. "Who told you I was married?"

"No one. But you carry a certain . . . How do I put it? A telling disquiet. Do you have kids?"

He thought of the thousands of prayers for conception that, unbeknownst to him, had vaporized into irrelevance the instant they'd left his mouth. "Working on it."

"If that's work, I'd love to know what play is," David said.

"What's her name?" Charlayne asked.

He told her.

"What's she like?"

He'd normally have punted the question but, watermelon drunk, he felt like humoring her. "Her father's a major Talmudic authority, one of the greatest of his generation."

"Impressive. But what's she like?"

"In my community we call someone like her a *balabusta*."

"I think it's pronounced 'ballbuster,'" David said. Nobody laughed.

"What's a *balabusta*?" Charlayne asked.

"It's Yiddish for 'good homemaker.'"

She raised an eyebrow.

"Not literally," he quickly added. "I mean, yes, literally, but also euphemistically. It means she's got all her ducks in a row, inside and outside the home."

It felt odd to discuss Sarah, particularly in this pastoral setting and particularly with Charlayne.

"I can see why you're so eager to get back to her," she said.

He shrugged. "She's my *beshert*."

Her eyes turned dewy. "Your destiny."

"My destiny."

— CHAPTER 10 —

NOT LONG AFTER GETTING BACK ON THE INTERSTATE, THEY SAW A BILLBOARD FEATURING JIM MORRISON IN HIS ICONIC "Young Lion" pose. His eyes were balls of orange flame. Below the image were the words "BABY LIGHT MY FIREWORKS in 30 Miles."

"You know," Charlayne said, "when the intelligentsia ridicule the South, I always tell them, 'Withhold judgment until you've lit up a mess of fireworks in a Mississippi parking lot.'"

"Have you?" Mayer asked.

"I have not. This is actually my first time in the backcountry."

"And?" David asked.

"Pleasant, but . . . let's give it a shot in the arm." She reached for the radio console—tuned to Bob Dylan croaking out a particularly dismal live recording of "The Groom's Still Waiting at the Altar"—and punched the tuner to FM, hitting paydirt on the first clear frequency.

When hope is gone and the night is endless
I remember your eyes and I see us together
Running hand in hand, making footprints in the sand,
I walk with you, I walk with you

Charlayne cranked the volume and harmonized rhapsodically.

Dancing past last call, making up our own songs
Climbing up rooftops, howling at the moon

Two fools breaking rules, skinny-dipping in the pool
I walk with you, I walk with you

Mayer felt movement on his thigh and saw Popeye with his paws over his ears. Charlayne saw it too, and disintegrated into laughter. "I hear you, Pop, but I can't help it. This song makes me feel like I'm sixteen and in love for the first time."

That last sentiment made the Belkins exchange wide-eyed glances in the rearview.

"Extra points 'cause of Dominic's backstory," she added.

Mayer remembered the news clip on TV that morning showing the wheelchair-bound Dominic Day serenading seventy-four thousand delirious girls and their grin-and-bear-it moms and dads. "What's his backstory?"

"Oh my God, you don't know? When he was eight or nine, he was in a car with his parents and baby sister. A deer came out of nowhere and his dad swerved, and the car ended up upside down at the bottom of a ravine. When a rescue team found them three days later, Dominic was the only one still alive."

"Man," Mayer said.

"Puts things in perspective, doesn't it?"

The earwormy chorus repeated over and over. Mayer found the lyrics puerile and cloying, but he had to admit the rousing, urgent hook had a way of getting in one's bloodstream.

"Oh shit!" David said, grinning at the rearview. Charlayne spun around and flashed a triumphant smile.

"What?" Mayer said.

"You were singing," she said.

"No I wasn't."

"You absolutely were," David said. "And it was magnificent."

Charlayne raised her arms and did the seat belt boogie. "C'mon, Hawkeye, let's live like there's no tomorrow and no yesterday."

Mayer felt his face burning. "No."

"C'mon!"

"No!"

David and Charlayne went ahead without him, chorusing so stirringly that for a minute you could almost believe Dominic Day might one day walk again.

THE SUN WAS liquid red on the horizon when David peeled off the interstate twenty miles from the Alabama border. He followed a country road eastbound through a commercial district fallen into decay. Plywood paned windows and doorways. Two-foot-tall weeds propagated from sidewalk cracks. Even the graffiti looked forsaken, washed out over untold rainy seasons.

"I'll bite," Charlayne said. "Where are you taking us, Dave?"

"You said you wanted to see the real South."

"Did I?"

Gravel smacked Daisy's undercarriage like birdshot. She passed a field of rusting auto parts, where a sad-looking mutt sniffed at a pile of fast-food cardboard packaging. She passed a discount liquor store, an indoor flea market and a Papa Luigi's Pizza—all shuttered. She passed a gas station getting swallowed by vegetation, and Mayer could have sworn he saw a wild boar foraging in a pokeweed patch between two pump islands.

David leaned over the dash, his nose almost touching the windshield. "Where the hell is it?"

"Where's what?" Charlayne asked, a shadow of unease in her voice.

The scenery abruptly turned bucolic. For a mile and a half, they drove through cow pastures and sugarcane acreage, David's eyes metronoming the horizon. They passed a Confederate graveyard of listing headstones half-concealed in tall grass. Finally, David smacked the wheel with his palm. "Hell with it, I'm turning back."

"Hell with what?" Charlayne said. "You're starting to unsettle me, Dave."

"Sorry. I had a surprise for you guys, but . . ." His sentence faded out when he saw a flicker of light at his one o'clock. "Hello."

A quarter mile up the road was an old warehouse. A banner hung loosely across the front facade. It read "BABY LIGHT MY FIREWORKS." Charlayne let out a Minnie Mouse squeal and clapped her hands.

"Surprise!" David said.

"You idiot." She gave his arm an affectionate squeeze.

The building looked like a decommissioned Army barracks, with cinderblock walls and a corrugated steel roof. But the lights were on and there was a Chevy Silverado parked by a side entrance. The air was funky with cordite. Charlayne hit the ground running the moment Daisy came to a full stop and was inside the store before you could say Claude Ruggieri.

"Our kind of girl, right?" David said.

"Have you seen my yarmulke?" Mayer asked. "I took it off just before the state trooper came up to talk to us, and haven't seen it since."

"No idea. Hey, what's with Popeye?"

The dog was whimpering like he hadn't whimpered since Biloxi. His ears were perked, the hairs on his spine upright.

"Must be the smell in the air," Mayer said. "I bet his previous owner had guns."

David tried to rub Popeye's head, but the animal rebuffed him, bobbing and weaving and never taking his eye off the store.

"Hey, Ese?"

"Yeah?"

"Letting Charlayne sleep in our bed? That was really shitty of me."

Mayer scratched a mosquito bite on his ankle. "No way to undo it. Let's just put it behind us."

"So we're cool?"

"Don't push it." He opened his door.

"Ese?"

Mayer waited.

"Don't go back to Mom's."

He sighed. "I have to. Sarah already bought her plane ticket."

"I bet it's refundable."

"That's not the issue."

They both got out of the car. David said, "Tell her you've got, I dunno, round-the-clock diarrhea. And you're pretty sure it's contagious."

"First of all, ew. Second, if I have any chance of winning her back, it's got to be done honestly. You can't build a relationship on lies."

The elder brother lifted a finger like he had a rejoinder, but all he emitted was an exhalation. "Okay. I'll have you in New Moab before noon tomorrow."

"I appreciate that."

David looked at Popeye. "C'mon, Pop." The dog didn't move. He clapped his hands twice together, but the dog still didn't move.

"Huh. What do you think we should do?"

"Tie him up by his leash somewhere?" Mayer said.

"No way. That's how we found him, remember?"

After a brief discussion, they agreed to leave Popeye in the car with the windows down. He seemed to enjoy the back seat anyway, and a gentle breeze kept the temperature near tolerable. But he whined pitifully when the brothers left him.

"We'll be back before you know it," David called over his shoulder.

LATER, AT THE hospital, Mayer would recall how that first step into BABY LIGHT MY FIREWORKS reminded him of Dorothy's iconic first step into the Technicolor Land of Oz. On shelves stacked fourteen feet high were what had to be every make and model of pyrotechnic known to man: fountains, ground spinners, sparklers, Roman candles, missiles, bottle rockets, yellow jackets, cherry bombs, aerial repeaters, beehives, flying fish, artillery shells, mortars, comets, good old-fashioned firecrackers, and all the subclasses and sub-subclasses thereof.

In New Moab, the boys' access to fireworks was limited to whatever Mr. Li kept in a back room at his corner store at Dixieland and Stephens—mostly Cold War-era surplus for which all sales were final. Whereas *this* embarrassment of riches, well. In open-mouthed ebullience Mayer rounded aisle after aisle of splashy packages with evocative names—"Storm Force"; "Destiny"; "Beast"; "Red, White, BOOM!"; "Grounds for Divorce." There were chickens that laid explosive eggs, tanks that shot off patriotic sparks, exploding Supreme Leaders of North Korea.

So enraptured was he that, coming out of aisle four, he nearly collided with a shopping cart teetering with goods. When his eyes met those of the cart's operator he had to smile; at last, he and his brother had found common ground. "Hell of an upgrade from old Mr. Li's, eh?" David said.

Mayer inspected the chest-level pile. "Think this will hold us?"

"Maybe for twenty minutes."

Charlayne emerged from aisle seven and started toward the Belkins. The look on her face at seeing the overloaded cart sent the boys into peals of laughter. "I had a feeling all along you guys were terrorists," she said.

"Now that you mention it, our mom used to call us that," Mayer said.

"Let's get out of here," David said. "The pyro in me is itching to raise hell."

The cashier was forty or so, bald, with a doughnut of hair grown long and tied in a greasy ponytail. His pallor was waxy, his eyes a shade lighter than black. His yellow T-shirt had once been white.

"You may close early today, huh?" David said companionably, beckoning to his overloaded cart.

Making no indication he'd heard the remark, the clerk stared at Charlayne with an odd expression.

"Hello?" David said.

Eyes glued on Charlayne, the guy stooped to pick up an old Folgers coffee can off the floor. He spat a brown gob into it and set it back down. Uncomfortable, Charlayne let her own gaze drop onto a string of plastic flags with southern crosses hanging from the counter edge.

"Over here, cowboy," David said.

The clerk snapped to. He glanced at the cart, then at David. "Well? You wanna get rung up or just stand there till kingdom come?"

David looked like he had a retort ready, but kept it in the chamber and started transferring merchandise from cart to counter. The man slid the packages across the barcode reader and shoved them to the bagging area. Mayer stepped forward to assist, but froze upon seeing the letters "AB" tattooed in blue-gray ink on the guy's hairy forearm. A cardboard clatter broke his trance and he looked at the bagging area, where overaccumulation was sending boxes overboard. He told the clerk to hold it.

David paused unloading the cart to ebb the logjam, but the clerk kept shoving packages into the pile as if on autopilot, sending several more to the floor. As the boys stooped to rescue what had fallen, the counterman took the opportunity to lock eyes with Charlayne and slowly run his liver-colored tongue across his lips. He then whipped a pack of arrowheads across the counter, knocking three more items to the floor.

"What the hell, man?" David said.

"This is a self-bagging operation. Ain't my fault if you just leave 'em there to fall off."

"You never said it was self-bag."

"You never asked."

David's jaw hardened but, still giddy about bringing in the Fourth of July early, he let it go. He asked his brother to bag what had been scanned. But before Mayer could begin, the clerk slammed another box into the pile, knocking off two more. Mayer stooped to pick everything up, but David told him to halt. "What's your name?" he asked the counterman.

"Huh?"

"Huh?" he aped. "Your name."

"Clete."

"As in Cletus? I don't know what your problem is, Cletus, but let's expedite the bullshit so we can get on with lighting these fireworks and you can go back to, I don't know, raping livestock. Be a good guy and pick up what you dropped, and we'll pay and be out of your hair—or what's left of it."

Clete swirled dip around his cheek. "You mean what you dropped on account of not bagging."

A pale blue vein rose down the center of David's forehead. He closed his eyes and the vein sank back down. "I'll tell you what: let me speak to your boss."

Clete hooted, a jarring sound. "That's my pop. But he ain't around."

"Say that again?"

"He ain't around."

"You're telling me your pop leaves you alone to run this place?"

"My pop don't give a fart. Store's been nothin' but a pain in his ass since he won it in a dice game." This information appeared to have a wilting effect on David, which in turn enlivened the counterman.

"Cletus?" David said.

"That's my name."

"Pick that shit up off the floor or so help me God."

"Nope."

David's forehead vein reappeared, pulsing visibly in the light of the high bay directly above. "Pick that shit up off the floor, goddamnit. I won't tell you again."

Clete rocked back on his heels and grinned at Charlayne. "Better get your oil driller to a hospital," he said, "before that nasty-ass blood vessel on his head pops all over my floor."

"You did *not* just say that to me, you redneck motherfucker," she seethed. "I'm gonna—"

But before she could finish her sentence, David belted out a bitter roar and arm-swept the counter, scattering pyrotechnics everywhere. He picked up a Roman candle at his feet and pitched it at a display of novelty fireworks, knocking more than half the items to the floor. Mayer took his brother by the elbow, but David jerked free. "Fuck that. Fuck that. He's gonna pick up every last one *and* bag 'em, and he's gonna smile like Shirley Temple while he does it."

Clete hooked a finger in the corner of his mouth in mock consideration. "I've got a better idea," he said. "You clean it up. Then say sorry. Then get outta my store."

"Sorry!" David said, apoplectic. "For what?"

"For making a mess." He jutted his chin at Charlayne. "And for letting that in here without a leash."

"The fuck?" Charlayne shouted, fists clenched at her sides.

Mayer, suddenly madder than he'd realized himself capable, stuck a finger into Clete's face. "You get down on two knees and apologize profusely, *imploringly,* you purple-gummed son of a—"

His words died when David lunged over the counter and got a fistful of Clete's T-shirt. Clete twisted free, kicking over the coffee can of tobacco sludge. David vaulted onto the counter and squatted to spring for a tackle, but the storekeeper moved faster, planting his hands on his foe's chest and shoving. With nothing to grab onto, David careened backward, pinwheeling his arms. He hit the floor with a meaty thud.

Instantly Charlayne was at his side, one hand beneath his neck and the other on his chest. "Are you okay?"

"Been better," he rasped.

There was a mechanical *ch-chunk.* The two looked up and into the eye of a Winchester pump-action shotgun.

"Jesus," David said.

"Hey!" Clete trumpeted. "Do not blaspheme here."

"You're gonna shoot us now?"

"It's my constitutional right to defend myself. You trashed my store and assaulted me."

"Or," Mayer piped up, "we could just leave."

"Yes, let's do that," Charlayne said.

"Nobody leavin' till I get a sorry from this somebitch," Clete said.

Now it was David who grinned. "Fuck you, ghettobilly."

Clete swung the Winchester at a whitewashed plaster wall and pulled the trigger, peppering it with buckshot. The boom reverberated up and down the aisles.

"You'll go to jail for this," David said.

Clete burst out laughing. "What do you think this is, Massachusetts? Half the police force out here is cousins of mine. My uncle's county sheriff."

"Mark my word, the ACLU and NAACP are gonna play tug-of-war with your small intestine."

"Still waiting on that apology."

"Dave, just . . . please?" Charlayne said.

He looked at her, horrified.

"I'm not getting shot," she said, "much less by someone so unworthy."

The two argued with their eyes, his imploring, hers full of reason. Mayer knew what was coming and couldn't bear to watch. His eyes settled on Clete's phone, which lay screen-up by the register. The wallpaper was a picture of two toddler girls, their hair done up in pigtails, the sweetness on their round faces utterly incongruous with the situation at hand.

David coughed up the two words Clete wanted to hear.

"I didn't quite get that," Cletus said.

David bit down hard on his lower lip. Charlayne touched his elbow. "Please, Dave."

"I'm sorry," he said through molten teeth.

Clete smiled. "Was that so hard?"

"Can we go now?" Charlayne asked.

"You bet."

She took David's elbow to help him up but he shook her off. He brushed the dirt off the seat of his pants. They started for the exit.

"But first you gotta clean up the mess you made."

David made a slow spin, the heel of one shoe scraping the floor. The Winchester was still trained on him.

"Say that again."

"Get to it now. Go on."

David's blood vessel got so engorged that Mayer feared it really would pop.

"I will not—"

Ch-chunk, went the pump action.

Charlayne touched the center of his back. "Play the long game, Dave. Play the long game."

They looked into each other's eyes. From where he stood, Mayer could only see his brother's face, and it was like watching someone age ten years in ten seconds. The cords in his neck went slack and his proud chest deflated. Wordlessly, he shuffled to the mess on the floor by the counter. When he cleaned that up, he got to work on the novelty fireworks. Clete kept the gun at hip level.

"Alright?" David asked impotently.

"You'd make a hell of a stock clerk," Clete said. "We've got applications."

David shot him a glare that had no more venom than a dead rattlesnake. His shoes scuffed the floor as he made his way to the exit. He turned one last time at the door.

"I'm giving you the shittiest Yelp review you've ever seen."

CHARLAYNE MARCHED TO the exit with a servicewoman's posture, chin up and back ramrod straight. Mayer meant to follow, but his shoes seemed to have melted to the floor.

"Skedaddle," Clete said.

He put his back into it and got his feet moving. He caught up to Charlayne, who had paused to wait for him. They walked in step, crushingly aware of all that had changed in a matter of minutes. They would get back in the car, and then on to New Moab and then Springer Mountain. But the road trip was over, courtesy of a sadist who held all the cards. It was intolerable.

Just before they reached the door, Patsy Cline's "Back in Baby's Arms" started up from a transistor radio behind the counter. The radio had been on the whole time, but Mayer hadn't paid attention—until now, because he happened to know this song well.

He closed his eyes and he was Marty again, pushing a shopping cart at Walmart while Ida Mae loaded it with canned goods. When "Back in Baby's Arms" came through the aisle speakers, her eyes became stricken. She dropped a can of pork and beans on the floor, put her hands over her face and wept. That morning, a dimple-chinned trucker named Iry Bullard had stormed out of the house, but not before blackening her eye. He'd had the same "AB" tattoo on his forearm as Clete, scrawled in the same Germanic lettering. This had been their song.

Mayer turned around at the door. "How long were you in for?" he asked.

"Huh?" Clete said.

Mayer touched his own forearm, then pointed at Clete's. Clete pushed chaw back and forth behind his lip. "Five years at Parchman Farm."

"What for?"

"Dealing."

Charlayne turned at the doorway.

"Dealing what?" Mayer asked.

"Crystal meth, mostly." He raised the shotgun so it was level with Mayer's heart. "You got a problem with that?"

It was a thought-provoking question. Did Mayer have a problem with wolves ganging up on their omega, praying mantises decapitating their mates, or mother rats eating their babies? Clete was an animal in his natural habitat, Mayer an animal out of his element, and God was letting nature handle the rest. If Mayer were a Jew, he could write off this whole ugly business as *bitul Torah*, a waste of time, and just walk away with his honor intact. But he was a goy—and damned if he wasn't the better goy.

"I asked you something," Clete said.

"I was just thinking," Mayer said. "A little while ago, you told my brother not to blaspheme. Are you a God-fearing man?"

Clete made no reply.

"You know, in Genesis," Mayer said, "God explains why he chose Abraham as the forefather of a mighty nation: 'For I have known him so that he commands his son and his daughters after him, that they keep the way of God to perform righteousness and justice.'"

"Alright," Clete said.

"The key words are 'so that he commands,' or teaches. God knew he could trust Abraham to teach his children the ways of righteousness, and make sure that his children did the same to their children, and so on. Similarly, the Bible states in Deuteronomy, 'And teach them to your children to speak with them when you sit in your house and when you walk on the way and when you lie down and when you rise up.'"

He glanced at the phone on the counter. His rival saw this and did likewise, and the skin around his cheekbones turned pink. "You see where I'm going with this, don't you?" Mayer said.

"Hawkeye?" Charlayne said, but she might as well have spoken to the wall.

"How," the counterfeit Jew said, "will you ever explain your actions to your daughters when they're old enough to ask?"

At this, a flush rose up Clete's face, cresting like a port-wine stain at his dome. "Fuck you know about my girls?"

Mayer lifted his palms. "Nothing, really. Only that they're innocent and imaginative and eager for new experiences, that any kid they meet in the morning could be their best friend by nightfall, that they believe they can be anything they want to be in life." He licked his dry lips, wanting nothing more in the world than a Chesterfield. "That to them, you are God."

Clete squeezed the gun's forestock so hard it shook, and when he spoke, brown spittle flew from between his lips. "I'll shoot your nuts off. You have no right to talk about my family. No right!"

"In the twelfth century," Mayer said, "there lived a holy man in Spain by the name of Bachya ibn Paquda. You know what he wrote about children?"

The gunman's eyes narrowed to slits.

"He wrote that children are unable to distinguish between good and evil. It's up to the parents to show them the difference."

"Don't you fuckin' tell me I can't teach my girls right from wrong."

"To teach with words is good; to teach by example is profound. Maybe you've heard the old theory that girls end up marrying their fathers. I don't know if it's true or not, but—"

"I'm counting to three, and then I will blow your brains out," Clete said. "I swear to the Lord Jesus Christ."

"Mayer," Charlayne said.

"One," Clete said.

"There was a holy man named Hillel who lived in Jerusalem more than two thousand years ago," Mayer said. "A man who had no fear of God said to him, 'I've got a challenge for you: if you can teach me the entire Bible while standing on one foot, I'll give myself over to the Almighty.' And Hillel said, 'Alright,' and he got on one foot."

"Two."

Mayer felt Charlayne's hand on his shoulder, but she made no effort to pull him back.

"Hillel told him, 'What is hateful to you, do not do to your neighbor.'"

Clete, his glare unremitting, his rifle sight never leaving Mayer's forehead, said, "Love thy neighbor as thyself."

"That's right."

"Gospel of Matthew, 22:39."

"Sure."

Something softened around the edge of the man's eyes. It wasn't much, but for the guy on the wrong side of a shotgun barrel, it was like a sliver of sun peeking through a hurricane.

"Three."

Mayer closed his eyes. Charlayne dug her fingers into his deltoid. "Jolene" came on the radio, and as absurd as the sentiment was at a time like this, he thought he could do worse than Dolly Parton as the last voice he ever heard.

He opened his eyes, and when he did, Clete burst out laughing. "You are one crazy somebitch," he said, "but you've got balls of steel—both of you in fact."

Before Mayer could make sense of what was happening, Clete dropped the bombshell. "Tell you what, ma'am. In the spirit of Hillel or Matthew or whoever, I'm sorry. I shouldn't've said what I said about you."

He started laughing again, the Winchester balanced in the crook of his elbow, the business end almost touching the floor. Mayer and Charlayne each had the identical notion that fascism might not be the guy's biggest problem. She gave Clete a faltering nod. This stoked his good humor, and his laughter renewed afresh. He wiped his tears with the heel of his hand. He sniffled a few times before casting a sheepish glance at his patrons, then at the puddle of tobacco juice at his feet. After a moment's consideration, he spat into it. He then eyed the merchandise on the counter and cleared his throat. "You still wanna buy this stuff, or—?"

A thundering boom shattered the equanimity of the moment. Three startled faces turned to the source of the disturbance, the side door, which had been kicked open with such force that the doorknob punched a hole in the adjacent wall. A man's silhouette filled the doorframe, his shaved dome eclipsing the setting sun. He held a long metallic tube in an at-ease position against his shoulder.

"David?" Mayer said.

The elder Belkin stepped forward, his brows arched at a savage angle, the corners of his mouth curved into a deranged smile. Locking his gaze on a stupefied Clete, David pulled out his Zippo and flipped the lid. He flicked the wheel and touched the flame to a piece of blue string hanging from one end of the tube. It sprang to life with a hiss and David took a knee, raising the end of the tube until it was zeroed on the enemy.

"Dave, no!" Charlayne screamed.

"Jesus Christ!" Clete cried and dove to the floor.

What followed took less than a second, but later, at the hospital, Mayer found he could replay the scene in his head in super slo-mo and ultra hi-def. There was a *foomp* and something the size of an aspirin tablet spiraled out of the tube. The pill grew to the radius of a dinner plate, then a flying saucer sled, then a satellite dish. A microsecond later, there was a tremendous clatter behind him and he spun around. The novelty fireworks display had disintegrated into a squall of shredded cardboard and plastic. The skin on his left temple burned as if it had been stamped with a branding iron.

"Mayer, get down!" Charlayne cried.

There was a ball of orange flame, and Mayer was thrown flat on his back. His eyes burned and his ears rang. Acrid smoke filled his nose and throat. All around him was a cacophony of coughing and sputtering and cursing. Then came a rapid *pop-pop-pop-pop-pop*, like automatic assault fire, and in his confusion he thought the store really was under assault. Stars of green, purple and orange fanned in every direction. He tucked his head between his forearms and waited until, at last, all went quiet—at which point a prone David lifted his head and jubilantly exclaimed, "Holy shit! Did you see that?"

Then a string of kettle-corn pops rang out from the smoldering novelty pile, followed by another string, and another, and then dozens at once. Clete vaulted over the counter with a fire extinguisher and doused the mess. As the white powder settled, a sharp report sounded from aisle four and a softball-size hole appeared in the ceiling.

"Goddamnit, you idiot!" Clete shouted.

He raced to aisle four with the extinguisher, and just as he arrived three reports like a .44 Magnum went off in aisle six. Diagnosing the latter noise as the more critical problem, he raced toward its source—but never made it. A five-hundred-gram aerial cake detonated in aisle one, loud as an IED. Bits of rusted metal rained down from the ceiling. Clete dropped to the floor and shouted words no one could decipher in the rapidly amplifying clamor. Then a crate of smoke bombs exploded.

Just like that, BABY LIGHT MY FIREWORKS was the front line for a dozen armies firing everything they had at the same time. Missiles and mortars turned the roof into Swiss cheese. Comets and aerial repeaters ricocheted off walls and floor before bursting into stars that ricocheted some more. Lightbulbs shattered. Thick green vapor lit up like sheet lightning. From deep in the bowels of the store a low hum rose to a high whine and—*kaBOOM!* Two roof panels blew sky high. Air flooded in, fueling fires that ignited more pyrotechnics that started more fires.

Mayer felt a hand grab the back of his shirt. He opened his eyes to David's face within kissing distance of his own. There was a trickle of crimson running down one temple, rivulets of perspiration cutting paths on his soot-blackened face. He looked as happy as Mayer had ever seen him.

"Come on!"

The elder Belkin leopard-crawled toward the exit, one forearm in front of the other. The younger did likewise, the downpour of sparks and bits of hot steel singeing his shirt. The boys' corridor to safety—fenced to the right by a wall of flame, the left by an actual wall—was closing fast. The linoleum floor blistered and popped six inches from Mayer's right elbow. The furnace air scalded his lungs.

He raised his head to see how much further he had to go. Beyond the exit was Charlayne's terror-stricken face, squinting into the smoke for signs of life. A moment later, David was beside her. She grabbed him around the middle and he wrapped his arms around her shoulders. Mayer doubled down like he was at Omaha Beach, desperate to reach cover before his head got blown off. And then from behind him he heard a feline scream that liquefied his viscera.

Clete.

He'd forgotten all about the cretin responsible for this nightmare—the first half of it, anyway. He flipped over and propped himself on his elbows. What he saw wasn't Clete, but a satanic figure forged of smoke and lit up like a jack-o'-lantern. It had two milky yellow sockets for eyes, a gaping blue mouth, and a pointy green hat perched between two twisted ram's horns.

What are these rituals to you? it teased.

Suddenly all fear abandoned Mayer and rage filled the void. He got to his feet and charged the dybbuk, lowering his shoulder just before impact. There was no impact, only a pop and a brilliant flash of green, and the malevolent spirit diffused. Something white-hot and needle-sharp pierced Mayer's right eye. He dropped to his knees and screamed until smoke took away his breath.

— CHAPTER 11 —

MAYER TRIED OPENING HIS EYES AND ONLY HALF SUCCEEDED; TAPE AND GAUZE SEALED SHUT THE RIGHT ONE. HE WAS in a hospital bed walled by pink curtain dividers. Black granules coated his skin and compacted under his fingernails. He smelled like an incinerator.

His brother snored in a chair beside him, his malodorous bare feet propped on the bed. He'd scrubbed his face and scalp, but otherwise looked like a chimney sweep. There was a Band-Aid on one temple and dots of dried blood on his shirt.

Mayer tried to say his brother's name. The word gusted out of him like a bellows. He flexed his larynx and managed to bray it out on the second try. David's eyes popped open.

"Ese! Great to see you up."

The patient passed a dry tongue between cracked lips. "Where are we?"

"The hospital."

He blinked his blinkable eye.

"Oh," David said. "Eutaw, Alabama."

"Where's Charlayne?"

"Getting coffee. Popeye's out front; I paid the security guard forty bucks to keep an eye on him. Speaking of eyes, how are you feeling?"

"What happened to me?" Mayer asked.

"Before or after you got blasted?"

"I guess after."

"Well, Char and I started shouting your name but you weren't answering, so I went back in for you. It was like the Fourth of July in Hades. Smoke was everywhere. I could hardly hear my own voice with all that racket. I got on all fours and started feeling around for you."

"How long before you found me?"

"I didn't. Popeye beat me to it."

"Popeye?"

"Just followed his nose. Grabbed you with his teeth and dragged you out, like damned Lassie."

Mayer put his head on his pillow and stared at the LED light humming above him. From everywhere sounded the *beep-beep* of vital-sign monitors, the Darth Vader whoosh of ventilators, the gurgly snores of sleeping patients. "Wait a minute," he said. "Why are we in Alabama? There was no hospital closer?"

"There was. But Charlayne and I thought it best to get out of Mississippi."

"What happened to Clete?"

"He and his truck were long gone before we even got in the car."

"Why don't I remember any of this?"

David broke eye contact. "I gave you something."

"Something?"

"I had to. You were screaming like somebody'd rammed a morning star up your ass."

On the other side of the curtain, a doctor asked a patient where it hurt. The patient said everywhere.

"David?"

"Yeah?"

"What you did back there, firing that mortar at Clete?"

His brother leaned forward, an eager gleam in his eye. "Uh-huh?"

"That was the stupidest thing I've ever seen anyone do in my life."

The gleam extinguished.

"What were you thinking?" Mayer said. "No, I'm seriously asking, because a part of me is worried that you don't know what an idiot you are."

"I found the bazooka in the back of Clete's truck and figured, you know—hashtaga pratis or whatever. Divine intervention."

"*Hashgacha.* But why fire it in the store? Why fire it at all?"

"Did you not see the shotgun aimed at our asses?" David asked.

"I talked him down, you ninny! If you'd taken two seconds to—" Mayer broke into a series of rib-fracturing coughs. When he recovered, he rasped, "You almost killed me. You almost killed everyone, including yourself. What were you thinking?"

"Obviously I wasn't," David said sullenly.

Mayer turned his face away.

"I said I was sorry."

"No you didn't!"

The curtain opened, and Charlayne came forward with a cup tray holding three coffees. She was markedly less grimy than the boys, but still the worse for wear; a streak of soot across her hairline tapered her forehead to the breadth of a yardstick. Her eyes were bloodshot and an earring was missing. On seeing the patient awake, she set the tray on the overbed table. Before Mayer knew what was happening, she kissed him on the mouth. His reaction made her laugh; he looked like a cochlear implant patient hearing Mozart for the first time.

"How are you feeling, Hawkeye?" she asked.

He cleared his throat. "Okay. A shower wouldn't hurt."

"You're telling me."

"Do I still have my eyeball?"

"Yes—miraculously, considering," she said.

"Does it still work? What did the doctor say?"

Charlayne took a beat longer to answer than he'd have liked. "We only spoke to him for a minute after the procedure, but I just saw him at the triage desk. Let me see if I can grab him."

"I'll do it," the elder brother said.

When David was out of earshot, Charlayne said, "He feels really bad about your eye."

"I wouldn't know," Mayer said.

She pulled back the tab on a coffee lid and offered it to him. He said no thanks, so she took a sip. "You might not know this, but all Dave wants is to impress you."

"I'd hate to see him disappoint me."

She sat on the bed, the seat of her shorts brushing his wrist. "I never thought I'd live to see a white supremacist apologize to a woman of color."

"Me neither," Mayer said.

"And here I had you pegged as a mild-mannered bird-watcher with a weakness for snack crackers. I hope Sarah gets to see the other side of you once in a while."

"How come?"

"It's damned sexy."

Butterflies fluttered in his chest. Then an unpleasant thought moved in like bug fogger, and the butterflies died. "Oh no."

"What?"

"Sarah's flying to Atlanta tomorrow to spend Shabbos—the Sabbath— with me at my mother's house."

"I thought you were just going there to tie up loose ends."

"It's a big loose end."

"I see," Charlayne said. "How'll you explain your eye?"

"Exactly. The first thing she'll say when she sees me is 'What happened?' I won't get two sentences in before she turns right around and goes back to the airport."

Charlayne swept a ringlet of hair away from her face. "Look, while you were sleeping Dave filled me in on your, um, marital setback."

Mayer said nothing.

"You're worried she'll be upset. I get that. But why not give her the benefit of the doubt? You suffered an injury after all. And given the terrible position your mother put you in, maybe she'll be sympathetic."

The curtain swished open and David entered, leading a weary-eyed medical resident wearing green scrubs and black Crocs. "David Chan, MD" was embroidered on his breast pocket.

"Good morning, Mr. . . ."

"Belkin."

"Glad to see you're up. How are you feeling?"

"Let's cut the coffee talk, doc," David interjected. "What's the damage?"

Chan gave David an irritated look before returning to his patient. "The good news is the impact to your eye was a glancing blow, not a direct hit. Your sclera—that's the white part—took the impact."

"That's great!" David said.

Chan gave David a look that said *strike two*. "Still, glancing blow or not, a fifteen-hundred-degree projectile hit you at the speed of a jet fighter. It left a small but dense field of debris that we had to pick out piece by piece."

"What's the prognosis?" Mayer said.

"Well, I examined the interior of your eye and found no damage at all. You'll likely come out of this with only scarring."

"No blindness?"

"No blindness, on the condition you do your part to fight off inflammation and infection," Chan said. "You want to avoid getting post-traumatic iritis—inflammation inside the eye—which leads to redness, pain and light sensitivity, and can be very bad if not treated. Much worse would be endophthalmitis, a full-blown inner-eye infection that *can* lead to blindness."

"Yikes," Charlayne said.

"In all likelihood you'll be fine," the doctor said. "I'm prescribing you a combination antibiotic-steroid eye ointment. Take Motrin or Tylenol for pain. Will you still be in town tomorrow?"

Mayer looked at his companions. "We weren't planning on it."

"Well, make sure to see an ophthalmologist wherever you plan to be tomorrow. In the meantime, take your ointment morning and evening and change the dressing frequently."

Mayer thanked him.

Dr. Chan turned to leave, paused and turned back. "May I give you a PSA?"

"Please."

"Act your age from now on."

WHILE CHARLAYNE FILLED the prescriptions, Mayer put on his fetid clothing. "Where's my phone?" he asked.

David dug through his pockets and handed over the device. There were four missed calls, three from Sarah and one from Yossi. He put it away.

"Charlayne tells me you used your old Jedi mind trick on that Aryan," David said.

Mayer said nothing.

"I knew you still had it."

"Hey, David?"

"Yeah."

"Please shut up."

For a minute they sat listening to heart monitors beeping, shoes scuffing, medical personnel speaking in rapid-fire jargon. "You know something?" Mayer said. "Yesterday marked the first day since our bar mitzvahs that I didn't put on tefillin."

David nodded somberly.

"Your cockamamie scheme to bring back my inner child has just about killed my chances of getting my life back," Mayer said. "Think about that."

IT WAS FIVE fifty-eight in the morning when Charlayne wheeled Mayer out of the hospital. The sun was wide-awake and ready to rumble. David had

GOYHOOD

parked at the curb and kept the car on. His seat was back and he'd dozed off with a joint sticking out of his mouth. Popeye, on seeing his friends, lapped at the rear passenger window.

Mayer took shotgun at Charlayne's insistence. Popeye climbed halfway between the front seats to give the injured man's face a tongue bath. Mayer grinned and bore it. "Guess I owe you one, huh, boy?"

"Anybody else hungry?" David said.

"I'd eat at Arby's, I'm so famished," Charlayne said, "but if I don't shower in the next thirty minutes I might actually die."

"I'd check that inclination if you're going Sacagawea for six months."

She stuck out her tongue at him.

They found a motel in town called the C'mon Inn. It had an old Miami Beach aesthetic, with a pink stucco exterior and twin palm trees abutting the entrance. The desk clerk raised an eyebrow at their grungy appearance, and another eyebrow when David requested one room for three adults. But she didn't say no to his credit card—nor a folded twenty to turn a blind eye to Popeye.

While Charlayne showered, the boys laid out new clothes—clean denim and a plaid summer shirt for Mayer, pale green chinos and a deep-necked Henley for David. Charlayne came out of the bathroom in a cloud of steam, Mayer noting that her skin-to-fabric ratio favored skin by a landslide.

"All yours, Ese," David said.

"No, you. Sarah's been trying to reach me."

"Right." He started for the shower.

"By the way," Mayer said, "I still can't find my yarmulke. Have you seen it?"

"Nope. I wouldn't hold out high hopes after where we've been." He went into the bathroom and closed the door. A half minute later the water started running.

Charlayne found her vanity bag. "I'll step out to give you privacy."

"Thanks, but maybe stay. Please."

Her lips parted slightly. "Okay."

She emptied the bag on the dresser. Mayer sat on the bed, facing the window, and Popeye hopped up next to him. He rubbed the canine's thick neck and looked out the window at the motel swimming pool. A little girl with beaded braids and arm floats splashed around in the blue-green water. A woman in a one-piece and straw hat reclined on a pool chair.

He dialed. Sarah picked up on the first ring.

"Mayer."

"I'm sorry," he said.

"Where have you been?"

He took a handful of Popeye's scruff. "Sleeping."

"You've been doing a lot of that lately."

"Yes."

"What's wrong with your voice?"

He touched his smoke-raw throat. "Never mind my voice. How are you?"

"*Baruch Hashem*," she said. "I made rugelach. I'll bring some tomorrow."

"Yum." He felt the reflection of Charlayne's eyes in the dresser mirror.

"And you?" Sarah asked. "How are you getting by in shiva?"

Her tone was placid—too placid? He squeezed Popeye's scruff harder. "Hanging in there."

"Hanging in there," she repeated. "That's new."

"Oh yeah?"

"I see you've gotten back your Southern accent as well."

"You seemed to like it when we first met. I figured I'd give it another go."

"'I figured.' 'Another go.' Have you got any more folksy phrases?"

He pantomimed a laugh. The little girl climbed out of the pool and started shouting and arm-flapping at the woman. Once she had her attention, she cannonballed back in with a mighty splash.

"The airline told me your suitcase was signed for this morning," Sarah said. "One less thing to worry about."

"Yes it was, *Baruch Hashem*." He made a mental note to thank Yossi for remembering this time.

"You have enough clothing to last you for the rest of shiva, but I can bring extra underwear if you need."

Mayer took an extended breath. "Do me a favor. Cancel your ticket."

"Oh?"

"The thought means the world to me. But cancel the ticket. It's been a difficult couple of days, and I just need . . ."

"You need . . ."

He swallowed. "Space."

Popeye whimpered, and Mayer realized he was digging his nails into the dog's skin. He let go and rubbed the area. "Look, my mother's passing—it started a whole *meshugas*."

"Do tell."

"I'd rather not. It's taken a lot out of me. That's why all the sleeping."

"Be more specific," Sarah said.

"Not on the phone. I'll tell you everything when I'm back in New York, okay?"

She didn't answer. He took the phone from his ear to see if they were still connected.

"Last night," she said, breaking the silence, "I was in bed thinking about my flight and all the planning involved—the food, the packing, the ride to the airport."

"*Schefele*—"

"Don't interrupt. Mostly I was thinking about being so high off the ground. What if there was an engine malfunction? What if the plane hit a flock of geese, *chas v'shalom*, and the pilot had to land in the Hudson River? For hours I tossed and turned, thinking about these things. Finally I said, 'If I don't find a way to distract myself, I'll never get to sleep.'"

"Right."

"I tried calling you—you've always been good at getting me to sleep—but you didn't pick up. So I decided to look at Instagram. It was a good decision. It calmed me down right away. I started to get drowsy."

"That's good."

"I decided, let me watch one more video."

Without knowing why, Mayer felt his skin prickle as though a stranger had snuck up behind him and blown a puff of air on the back of his neck.

"The one I watched was shot at an outdoor café," she said. "In the beginning, you see the crowd eating, schmoozing, having a good time. Then a car stops at a traffic light just beyond the tables. Its windows are down and the radio is playing at full volume. It's extremely loud. Everyone gets annoyed—everyone except these people at one table. They start dancing in their chairs."

Mayer felt his stomach constrict. "Sarah."

"Wait, here's the best part. There's a chain reaction. People at the other tables start dancing too. It's kind of like a . . . what do you call it? Flash mob."

Mayer took deep breaths to quell his thrashing heart. It didn't work.

"Pretty soon the whole crowd's in on it—except for one guy at the table where it all started. He has this look on his face like, *What planet am I on?*"

His eye started to throb as if his overexerted heart had flushed out the anesthetic. After a prolonged silence he realized he had the floor. "You don't know the half of it, Sarah. A tenth of it. These past two days have been the most difficult of my life. I'd call it a nightmare, but nightmares you wake up from. I was going to tell you the whole story tomorrow."

"I thought I wasn't coming tomorrow."

"Yes, but only because—"

"Because I'd ruin your vacation, Mr. 'Hanging in there'?"

His face burned as if from fever. A hand touched his shoulder and he looked up at Charlayne.

"Seeing you in that video reminded me of something I hadn't thought about in a long time," Sarah said. "You were the only boy my father ever offered up to me. He told me, 'Take him or leave him—but either way, you leave my house.'"

Mayer ran a sandpaper tongue across his lips.

"I was nervous to meet you," she went on. "You were the first boy I'd ever had a real conversation with. You still had a trace of that accent, and some-thing else too—a presence that I was unfamiliar with. I was scared of you at first, if I'm being honest."

She laughed, a tinny sound that made his skin crawl.

"What a lamb you turned out to be: inoffensive, obedient, predictable. In fact, I can't remember a time you ever made a real impression on me, good or bad—until that video showed up in my feed."

Mayer pressed a finger to his eyepatch. It was like being jabbed in the eye with a cattle prod. Charlayne stepped away to get something.

"For eighteen years you cultivated your daily routine like a fragile plant that needs exact amounts of sun and water to stay alive. I thought you were just being neurotic, but look what happened: you put your guard down for one day and your mamzer brother talked you into dressing like a goy without even a yarmulke, and eating at a *treif* restaurant."

"It was kosher," Mayer said flaccidly.

"Oh, by the way, nobody signed for your suitcase this morning. I made that up just to see what you'd say."

Charlayne reappeared with a tiny white pill in her palm and a bottle of water. He accepted the pill and declined the water.

"I am curious about one thing," Sarah said.

"What's that?"

"Who's the *schvartze?*"

SARAH DIDN'T SAY "It's over," but Mayer heard it in her tone just before she ended the call. "We'll talk when you get back." *Click.* He never even got a chance to tell her about Ida Mae's letter.

Yet in the shower for some reason—perhaps it was the catharsis of watching the sooty water circle the drain—he found himself thinking not of Sarah but her grandfather, whom he'd never met. Reb Avraham, as people knew him, was a renowned Torah scholar, supermarket tycoon, philanthropist, and—arguably most notably—father of *HaGaon HaRav* Yaakov Drezner. His death at eighty-nine was newsy enough to earn him an obituary in the *New York Times*—an irony, as he'd never read the *Times*, had never even heard of it, despite living in Brooklyn for sixty-two years. Yet what he lacked in worldly sophistication he made up for in cutthroat entrepreneurialism, expanding his mini-mart in Williamsburg into a chain of kosher supermarkets in six cities.

From 1951 to 1994, six days a week, twelve hours a day, he ran his business from the counter of his corner grocery on Hooper Street and Lee Avenue, ordering inventory from his Yiddish-speaking suppliers and balancing eight-figure sums in dime-store composition notebooks. After closing each night, he went upstairs to the second-floor apartment he shared with his second wife and their seven children. He ate his one meal of the day and slept for two hours. At eleven he got out of bed, dressed, and walked to the *beis medrash* down the block to study Talmud until dawn. Then he bathed at the mikvah, davened and went to work. When he retired at seventy-nine, he slackened his routine to fourteen hours a day of Talmud study broken up by phone calls to the men who managed his stores, investments and charities. And he slept for three hours a night instead of two.

Yet remarkable as Reb Avraham's life was from 1951 onward, it was the events prior that garnered him the notoriety requisite for a Gray Lady obituary. Before immigrating to New York, he lived at a German displaced-persons camp, and before that, Birkenau. Assigned to the Sonderkommando unit, his duties included prying gold-filled molars from the mouths of the dead, piling the bodies on carts, wheeling them to crematoria and stacking them head-to-foot. Rumors were that on his first shift, he stacked his first wife and three children, a claim he neither confirmed nor denied.

Only a handful of Sonderkommando survived to see Birkenau liberated. Of these, most had been on the job for a few months or less. Reb Avraham was in the unit for two years. His ticket to survival was his yeoman's work ethic; he was so industrious and scrupulous that he became a sort of mascot for his SS overseers. Commandant Höss himself dubbed him "Maschinenmensch" after the robot played by Brigitte Helm in *Metropolis*.

Generations of Yiddish-speaking children in Williamsburg whispered Reb Avraham's macabre wartime nickname when they saw him coming up the street, scattering like birds when he got near. Old wives said if you looked into his eyes, his soul would look back at you and drive you insane.

There were varying theological interpretations of the Holocaust. Some scholars maintained it was God's divine retribution against the Jews for rejecting their birthright; secular theologians accused God of parental neglect, turning the other cheek to the cruelty inflicted on his children; other thinkers rejected rationalization altogether, for there was no precedent in the Torah for such a calamity.

Reb Avraham championed the first approach, that the Almighty weaponized the goyim against K'lal Yisroel for forsaking him. His survivor's debt could only be paid by a life of piety and repentance, and urging others to do likewise, lest there be a second retaliation. This was the doctrine he imparted to his children every day of their young lives, and they to theirs.

DOLORES'S DINETTE IN Tuscaloosa was a tribute to 1950s kitsch—a soda jerk hat on every worker's head, fourteen kinds of pie rotating in a glass case, nary a table without a jukebox. Dolores herself, an immense-breasted African American woman with a voice like a diesel train, rang up orders on a cash register with a wooden hand crank. The place was jam-packed when the quintet—including Ida Mae—arrived for breakfast, but they managed to nab an empty booth just outside the kitchen. From it wafted aromas of fried chicken, pancakes, eggs, onions, bacon, cinnamon buns, coffee and warm butter.

"This place is awesome," David said, admiring a shrine to the Crimson Tide on the wall. "Aren't you gonna Instagram, Char?"

"Nah," she said languidly; her sleepless night at the hospital was catching up to her. David, on the other hand, was bursting with energy. He ordered for them both the house specialty, fried chicken and waffles with sides of turnip greens and lima beans. For Popeye he ordered chicken-fried steak.

Mayer wanted only black coffee and a bowl of applesauce. His appetite, intermittent since New Orleans, hadn't come back at all since his injury. Between his meager caloric intake and unremitting perspiration, he could feel himself starting to waste away—yet he couldn't bring himself to fight it. His body and soul had always been in tandem, and he couldn't nourish one without nourishing the other. What was food if he couldn't even say a blessing over it?

After a waitress poured their water, Charlayne propped her chin in one hand and speared the ice in her glass with the other.

"You okay?" David said.

"I've got Maine on the brain. I'll need crampons by the time I get there. *If* I get there."

For both brothers, recent events had eclipsed Charlayne's imminent migration into the Appalachian wilderness. If they made good time to Springer Mountain, she could be on the trail by midday.

"Why not cut your losses and wait till spring?" David asked.

"Can't."

"Why?"

Evidently unaware she was doing it, she started rubbing at the shiny white lines on her wrist like they were a patch of eczema. "I just can't, okay?"

The waitress came back with an array of plates, all steaming. Mayer watched, amused, as Popeye made quick work of his steak. All the TLC the dog had received lately had done a body good: his protruding ribs were receding a little, his coat had a healthy gloss and the gash on his nose was starting

174

to scab over. His one working eye seemed to glow with perpetual wonder at all that was good on Earth.

David doused his meal in pancake syrup. He skewered a chunk of chicken breast and waffle and shoved it in his cheek. "Oh, Ese," he moaned ecstatically, "please, let this be your one."

"My one?"

"Your one indulgence before you convert."

"No desire."

Charlayne tore off a small piece of white meat and worked it between her front teeth.

"Not hungry either?" David said.

"Not really."

He washed his mouthful down with coffee and took another bite. "So, Char, what made you want to hike the AT anyway? You never told us."

"You never asked."

"I'm asking now."

"It's a fairly common aspiration," she said.

"Yeah, if you're just out of college," David said.

"I'll have you know that the mean age of thru-hikers is thirty-four."

"It just seems off-brand, is all I'm saying."

"What do you mean?"

David swallowed. "Your Instagram is all about street musicians and margaritas and farm-to-table meals, and the rare bikini thirst trap."

"Maybe I'm looking to reinvent myself," Charlayne said.

"There are ways to reinvent yourself that don't involve blisters and bug bites and giardia—not to mention crippling loneliness."

Mayer reached for his coffee and knocked over a water glass situated in the dark half of his visual field. They all sprang up and mopped the puddle with napkins. When they were seated again, David said, "Look, Char, ditch the trail and ride with us to New York. It'll be a gas."

"Why are you trying to talk me out of this?" she said. "You're the one always proselytizing roads less traveled by."

"Yeah, the Jack Kerouac kind, not James Dickey."

Charlayne didn't reply.

"You gonna eat that?"

She pushed her plate across the table and he got to work. She propped her heavy head in two hands and the charm bracelet slid up her arm, giving Mayer his first clear view of her scarred wrist. It wasn't a healed laceration after all, but a lasered-off tattoo. The morning sun illuminated the shiny surface, revealing a word in slanted script.

Adam.

— CHAPTER 12 —

CHARLAYNE UNROLLED AN INFLATABLE MAT ATOP
ALL HER CAMPING PARAPHERNALIA AND LAID OUT HER SLEEPING BAG
on the mat, creating a surprisingly sizable and comfortable bed. Spooning
Popeye's compact body like a teddy bear, she closed her eyes. In less than a
minute her breaths were slow and deep.

"She sat up with you all night," David said.

"Really?"

"I told you, Char's good people."

Mayer palmed his left eye and faced the rising sun. Orange embers illuminated the dark behind the tape and gauze—an encouraging, albeit painful,
sign. "Do you have extra sunglasses?" he asked.

David opened the center console and took out a pair of Wayfarers. Mayer
tried them on. The nose pads wouldn't hold to the medical tape, so he gave
them back.

Two blocks ahead, a sign pointed to the I-20 ramp. To their immediate
right was a used car lot, in front of which stood a fan-propelled tube man. Its
torso pitched, its arms flailed, its head whipped. Mayer had never seen one of
these, and its purpose puzzled him; what prospective customers did the deal-
ership hope to lure with the likeness of a drowning man?

He turned to his brother. "David?"

"Yeah?"

"Think you can ever forgive Mom?"

The elder took a packet of Big League Chew from a cupholder and stuffed
a purple wad in his cheek. "I kind of hate to say it, but I already have."

"No kidding?" Mayer said.

"Look, Mom was a train wreck, but she loved us. And we're not totally blameless either."

"Because we never checked our genealogy."

"She grew up on a hog farm, for Chrissakes."

"There are Jews in the world who've grown up on hog farms."

David got on the ramp to the highway bound for Birmingham. "Her grampa was a goose-stepper, bro. How hard would it have been to do a background check?"

He was right: they'd had every reason to probe their mother's background, which, if you got right down to it, they knew nothing about; when she'd tell the boys about life on the family farm—and only when cajoled—her stories were shamelessly plagiaristic. In one, she fell off a rail fence into a pigpen and one of the farmhands jumped in and scooped her out. In another, she rescued a runt piglet from the chopping block and raised it to win blue ribbon at the Claiborne County fair.

"I don't remember her once saying 'Jew' until the day Rabbi Kugel came to our house," David said. "After that, it was nonstop 'Jew this,' 'Jew that.'"

"Yossi was probably the first man she ever met who didn't want anything from her," Mayer said.

"Well, she rode that gravy train to the end of the line, didn't she? And we went along with it."

"We were just gullible kids."

"No, I was just gullible," David said. "You thought God was speaking to you through Mom."

Mayer whipped his head to the left so fast it made his eye hurt. "How did you know that?"

"Maybe you forgot, but you'd become a big skeptic at the time, especially when it came to Mom. So when you ate up her Jew story without batting an eye, I figured you must've thought you got confirmation from a higher authority."

"Right," Mayer said, turning back to the unfurling highway.

"And when you take into account your 'revelation,' or whatever you want to call it, at the big menorah earlier that day—"

"Stop," Mayer said, swiveling his head leftward again. "You're playing with me. We spoke about this before and I just forgot, right?"

David blew a purple bubble that popped onto his nose. He unfastened it with his tongue. "I'm not as dumb as I look, Ese."

This made the younger brother laugh, which made the elder laugh, and they laughed together for the next mile and a quarter. When Mayer got his breath back, he said, "Hey, Dave?"

"Yeah?"

"Sorry for bailing on you when we were kids."

David's smile tightened. "It's alright. You found your calling, Ese. Most people never do."

"But to what end? I was living like Shimon bar Yochai in the cave—only bar Yochai used the time to write the Zohar. I never wrote a book. I never taught a class. I never got involved with my community or volunteered for a charitable cause. I just learned and learned and learned Torah—selflessly, I told myself, but in hindsight who benefited but me? Meanwhile, you were stuck in New Moab with Mom."

"Not the whole time," David said. "Eventually I moved to Atlanta—and did alright for myself, if I may say so."

"Yes, you figured it out on your own. I'm proud of you."

David's nose reddened. He wiped the corners of his eyes. "Hey, tell you what," he said. "If you and Sarah are really splitsville, come live with me. I've got an extra bedroom and bathroom. All yours."

Mayer looked out his window at a freight train of at least two hundred cars running parallel to the road about a mile away.

"I'll even kasher the kitchen, buy separate dishes for meat and dairy. Atlanta's got a pretty big Jewish community—not New York big, but still.

There's an Orthodox shul like two blocks from me."

"I appreciate this, truly," Mayer said, "but given our conflicting lifestyles . . ."

"Give me the benefit of the doubt, bro. What makes you so sure I don't want to convert too?"

Mayer grunted.

"I'm serious. I'm definitely considering it."

"Oh yeah?"

"Look," David said, "obviously I was never a gold-medal Jew—hell, green-ribbon Jew—but I always thought it was cool being a part of an ancient order, like the Knights Templar or something."

"Odd analogy."

"You know what I mean."

"A *giyur* is typically a major undertaking," Mayer said. "Most people need at least a year of intensive schooling first, and then they have to convince the *beis din* that they'll commit themselves to service to God."

"I can handle that," David said. Suddenly he stopped chewing his gum. "Wait, I don't have to get circumcised again, right?"

"You'd have to get what's called a *hatafas dam bris*, where the mohel would draw a single drop of blood in the area where the foreskin was."

"Is that what you're doing on Sunday?"

"It won't be the first time."

"Really?"

"I did it right after I moved to New York."

"Does it hurt?"

"A bit."

A tractor trailer hauling chickens passed them on the left, the miserable birds huddling together against the wind. David put on Dusty Springfield, who sang, in succession, "Yesterday When I Was Young," "In the Middle of Nowhere" and "I Can't Make It Alone."

"That's some cherry-picked soundtrack," Mayer said.

"Look," David said, "remember us talking about this trip being a kind of *Rumspringa?*"

"Yeah."

"I've been on *Rumspringa* my whole life, okay? I've tried every drug on the market, and I mean *every* drug. I've slept with more women than Robert Plant. I have a daughter I've never met. I once got beat over the head with a tire iron and spent two months in a coma."

"You've told me all this before."

"Did I tell you I once made and lost a million and a half dollars at a craps table in Monaco? Did I tell you I was once so hard up for cash in Chihuahua that I played Russian roulette—*actual* Russian roulette?"

Mayer shook his head, his eye fixed on—but not really seeing—a jetliner cutting a vapor trail across the sky.

"I should have died six times. Instead, I'm rolling in dough because one of my harebrained schemes actually paid off. I can finally afford all the drugs and women I could ever want—and I want none. You wanna know what I do with my spare time, which is basically all my time? I shoot pool in my big apartment by myself, wondering what I'm supposed to do now that I've made it. And you know what else?"

"What?"

"It gets so depressing that sometimes I think about jumping off my balcony."

Mayer gawked at him. "But you're the happiest guy I know."

"I'm on the brink, Ese. Or was on the brink, until . . ." He reached across the divider and tapped the urn lid. "I've never been religious. I've never even been spiritual. But when I line up the events of the past couple of days, I see patterns, and the patterns tell me there's providence at work right now. I'm absolutely sure of it."

DAVID EXITED THE interstate in Villa Rica, Georgia, to refuel, restock on victuals, and—his words—rock a deuce. He found an outlet for all three at a QuikTrip gas station.

Mayer had taken two Tylenol after his eye flared up a half hour ago, but was still having pain so he swallowed a third. Charlayne sat up and stretched. "I slept like the dead. How long was I out?"

"About three hours."

David let the dog run off to do his business. Ida Mae stayed in the car. Everyone else went into the QuikTrip, where Charlayne helped Mayer with his eye ointment. "It actually doesn't look too bad," she said. "I mean it's nasty, but not infected-looking."

David was taking his time in the bathroom, so they went outside again. They sat at a picnic table with an umbrella, where Popeye had already taken refuge from the sun. Nearby, a weather-beaten hound dog lay in the shade of a dilapidated food truck, indifferent to the horseflies flying figure eights around its head.

"Well, Hawkeye?"

"Well?"

"How are you coping?"

"With losing my chance at ever getting my life back? Trying not to think about it."

"Sorry. I'll shut up."

"It's okay," Mayer said. "The sooner I face the mess I've made of things, the better."

"I've been thinking about that mess," she said. "I'd be angry at my husband, too, if I caught him someplace other than where he said he was. On the other hand, there's a big difference between getting caught eating beignets at Café Du Monde and, say, snorting coke off a stripper's ass."

Mayer stared at a silver-dollar-sized knot on a table plank. It was crammed with three pieces of bubble gum, each a different shade of beige. "I hear you, but these things are relative. Where I come from, going to a café without a yarmulke is a major transgression."

"Against whom?"

He grinned, despite himself. "Good question—for another time. For our purposes, let's just say Sarah doesn't do well with mistakes. Early in our marriage, I left a gob of toothpaste in the sink. I never did it again."

Charlayne smiled. "My mother could have taken a lesson from her."

"Once I ran a bath and forgot to turn it off. The water leaked through the dining room ceiling."

"Oh boy."

"I didn't see my wife for three weeks."

The mirth drained from Charlayne's face. "She kicked you out?"

"Oh, no, what I mean is I saw her every day. We ate dinner at the same table. We slept in the same room. But she wasn't there."

"Explain."

"I call it her invisible dome. She's been living in it for as long as I've known her. It's no big deal; some people need their personal space. But once in a while, I make a mistake. Leaving the bathtub running might have been the worst mistake I ever made. The invisible dome went from plastic wrap to airplane window glass."

"That sounds awful," Charlayne said.

"It wasn't fun."

"How did you guys meet, anyway?"

"Let's save that story for a rainy day."

"There's got to be an abridged version."

"Not really."

"Try?"

Mayer put his hands on his knees and sighed again, wishing he hadn't engaged, but also strangely compelled to satisfy Charlayne's curiosity—and, to be honest, his own desire to tell.

MAYER HAD NEVER exchanged a word with the *rosh yeshiva* when he was summoned to his office one November day in his second year of post–high school studies.

"Are you sure?" he asked the Rav's secretary, a newly ordained rabbi named Ostreicher, who'd come to fetch him. That the Rav knew Mayer's name out of a thousand names was flattering; that he wanted to meet with him was disquieting.

As he followed Rabbi Ostreicher to the *rosh yeshiva's* office, he racked his brain for an alibi—but in defense of what accusation? Had he made an unintended off-color remark to one of his *rebbeim*? Had one of his dormmates accused him of stealing nosh—or, *chas v'shalom*, money?

The door to the Rav's office was open. It was a small and functional space with a library of yeshiva standards and obscure antiquarians. The *gadol* sat at a plain metal desk, two fingers moving vertically down a page of Talmud. Slight of frame with a long, squared-off beard, he wore a black kaftan and a round-rimmed hat. The thickness of his glasses made Mayer think of camera lenses.

The young rabbi rapped on the door. The Rav did not look up, but raised a finger with his free hand while the other continued down the page. At every line or two, he'd pause to consult with Rashi on the inner margin and the tosafists on the outer. He did this with incredible speed.

His apprehension notwithstanding, Mayer delighted in the rare opportunity to see the master learn a whole *blatt* of Gemara in the time it took him to learn three lines. Rav Drezner's photographic memory, laser focus and Einsteinian intellect earned him the title *Gadol Hador*—one of the greatest of his generation. His Torah lectures were breathtaking spectacles whereupon he plucked opinions from dozens of sources spanning two thousand years, then wove them into a tapestry of astonishing symmetry—all without so much as a notecard in front of him.

When the Rav came to the last line of Gemara, he looked at the two men. "Ah. *Shalom aleichem*, Reb Belkin."

"*Aleichem shalom*," Mayer replied, honored and mortified to hear the *gadol* say his name.

The Rav lifted his fingers and the secretary left them. He beckoned Mayer to sit across from him. The young man did, and as he stared at his clammy hands, he felt the older man's eyes bore into him.

"Your *rebbeim* have told me of your achievements in the *beis medrash* since you enrolled here," the Rav said. "*Shkoyach*."

Mayer gave a slight nod of gratitude.

"They have also spoken of your dedication to *Avodas Hashem*—all the more impressive in light of your humble beginnings in Georgia."

Startled, Mayer looked up. He saw the faintest tremor of amusement at the corners of the Rav's mouth. "For a boy with your background, it is no small feat to assume a *Torahdik* life, much less reach your *madregah*."

"*Baruch Hashem*." Needing somewhere to anchor his restless eyes, he settled on a circa-1970s Western Electric telephone on the desk.

"As for why I summoned you here, Reb Belkin of Georgia," Rav Drezner said. "Have you started making inquiries into a *shidduch*?"

A marriage partner? The young man came perilously close to asking the *rosh yeshiva* to repeat himself. "No, Rav."

"I have started making inquiries for my daughter. Would you be interested in meeting her?"

Mayer's head instantly became waterlogged. If only he'd had time to wring out his thoughts.

"*Nu?*"

With great effort he managed to say, "What a *zechus*! I'm honored just for the opportunity."

"*Geshmak!*" The Rav clapped his hands once. "You will be contacted about where and when." With that, he went back to his Gemara. An inordinate length of time passed before Mayer realized the meeting was over.

THAT SUNDAY HE arrived at the wrought iron gates of the Rav's townhouse in Borough Park. It had a slate and granite exterior, bowed windows and a mansard roof. The square footage easily quadrupled that of his house in

New Moab and outvalued it by a factor of forty.

A uniformed valet received him at the marble entryway and led him to a drawing room twenty times bigger than his dorm room. He was told to make himself comfortable on a chaise longue upholstered in lime-green velvet. When the valet left, Mayer took a furtive look around. The furniture was Victorian, the chandelier Swarovski, the rug Turkish. The massive fireplace was sequoia marble and too clean to ever have been used.

To his right, beyond two round columns, was a grand marble staircase. Two slender women of striking refinement descended. Both wore button-down blouses and ankle-length skirts. Mrs. Drezner augmented her look with a pearl necklace, a lustrous sheitel and impeccable makeup. Sarah had a plain bob and wore no makeup—but she stole Mayer's heart in a second. She had a long and graceful neck, alabaster skin, mischievously arched brows and midnight eyes that conveyed . . . what? Curiosity? Detached interest? She could have been da Vinci's muse.

Mrs. Drezner beckoned her daughter to sit in a parlor chair perpendicular to the chaise longue. She thanked Mayer for coming and asked if she could bring him tea or coffee. He declined graciously, and she, with a slight bow, left the two alone. The valet, acting as chaperone, sat on a folding chair in a corner and read a Spanish gossip magazine.

Sarah folded her hands in her lap and waited for the conversation to begin. Mayer shuffled through prompts he'd prepared in his head. *Where did you go to high school? Did you like it? Who was your favorite teacher? Do you have hobbies? Professional aspirations?* Now that he'd seen the girl—and her house—each prompt seemed more pedestrian than the last. But what alternative—quiz her on *Ethics of the Fathers?* Seconds ticked by. They still hadn't made eye contact. He could feel the valet staring at him.

He blurted out the first thing that came to his head. "This is a beautiful house."

"Thank you."

As he scrimmaged for a follow-up, Mrs. Drezner reappeared like the angel of mercy Tzadkiel with a sterling tray bearing a pot of tea, two china teacups and some pound cake. She set it on the coffee table and retreated wordlessly. Grateful for something to do, Mayer filled each cup. He glanced to his right to see Mrs. Drezner go upstairs, her flats silent on the marble steps.

"So," he said, "where did you go to high school?"

She told him.

"Did you like it?"

"Not especially."

He steeled himself to make another inquiry, but she surprised him with her own. "Your accent."

His teacup halted just below his lips. "Pardon me?"

"Is that how all people from Georgia sound?"

He blinked.

"I don't mean to offend," she said. "Just wondering."

"Oh no, it's just—I didn't know I had one."

"You definitely do." She picked up her teacup. "I've never met anyone from Georgia. Is it different?"

"Different than here? I'd say so, yes, it's very different."

"How?" She held her cup in two hands.

He made a dismissive gesture. "Oh, it's real *galus* down there—where I'm from, anyway."

"Isn't *galus*, by definition, anywhere that's outside of Israel?"

"Consider Brooklyn the exception. There's a shul on every block, kosher food everywhere. Everyone's *tzniusdik*—that's a big one; most places you go in America, there's a tremendous lack of modesty. Trust me, it's a real privilege to grow up here. I'm jealous of you."

Something in her face tightened, and for a moment he feared he'd overstepped with the "jealous" remark. Then her face relaxed and she asked, "So how does a boy from *galus* end up in Eden?"

"It's a long story."

She nodded for him to continue. Buying time to organize his thoughts, he made a production of selecting a piece of cake from the tray, making a blessing, biting off a corner and chewing thoughtfully. Then, in as few sentences as possible, he gave the crux of how he found Yiddishkeit—or rather how Yiddishkeit found him—by way of Rabbi Kugel, the Chabad emissary in Moab. When the story shifted to Brooklyn, he slowed the tempo, weaving in pathos and elucidation. The more he spoke, the more he became swept up in his own narrative. He crescendoed with the exhilarating evening he sat through his first lecture by Rav Drezner—his "I've made it" moment.

Sarah's reaction, a small nod and a tight smile, disheartened him. A thick silence filled the room. "Yes, it's been quite a journey," he said. More silence, broken only by flipping pages of the valet's magazine. Mayer felt the night slipping through his fingers. What had he done wrong?

"I've never met anyone from Georgia," Sarah said a second time. "Tell me more about that."

"What would you like to know?"

"I don't know. Anything. What did your house look like? Who were your friends? What did you enjoy doing?"

"Well, there wasn't a lot to do. We had to invent our own fun."

She perked. "What do you mean?"

"You really want to hear about this?"

"Why else would I ask?"

Haltingly at first, then with some energy, he gave a few of the wholesomer anecdotes from his childhood. He made no mention of Ida Mae's boyfriends or sadists with jacked-up air guns—and inadvertently sketched a bucolic picture of small-town life in the pre-internet age.

"So different," Sarah said. Her lips parted, revealing perfect teeth. He'd have married her for her teeth alone.

"You can take your hat off if you want," she said.

"Do you want me to?"

"I can hardly see your face."

His neck turned fuchsia. He took off his hat and put it beside him.

"I like these stories," she said. "Tell me more."

HIS FIRST THOUGHT upon waking the next morning was he'd prattled on too long about his childhood without asking any questions in exchange. Conversation was a game of volleyball, not paddleball. Who did he think he was, a visiting lecturer?

The hours crawled without word from the Rav. He tried learning Talmud. The words on the page were a school of minnows, so he stared at the big clock on the east wall of the *beis medrash*. He didn't trust the clock; the second hand had to be taking at least ninety seconds per revolution. He skipped lunch and went for a walk on Ocean Parkway, replaying last night in his head on loop. He kept coming back to a moment, about an hour in, when he'd let his guard down and settled into a half recline with one leg crossed over the other. His pant leg rose up, revealing a wedge of calf. It felt right at the time, and Sarah appeared impartial. But now it stood out as the defining moment of the night. He'd blown it.

The next day was a day of mourning. He woke up convinced that *Hashem* had decreed he become a Drezner, then rescinded after replaying his dismal performance with Sarah. If this were ancient times, he'd wear a sackcloth and pour ashes on his head. When evening prayers came, he prayed with *kavanah* that God should heal his broken heart speedily—if for no other reason than so he could get back to his studies.

Miraculously, God answered his prayers. He awoke Friday morning clear-headed and convalesced. He now saw what an honor it was that the Rav had even considered him for Sarah. And who said the evening was a total wash? God willing, it was a learning experience for both of them, and each would find his and her respective *beshert* speedily. Fueled by positive thinking, he was productive all day in the *beis medrash*. An hour before sunset, Mayer closed his Gemara and made for the dormitory to get ready for Shabbos. One of the Rav's closest aides, an elderly scholar named Ostrovsky, intercepted him.

"The Rav needs to see you right away," he said in Yiddish.

Rav Drezner was at his desk, two fingers moving down a column of Gemara. "Ah, Reb Belkin from Georgia," he said dispassionately, and pointed to a chair. Rabbi Ostrovsky left them alone.

For the second time that week, Mayer found himself torn between apprehension and awe. The *rosh yeshiva*'s pace of learning was superhuman. This time, however, he didn't break at the bottom of the page, but flipped to the back of the volume to consult with the Maharshal, the Maharam, and other Early Modern Era commentators. With these he took his time, setting his elbows on either side of the Gemara and glaring at the tiny words, all the while stroking his beard.

Minutes passed. Then more minutes. Mayer stole an occasional glance across the desk. Rav Drezner's static posture was a portraitist's dream. Had he forgotten about the young bochur? Should Mayer clear his throat? If this went on much longer, he wouldn't have time for a pre-Shabbos shower, which, because his previous shower was last night, would mean thirty-six bathless hours. What's more, he had to pee.

His right knee started to bounce. He held it down, but this only awakened the other one, so he held both knees like a kid at his first job interview. Fifteen minutes passed. Twenty. Twenty-five. The Rav's eyes moved like the shadow on a sundial. If Mayer managed a one-minute shower, it would be a cold one; Ohr Lev's water tank was installed seventy years ago when there were half as many *talmidim*.

As he was summoning the courage to clear his throat—his bladder could only take so much—the Rav said, "Ah," and closed the Gemara with a thump. He looked at Mayer. "What did you think of my daughter?"

Anticipating this question days ago, should he be so lucky to be asked,

Mayer had praises at the ready revering Sarah as a model of virtue and purity—the ideal Jewish bride. "*Balabatish*," he fired off. "Truly a *ba'alas midos* with *yiras shamayim*."

To Mayer's consternation, the Rav didn't appear moved by the accolades. "She is an . . . *interesting* girl," he said, "cut of cloth different from my other daughters. She needs a husband with exceptional resolve and limitless patience. Such men are rare in Brooklyn, but—so I've heard—less rare out of town. Take Georgia, for instance. Perhaps the country air fosters cooler temperaments."

It took all of Mayer's power not to seize the arms of his chair and squeeze for dear life.

"If things proceed between the two of you, you'll continue learning at Ohr Lev?"

"Yes."

"You wouldn't transfer to a *beis medrash* in Lakewood, for instance? Or Monsey, or Chicago, or Yerushalayim?"

Question two gave him pause—not because he had a particular desire to live in any of these Orthodox strongholds, but because of its redundancy. Shouldn't his "yes" to the first question render the second unnecessary? Even more puzzling, the Rav listed four cities as examples when just one sufficed. Anyone familiar with his verbal style knew he meted out words as if they were wartime rations. Why put so fine a point on it?

"No," he said.

"I understand you are without family or funds in Brooklyn, so this is my offer: in exchange for your lifelong loyalty to Ohr Lev, I will provide you and my daughter with a comfortable home and see to it that all your financial needs are met. Is this acceptable?"

Now Mayer did grab the arms of his chair for fear of sliding off.

"*Nu?*" said the Rav.

"It . . . it would be an unbelievable *zechus*."

The Rav extended his hand across the desk and Mayer took it. It was like squeezing an overripe plum.

"Mazel tov. We'll make a *l'chaim* after Shabbos."

"A *l'chaim*," Mayer repeated hoarsely.

The Rav reopened his Gemara and, in an instant, was submerged.

"YOU LOSERS READY to roll?"

David was back at the pump island, arms loaded with sweet teas, a paper sack of boiled peanuts and a shopping bag of Doritos, Sugar Babies, Swee-Tarts and other junk.

"Give us a few?" Charlayne called back.

Making a face, he loaded up Daisy, climbed in, and parked in a disabled spot by the mini-mart door.

"How does he eat all that crap and stay fit?" Charlayne said.

"He's got our mother's genes," Mayer said. "Wait till he turns fifty."

"Anyway, your father-in-law."

"What about him?"

"I bet he gives great hugs."

Mayer laughed out loud. "Look," he said, "I wasn't exaggerating when I called Sarah a *balabusta*. She's a good woman."

"I didn't say she wasn't."

"She doesn't have it easy. She carries a deep . . ." He searched for the word. "Discontentment."

"What's she so discontented about?" Charlayne asked.

He raised his hands and let them drop.

"You don't know?" she said.

"Not entirely. I've always believed that, whatever it is, having children would fix it. Unfortunately, we've struggled to make that happen."

Charlayne said, "I don't have kids of my own. But my understanding is kids aren't great about staying outside invisible domes."

Mayer didn't reply. He reached down and gave Popeye a rub.

"Does she have sibs?" she asked.

"Seven."

"Where do they live?"

"All over," he said. "Israel, Chicago, New Jersey."

"Any in Brooklyn?"

He knew what she was getting at, and the reality was, he never found out exactly why the Rav was so vehement that they stay in Brooklyn. But over the years, he pieced together a bare-bones story about an incident from when Sarah was a counselor at a girls' summer camp in the Catskills. Her boss caught her and another female counselor doing . . . *something* . . . in a bunkhouse when everyone else was at a night activity. Only five people ever knew what that something was—the two girls, their boss, and Rav and Mrs. Drezner.

Daisy's horn blared again.

Charlayne said, "Let's get out of here before your brother has an embolism."

— CHAPTER 13 —

THE GOLD SPIRE ON BANK OF AMERICA PLAZA SHARK-
FINNED THE HORIZON. THEN CAME SUNTRUST PLAZA, ONE ATLANTIC
Center and the rest of Atlanta's skyscrapers. Though he and David had driven
through the Big Peach only two days ago, Mayer felt as if he were seeing it for
the first time.

They stopped for a late lunch at Little Bees Garage in the fashionable Old
Fourth Ward. David, Charlayne, Ida Mae and Popeye got a table while Mayer
ran across the street to a Publix for snack crackers and brisling sardines. He
ate standing over Daisy's trunk lid, then joined the others. They were having
cheeseburgers and sweet potato fries. It was lost on nobody that this was to
be Charlayne's last indoor meal for some time.

Back on the I-75, she asked if they could stop in New Moab to see the
Belkin homestead. Neither brother felt like it—now or ever again. Mayer had
already absolved himself from handling the sale of the house. He'd sign on the
dotted line and take whatever proceeds came his way, not that he expected
any. He wanted no keepsakes.

Traffic was light to Marietta, where they got on the I-575. Charlayne
and David chatted while Popeye slept. Mayer stared ahead at the asphalt corridor of pine-green walls. On the horizon hung a blue-gray haze that he first
thought to be the edge of a storm. But hadn't the weather report predicted
another day of pristine skies across the region?

Gradually the haze darkened and acquired contours, and when he realized what he was looking at, he felt an emotion that, had he seen *Pretty
Woman*, might have brought to mind Julia Roberts's iconic first night at the

opera. For all his love of nature, he'd never seen a mountain. The Blue Ridge range, of rugged rises and round, weathered tops, was as spectacular a first as one could ask for.

As they advanced, the mountains' hue tinted sage, then emerald, and finally sun-emblazoned shamrock. Their immensity evoked in Mayer's imagination beached Leviathans sleeping through the millennia, waiting for a second flood to wash them back to sea. Charlayne, her expression an amalgamation of anxiety and awe, hugged Popeye so tightly around the neck that one of his outer eyelids stretched to the cheekbone.

AFTER DRIVING THROUGH East Ellijay, they flanked the Cartecay River for about a mile before the road split off east. After another two miles, David got on Highway 52 into the Chattahoochee National Forest—in whose depths stood Springer Mountain, the southern terminus of the Appalachian Trail.

"How much longer?" Charlayne asked.

David glanced at his phone. "Forty minutes."

The scenery started out pastoral, mottled with apple orchards, greenhouses, farm stands, chicken coops, modest wood churches and inexpensive motels. Gradually, and then all at once, flora muscled in on the open spaces. There were loblolly and white pines, chestnut oaks, hickories, hemlocks and tulip trees inset with ferns, rhododendrons, azaleas, goldenrod and laurel. David rolled down the windows, welcoming in a chorus of untold avian varieties, accompanied by windblown leaves, groaning trunks, and gurgling distributaries of the Nottely River. Popeye wriggled out of Charlayne's grip and stuck his nose out the window.

"I'm just gonna come out and say it, Char," David said. "I think this is a mistake. Just give me the word and I'll turn around."

Charlayne said nothing.

"There are some excellent bed-and-breakfasts around here. Let's all sleep comfortably tonight. Pancakes and coffee for breakfast, then we regroup."

"No," she said.

They traveled southeast on a gravel road for seven miles. The mutual feeling in the car manifested itself in the mournful look in Popeye's one seeing eye. Daisy herself seemed to labor harder than she ought to up the rises, as if she knew each one brought her closer to goodbye.

A few minutes after three, David pulled into the Springer Mountain parking lot. That there were just two other cars here was a barometer of Charlayne's delinquency—and a harbinger of the price she'd pay in New England come autumn. She and Popeye got out first, the latter disappearing into some laurel bushes while the former walked up to a rectangular wooden trail sign staked in the ground. It said "SPRINGER MTN .9," with an arrow pointing leftward, in the direction from whence they'd come. To their right, the Appalachian Trail continued east.

"Less than a mile," she murmured. "Unreal."

"'Two roads diverged in a wood, and I—I took the one less traveled by,' " David said, reciting the penultimate two lines of Robert Frost's most celebrated poem.

"'And that has made all the difference,'" she said, capping it off.

David walked off to study a map tacked to a wood information board. A minute later he was back, holding a lit joint. He offered it to Charlayne, who gratefully accepted.

"Funny," he said. "I was expecting more fanfare when we got here."

"From who, the Lollipop Guild?" Mayer said. That sent David into peals of laughter. Charlayne popped Daisy's trunk and took out a plastic tarp folded in a rectangle. She spread it on the gravel lot and set to piling up her cargo. The Belkins chipped in, and before long she accepted the honor of crowning the heap with the Star of Bethlehem—the camping stove. It teetered, then rolled down the side and onto the gravel, stopping at her toes.

She stared at it for several seconds. "I can't do this."

"What?" David said.

"You're right. I'm too late. I'll never make it."

David looked at the heap, then her.

"I'll get lost," she said. "I don't know how to use half this gear. The only hiking I've ever done is nature walks. I've never pooped outdoors in my life. And . . ."

She swatted at a black fly on her arm, missing by a mile.

". . . I hate bugs."

"I once squatted on a patch of poison ivy to relieve myself," David said. "Talk about a rite of passage."

Charlayne snorted a dispirited laugh. "What was I thinking?"

David touched the small of her back. She stepped away. "Help me put this stuff back in the car."

He scratched his upper lip. "Are you sure that's what you want?"

"What the hell," she said irascibly. "I finally come to my senses and now you're my rah-rah girl?"

"I just don't want you to give up because of me."

"No, I'm being smart for a change. Look, I'll tag along with you guys to New York. We'll barhop through Manhattan. I'll Instagram the shit out of it." She smiled as if a puppeteer were tugging at her mouth with strings.

David shrugged. "If that's what you want."

Just then a breeze blew by, and hundreds of leafroller caterpillars, heretofore unnoticed, swayed on silk strings. An avian screech sounded from high above. Charlayne's two eyes locked on Mayer's one.

"What?" David said.

"Broad-winged hawk," Charlayne said.

"Ah."

"Once in Hawk Ridge, I saw a kettle of broad-wings. There were hundreds. It was the most . . . What's that look on your face?"

"You captivate me," Mayer said.

"Why?"

"Because of all you've seen and all you will see. You're a student of the world. I never saw a kettle of hawks. I doubt I ever will."

"Why not?"

He backhanded the air. "*Bitul Torah.*"

"What's that?"

"Time wasted not studying Torah. But that's all in the past and . . . well, maybe the future too. Let's just worry about now."

Her lips started to quiver. She wiped the corner of an eye with a knuckle.

"Let's pack you up. Give David and me the honor of escorting you to Springer Mountain. It's only a mile and there's plenty of daylight left. Let's look at that first trail marker and make believe we've got the courage to walk past it and not stop till Maine."

Charlayne's throat bobbed. She stepped toward him. Suddenly, Popeye bounded out of the brush, covered in pricklers and holding what remained of a vole in his teeth. They cleaned him off. Then they got packing.

TO EVERYONE'S SURPRISE and relief, the packing took only half an hour. The rucksack's myriad pockets, compartments and straps held a physics-defying amount of gear. It helped that Charlayne only needed about a third of what she'd brought along; one headlamp, not three, would suffice. Nor did she need half a gallon of cooking fuel or a gallon of water.

While the Belkins cinched, zipped and tied the rucksack, Charlayne went behind an oak tree. She came back wearing blue nylon shorts and a matching tank, hiking boots and padded socks. Her hair was tied back with a red bandanna, a blue one around her neck.

David put a finger in each corner of his mouth and whistled.

"Shut up." She tossed her civilian attire in the trunk with the other nonessentials, then examined the rucksack, which the brothers had leaned upright against a tree.

"It looks like an engorged sea cucumber," she said.

"Try it on," David said.

She took the grab handle in two hands, bent her knees and heaved. She got it to chest level and tried to thread an arm through a shoulder strap, but the weight proved too much for her other arm and she dropped it. Mayer stepped forward to assist, but David halted him with a hand to the chest. She lifted the rucksack again by the grab handle and managed to get an arm through a strap. But when she tried to do likewise on the other side, she missed and the thing went horizontal, dangling from the crook of her elbow. She was forced to drop it again.

"Maybe if you—" David said. She cut him off with a look. Hands on hips, she brooded. After a brief spell, she picked the bag up once more by the grab handle and dragged it to the tree. Facing away from the pack, she squatted and snaked both arms into the straps. With a forward pivot and a weightlifter's heave, she stood, teetered, staggered, almost fell—and found her center of gravity. She pulled down the harness adjusters and secured the sternum and waist clips so that the pack was airtight against her back. She grabbed her trekking poles and wordlessly set down the path to Springer Mountain. When she realized no one was behind her, she turned and looked at the bewitched Belkins.

"Coming?"

WITH IDA MAE in the crook of his arm, David hiked in step with Charlayne, the two clearing roots and boulders with alacrity. Popeye, in his element, veered off the path for minutes at a time to chase whatever caught his fancy. Mayer took it slow. Years of nature deprivation—allayed only by rare trips to Brooklyn's Prospect Park, which, enchanting as its duck ponds and grassy meadows were, was no wilderness—had inflicted him with a kind of intrapsychic scurvy.

As soon as his companions were out of earshot, he sat on a lichen-covered boulder. He inhaled laurel, rhododendron, pine sap, wild mushrooms and rich, fertile earth. He listened to yawning trees, rustling leaves, multitudinous bird-calls, a burbling brook—and a rapid staccato roll from high above. Looking into the trees he saw it immediately: a red-headed woodpecker some forty feet up.

Melanerpes erythrocephalus.

It was strange and exhilarating to be so utterly in the present that to-morrow was an afterthought. In the *beis medrash,* tomorrow was now: learn Torah, accumulate spiritual currency, cash it in in the World to Come. That which didn't advance the goal was a distraction one trained himself to ignore. It had never occurred to him that perhaps God wanted him to stop learning once in a while and admire his artistry—that walking in the woods was not *bitul Torah* but an opportunity to worship.

Ruminating on this, he resumed his trek, hyper keen to every rustle of brush, every birdcall, every earthy aroma. Despite a one-eye handicap he managed to pick out gray squirrels, chipmunks, mice, voles, toads and, to his everlasting delight, a rattlesnake sunning itself on a bed of moss. He saw birds, of course—an American robin, a yellow-bellied flycatcher, a bluebird, two species of thrush, three species of sparrow, an osprey, a red-tailed hawk, a tanager and a purple martin. He sampled blueberries, huckleberries, sassafras and other wild edibles he and David foraged as kids when starved for fresh produce. The hike was easy and Mayer, even at a rubbernecker's pace, reached the summit in less than an hour. His eye was starting to ache, so he dug into his pocket for his medication. Neither it nor the Tylenol was there, or in any of his other pockets.

Charlayne and David were sitting on a rock with a plaque marking the spot as the southern terminus of the Appalachian Trail. They were joined at the hip, her head on his shoulder, sharing a joint while watching the mountain peaks through the leafy overhang. Popeye sat on the ground beside them, licking his muzzle.

"*Hashamayim m'saprim kavod el umaaseh yadav yagid harakia,*" Mayer said.

Charlayne looked behind her. "What does that mean?"

"'The heavens describe the glory of God, and the sky tells the work of his hands.' It's from Psalms."

David tossed him a bottle of water. He drained it, then sat cross-legged on a slab of rock which also had a plaque, this one depicting a rugged outdoorsman embarking on his two-thousand-mile trek northward. A valley breeze came over the mountaintop and cooled his damp shirt.

"There's a shelter just back the way we came," David said. "Char and I were talking about maybe sleeping there tonight."

Mayer palmed his angry eye.

"You okay?" David said.

"Little pain," he said.

"Did you take something for it?"

"I left my meds in the car."

"I'll run back for them," Charlayne said.

"It's okay," Mayer said. "It's mild. I can go a night without the meds."

Popeye came over and sniffed his face. Mayer was reassured—if a tad nauseated—to smell blood on his breath, as they'd brought no kibble. Charlayne joined them and looked down at the plaque of the outdoorsman.

"A footpath for those who seek fellowship with the wilderness," she read aloud.

Another breeze came, making Mayer shiver. Charlayne said, "Let's go check out that shelter."

THE SHELTER WAS a pitch-roofed shack in a clearing some two hundred yards off the trail. Nearby was a firepit with a pile of thick branches left by a prior occupant. There was also a wood picnic table, a privy and a bear-proof tool chest to store food.

Mayer, who was starting to get anxious about the growing pain in his eye, bristled when his phone vibrated. Was there no refuge from cell towers? He took it out, glanced at the screen and put it away. What Sarah wanted was already hers; she could stand to wait another day to learn this.

Charlayne spread her tent on the shelter floor, and Mayer helped pitch it. The polyester dome slept two, which meant someone would sleep under the stars. Charlayne crawled in and unrolled her sleeping bag, tucking her copy of *A Grief Observed* inside. Popeye got in, making himself comfortable on the downy bag.

David, in the interim, had gathered kindling and was building a little tee-pee of twigs and bark in the firepit. He put his Zippo to it, and as it burned, he reinforced the structure with larger twigs and small branches. The fire grew, and he fenced it in with sticks and lay branches across the top.

"When were you in the Boy Scouts?" Mayer asked.

"Never." The elder Belkin blew two gusts into the flames and they rose, licking the thatching. He added more branches.

"Then who taught you to do that?" Mayer asked.

David made a face as if to ask, *Is this a bit?* "You did, Ese."

"I?"

"In the pine barrens. We almost started a forest fire one time."

Mayer had no recollection. "Well, I'm glad I taught you one useful thing."

David's eyes flickered in the firelight. "You taught me everything I know worth knowing."

DAVID WHIPPED UP a pot of mac and cheese on the camping stove, then made hot chocolate. Mayer, wishing he'd taken Charlayne up on her offer to get his meds, had no appetite. They sat around the fire, watching the stars come out and talking like old friends. David told tales of his roller-coaster life, which alternately had Charlayne in stitches and open-mouthed horror.

As night squeezed in on dusk, the temperature fell and they all moved closer to the fire. The conversation took a somber turn on revisiting Ida Mae's suicide and its aftermath. But when they segued to the fireworks fiasco, even

Mayer laughed in defiance of his pain—then doubled over, palming his eye.

"Seriously bro, you okay?" David asked.

"Yeah."

"Hang on." David reached into his pocket and pulled out a Ziploc baggie containing three joints.

"I'm not smoking that," Mayer said.

"Then you're in for the longest night of your life." David put a joint in his mouth and lit it. "Two hits of this and you'll never want Tylenol again. Now pay attention."

He toked, holding the smoke in his lungs and blowing it out slowly. "Now you."

"David, leave the poor guy alone," Charlayne said.

"I'm trying to help him."

"You're making him uncomfortable."

"I'm not uncomfortable," Mayer said, "I'm just . . . oh, give me that." He took the joint, stuck it between his lips and drew deeply into his virgin lungs. Out came a bombardment of violent coughs, each igniting his eye socket like a combustion chamber in a stock-car engine. When it ceased, he pressed his palm to his eye patch and rocked back and forth, blubbering.

"Just let that soak in," David said. He pried the half-crushed joint from his brother's fingers, straightened it and passed it to Charlayne, who took a hit. Mayer shook his head when she offered it to him.

"Don't stop now, bro," David said.

The second time around, he managed to hold down the vapor for a whole two seconds before succumbing to another coughing fit. He rocked in his seat, whimpering and groaning. Gradually, the pain subsided and his attention shifted to the weirdly riveting sparks corkscrewing up from the embers. *Like gnats*, he thought. Then something else caught his eye—Charlayne's thighs flush together, her calves an inverted V. He looked at her face. Shadow and firelight fought for real estate on her lips, cheekbones, the bridge of her nose.

"You're beautiful," he said.

"And you are a sweet man."

"What are you thinking about?"

"That I suck."

He rested his chin on his hand, rapt. "How come?"

"I should have been in Virginia by now." She threw a twig into the fire. "I'm such a coward."

"False," David said. "You're a baller for going through with it anyway."

"Am I going through with it?"

"Are you not?"

She turned to Mayer. "How's your eye, sweetie?"

"Which one?"

She giggled, which made him giggle.

David said, "So, how 'bout as a parting gift you tell us what this is about."

"What what's about?" Charlayne said.

"Why the AT."

The smile stayed on her lips but disappeared from her eyes. "It's not a big secret or anything." She stretched out her legs then drew a line in the earth with her heel. "I mentioned I was married, right?"

"To Adam," Mayer said.

Her eyes rounded. "How did you know that?"

He tapped the underside of his wrist.

"Ah," she said. "Well played, Sherlock."

Mayer was thinking of Iry Bullard, who'd given his mother a shiner before leaving the house on Bragg Street and never coming back. "He did something bad to you," he said.

Charlayne raised her face to the empyrean. Mayer did, too, and was amazed by how many constellations he knew. There was Lupus, Ursa Minor, Sagittarius, the Little Dipper. And there was the North Star, which, until very recently, he'd called Sarah.

"When I was little," Charlayne said, "my parents taught me to never give a man the power to hurt me. And then I went ahead and did just that."

"Don't blame yourself," David said.

"I don't."

"Good, 'cause take it from someone who's given his share of women hell, we're not worth it."

She tossed another twig into the fire. "Adam and I were only fifteen when we fell in love, but even then we knew we were each other's . . . what's the word?"

"*Beshert*," Mayer said.

"How was I supposed to know how unlikely it is to meet your *beshert* at fifteen? I broke up with him in our freshman year of college because I didn't want to be tied down. It took dating an all-star loser lineup to realize my mistake."

"So what happened—he took you back?" David said.

"Yes."

"But he never forgave you."

She laughed. "Not only did he forgive me—he asked me to marry him."

Mayer stared blankly at her. David scratched his head.

"And then he cheated on you?"

"Cheat? Adam was a jellyfish around women. He was short and bald. And he had a speech impediment."

The Belkins exchanged glances. "Did he embezzle from you?" David asked.

She laughed again. "My eight-year-old nephew understands money better than he did."

"I'm stumped," Mayer said.

"Me too," David said.

She put her elbows on her knees and warmed her hands over the embers. "Bus accident."

It took a few seconds for the brothers to grasp her meaning. "When?" David said.

"Three years ago."

"I'm so sorry," Mayer said.

Charlayne gave a half smile. "We always joked about what an odd couple we were—like if Pam Grier married Smeagol."

David chuffed out a laugh.

"But our souls were one."

"*Ani l'dodi v'dodi li*," Mayer said, thinking of the words printed in gilded letters on the wedding album he and Sarah hadn't opened since Dubya was president.

"What does that mean?" Charlayne said.

"'I am to my beloved as my beloved is to me.' It's a quote from King Solomon in Song of Songs."

Her eyes misted over. "That."

The diminished fire crackled in defiance of its impending demise, embers the color of red coral.

"May I read you a passage from my book?" Charlayne asked.

"Let me get it," Mayer said.

A Grief Observed was falling apart, the cover more or less a folder for the detached leaves. Passages had been underlined in ballpoint. Margins were dense with notations.

"C. S. Lewis had a lot on his mind after the death of his wife, Joy Davidman—a Jew, incidentally—so he wrote it all down," Charlayne said. "Actually, this was Adam's copy. I found it when I was giving away his books. I've read it so many times I probably know it by heart."

She flipped through it, stopping at page ten. She read aloud.

"'I once read the sentence "I lay awake all night with a toothache, thinking about the toothache and about lying awake." That's true to life. Part of every misery is, so to speak, the misery's shadow or reflection: the fact that you don't merely suffer but have to keep on thinking about the fact that you suffer. I not only live each endless day in grief, but live each day thinking about living each day in grief.'"

She read it again to herself, savoring the syntax.

"He taught English," she said. "Adam, I mean. C. S. taught English too, at Oxford and Cambridge; Adam taught high school. He was so funny, especially when he wasn't trying to be. His students were shattered when—"

She closed the book abruptly. "Anyway, after Adam, I've been without a leg. That's my answer to C. S.'s toothache."

"I don't think I've ever felt that way about anyone in my life," David said. "No one I've ever slept with, anyway."

"Pity," Charlayne said.

"So why the Appalachian Trail?"

"Well, we both loved the outdoors. I just preferred my outdoors to be within driving distance of a Starbucks. He always wanted to do the AT with me. I'd be like, 'Sure, when we're retired.'"

She swallowed a rising lump. "So here I am, hoping if I can manage it on one leg, he'll let me have the other one back."

"Do you wish you'd never known him?" Mayer asked.

"What do you mean?"

"To have avoided the grief."

"Never." The embers reflected in her eyes like two terrace ponds under a harvest moon. "Everyone should be so lucky to love and be loved equally, at least once."

"Then why did you get the tattoo of his name removed?" David asked.

She looked at her wrist. "At first, the pain was so unbearable that I'd do anything to make it stop. The drugs they prescribed me barely helped. In my delirium I thought if I took his name off my body, my soul would get some relief. It didn't work, but that's where my head was at the time."

A few minutes ticked by—or a few seconds for all anyone knew; real and perceived time had gone their separate ways. Suddenly, a series of deep hoots pierced the quiet—*Hoo-h'HOO-hoo-hoo*.

Charlayne and Mayer looked at each other. Identical smiles broke on their faces.

Bubo virginianus; great horned owl.

"Oh, get a room," David said.

A SLIVER OF morning sun touched Mayer's eyelid. He opened it and saw hickory leaves on a taffy-blue veneer. He smelled wildflowers, sweet dead pine needles, clean soil, and wood char from the fire, which had burned itself out. He felt Charlayne's leg over his, her arm across his chest, her cheek on his shoulder. An incorrigible coil of her hair tickled his chin.

Never until now had he experienced a dream segueing into an identical reality.

He gingerly touched his eye bandage and grimaced. Not good, but at least he wasn't feverish. Nothing had happened last night with Charlayne; they'd laid out the tarp on some ferns and stared at the stars, drifting off without ever working out who'd sleep where. At some point in the night, she'd pulled her side of the tarp over the two of them. Waking up this way was the most intimate moment of his life.

His phone vibrated. Charlayne snorted and blinked twice, then nuzzled into the hollow of his neck. "Good morning, sunshine," she said.

The phone vibrated seven more times before it quit. Then came a zipper noise, and David's head poked out from between the tent flaps. He was red-eyed and puffy-faced, a joint tucked into the corner of his mouth. There was a dent like a question mark on his forehead.

"What happened to you?" Mayer asked.

"I must've used my shoe as a pillow," David said. Mayer and Charlayne broke into titters of laughter. The sound lured Popeye out of the tent and over to their tarp, where he was rewarded with a full-body scratchdown.

David joined them, Ida Mae in one hand and *A Grief Observed* in the other.

"How did you like it?" Charlayne asked, eyeing the book.

"I read it twice—before I passed out and when I woke up. You should give it a go, Ese."

"Oh?"

"The way he talks about God reminds me of what you're going through. Check this out."

He flipped the pages until he found what he was looking for: "'Not that I am (I think) in much danger of ceasing to believe in God. The real danger is of coming to believe such dreadful things about Him. The conclusion I dread is not "So there's no God after all," but "So this is what God's really like."'"

"Who's this guy again?" Mayer asked.

"C. S. Lewis." Charlayne said. "Ever read The Chronicles of Narnia?"

"I think the first one."

"C. S. was famously a Christian apologist, so the religious set was taken aback by how candid he got in *A Grief Observed*. He died two years later."

"I guess he finally figured it out in the end," Mayer said.

"Figured what out?"

"That God never gave two beans about him or his wife."

She looked askance at him. "You really think that?"

"I don't know. Hey, what's for breakfast?"

"No," Charlayne said, "do you really believe that his wife's death was just a random and meaningless act of God? That God didn't care about his pain?"

"Who cares what I think?"

Suddenly, clarity came to her eyes and they turned hard as marbles. "You think God didn't care how he felt because he wasn't Jewish?"

"Look, I'm not either."

"Neither am I. Neither is David. But you'll be soon enough. And what then?"

Mayer groped inwardly for a satisfactory response. "You have to understand," he said, "for more than two-thirds of my life I've been blind to gentiles. A non-Jew could walk right past me on the sidewalk, and I'd be aware of a physical human presence, obviously, but I wouldn't really *see*. They had no relevance to me. I could tell you exactly how many dinars you owed if your ox kicked a pebble that damaged your neighbor's clay jug. But on the subject of gentiles, I'm completely ignorant."

"For a guy who pleads ignorance, you've formed a pretty strong opinion of us," Charlayne said.

"What do you want me to say?"

Her long lashes fluttered. Tears glassed her eyes. "How about, 'Gentile or not, I'll never forget you.'"

David picked that moment to break into a coughing fit, cannabis smoke jetting from his mouth like backfire from an exhaust pipe.

"You okay?" Charlayne asked. He nodded, but went on hacking for another half minute, bent over and beating his chest with his fist.

When he settled down, Mayer pointed to the smoldering joint and said, "Hey, alright if I . . . ?"

David gave it to him. He took two light puffs, somehow avoiding coughing altogether. David went to the rucksack and removed a roll of toilet paper. "I'll be back in five"—he touched his lower abdomen—"ten minutes."

When he was gone, Charlayne said, "Can I make a suggestion, Hawkeye?"

"Go ahead."

"When you go back to your old-slash-new life, make it a point to ask God why he did this to you."

"I'm not sure what that means."

"It means don't dismiss everything that happened to you as meaningless. I know your worldview sees it that way, but I promise, God did this to you with full intent, and it was good intent. Ask him why."

"How do you know?" he asked.

"Because if I hadn't met you guys, I wouldn't be here. I'd be off to another city, lugging my camping gear and making excuses why I should hold off doing this for another year. It's a miracle I'm here. A miracle. You'll never know."

DAVID RETURNED WITH a considerably shrunken TP roll. "Serves me right for noshing on protein gels all night." He rummaged around the bear box until he found an assortment of energy bars and a Ziploc baggie of freeze-dried coffee. He built a fire, made a stovetop of thick branches and soon had a brew bubbling. Popeye perked to the sound of his breakfast rustling in the thicket, and he darted off to chase it down.

When everyone was fed, Charlayne surveyed her depleted stores. "Uh-oh."

"We'll resupply you when we get to the car," David said.

"Oh yeah, we have to go back that way, don't we? Then I should be good until Mountain Crossings."

David stomped out the fire, then excused himself for another trip to the privy. Charlayne rolled up the sleeping bag while Mayer dismantled the tent. When he lifted a corner to free a pole from a grommet, he saw on the floor a powder-yellow compact slightly smaller than a hockey puck. He picked it up and opened it to reveal a circular array of little white pills.

"This yours?" he asked Charlayne.

She grinned demurely. "Don't know why I brought that along. Wishful thinking, I guess."

"Better take it with you."

"Oh yeah?"

"Well, yeah. For your migraines."

Her brow knitted. "Migraines?"

"You don't get migraines?"

"Not really, why?"

Now they both looked confused. "Sarah's got a case just like it," he said. "She takes one every morning to ward off . . . are you okay?"

"Fine," she said quickly, before grabbing the compact and sticking it in her pocket.

THE TROOP HIKED back the way they'd come, light-footed and high-spirited—especially pot-happy Mayer. They reunited with Daisy just before eight and restocked Charlayne's provisions. David gifted her a baggie of his finest and promised another stash would be waiting for her at the post office in Hot Springs, North Carolina.

"I want you to have this," Charlayne said, holding *A Grief Observed* out to Mayer.

"I couldn't," he said.

"I have a feeling you need it more than me. Anyway, it's just on loan. I'll want it back when I see you again."

"In that case, let's raise the stakes." Mayer opened the car and took out *Field Guide to the Birds of North America*, which he handed to her. She stepped into him and wrapped her arms around his neck.

"I really mean it," she whispered. "Don't make this goodbye." She squeezed him so hard his breath caught in his throat. "I love you, Hawkeye."

Mayer nodded.

"Have that talk with God. And look after your brother. He smokes too much."

He nodded again. She kissed the corner of his mouth. Then she squatted to embrace Popeye. She spoke endearments into his ear and he lapped her cheek. She moved on to David, who handed her Ida Mae. She put her lips close to the pewter, whispered something and kissed it. Then she hooked her arm into David's and guided him some fifteen feet away. She spoke in tones too low for Mayer to hear, but he watched her lips—and was almost certain she said the word "migraine." David recoiled, his expression disbelieving. He tried to speak but she shushed him. She leaned into him and said something else. He responded, "Okay. Okay. Fine."

"What was that all about?" Mayer asked when they came back.

"I had to drop some hard knowledge on your brother," Charlayne said. "Now, don't be strangers. Send texts. Emails. Smoke signals. Whatever you have to do."

"You can count on it," David said.

She shrugged on her sack for the final time, expertly cinching the straps. She put a protein bar in each pocket and took a swig from her water bag. She gave her bootlaces a final check and looped her hands through the canvas straps of her trekking poles. She awaited the Belkins' verdict.

"You look ready to kick butt," Mayer said.

"We're proud of you, Charlayne Valentine," David said.

She beamed. "Until we meet again . . ."

"May God hold you in the palm of his hand," David said.

She turned to face the trail. She closed her eyes, filled her lungs and blew out. "And . . ." She took a halting step, stopped. She took a second step, a third. She broke into a stride. The Belkins and Popeye watched the massive ruck-sack bounce across the lot. They watched boots step off flat gravel and onto black, craggy earth.

She turned once more to face her friends, smiled and raised a fist in the air. The boys mirrored the gesture. She faced the trail again, ducked under some overhang, and was gone.

Neither brother nor the dog moved or spoke as her footfalls faded to silence. They stood like that for another minute, staring at the overhang.

"Well?" David finally said.

"Well, what?"

"Did you guys fuck last night or what?"

— CHAPTER 14 —

THE DEPLETED CREW TRAVELED NORTH TO BLUE
RIDGE, A SCENIC MOUNTAIN TOWN AT THE EDGE OF THE
Chattahoochee. Mayer craved fresh food, so they stopped at Walmart. He
fixed himself two tomato-and-onion sandwiches in the parking lot of a Waffle
House while the others went in for breakfast.

He found them at a corner booth. David was texting; Ida Mae held court
with the syrup dispensers; Popeye lazed under the table.

"What's up?"

The elder Belkin looked up from his iPhone. "My assistant's getting you
an appointment with an eye doctor in town."

"That's good news."

David had been on edge since he helped Mayer change his bandage and
apply fresh ointment at the Springer Mountain parking lot. He'd said the eye
reminded him of Rocky in the fifteenth round with Ivan Drago.

"How's it feel?" he now asked.

Mayer probed the new dressing with his fingers. "Warm."

"Does it hurt?"

"Yeah, but it's manageable. I took three Tylenol back up the road."

A waiter soon appeared bearing a waffle with whipped cream and pecans,
three scrambled eggs, bacon, sausage, and grits with cheese and onions—all
for David. There was coffee and OJ for both men, and three orders of sausage
and eggs for the dog.

David picked up a rasher of bacon and swung it like a movie hypnotist.

"Get that out of my face," Mayer said.

"You used to love bacon. You loved it more than me."

"The smell turns my stomach."

David shoved it in his mouth like a stick of Juicy Fruit and winced with pleasure. He regarded Ida Mae as he chewed. "Where do you think we should sprinkle her?"

"I don't follow."

"Remember what she said—how she wants her remains scattered somewhere that'll make her smile from the afterlife?"

"You actually want to honor that?"

"She's still our mother, Ese."

Mayer sipped coffee. "I find the concept grotesque."

"It's actually a pretty healing experience. I've done it a couple of times."

"Of course you have."

David's phone vibrated. "Great. You've got a twelve-thirty appointment with a Dr. Willoughby, right here in Blue Ridge." He looked at his Rolex. "That's in two hours. After we're done here, let's get a room somewhere and get cleaned up."

"That's the best idea I've heard in a long time."

The idea was so good, in fact, that David got the check early, with half his food uneaten. A thought came to Mayer as he watched his brother work out the tip. "You haven't done that thing in a while."

David signed the check and looked up. "What thing?"

"Swiping women on your phone."

"Huh, so I haven't," David said. He grabbed Ida Mae and stood to go.

"You didn't realize you'd stopped?" Mayer said.

David shrugged. "I guess I just stopped feeling lonely."

THE BLUE MOON Inn was a serviceable motel with a bluff stone exterior and mountain views. Mayer won Rock Paper Scissors for first shower. David got comfortable on the bed, flipping on *LIVE with Kelly and Mark* and lighting a joint.

"Maybe take it easy on that stuff," Mayer said. "You don't want to drift through life in a stupor."

"You've got it all wrong," David said. "I'm in life supreme."

In the shower, Mayer stuck a finger in each ear so his head filled with white noise from the spray. In his mind's eye he raked up all the fears, doubts, regrets and yearnings from his past, and set the heap on fire. The purge was sublime, emancipating—but one bygone memory escaped the blaze. It went airbound, somersaulted, descended. He caught it.

It was a Shabbos afternoon in late spring. The temperature was a perfect seventy-two, the trees in full bloom, air sweet from an earlier rainstorm. It was one of those rare moments when one forgot they were in the heart of New York's most paved borough. Mayer and Sarah walked and talked on Ocean Parkway. Though married only a few months, he knew all about her invisible dome and took pains not to breach it. But as they waited for the light at Ditmas Avenue, she, on a rare impulse, weaved her fingers through his. The unsolicited touch sent a surge of electricity through him, but he remained outwardly dispassionate for fear of spooking her.

A "tsk-tsk" sounded behind them. Sarah instantly pulled her hand away. They spun around and saw a *chassidishe alter bubbe* on a park bench. Her face was lined with deep fissures, her eyes slits of milky blue. Forked earlobes memorialized vanity's final losing battle with gravity. She crooked an admonishing finger at the couple and cried, "*Yeridas Hadoros!*" lamenting the indecency of the young.

She might have been right. But her *shpitzel* tilted so far to one side that it looked like a military side cap, and the young couple struggled to keep straight faces. The ancient woman wasn't having it; she bared her teeth at the impertinent pair. The teeth fell on her lap, and it was game over. Sarah and Mayer jackknifed in paroxysms of laughter. The walk signal came on, and they ran before the *alter bubbe* could cast the evil eye on them.

For the rest of the day, they couldn't flush the laughing bug. All either of them had to do was say "dentures" and they'd both fall to pieces. That night in bed, Mayer pretended twenty years had gone by and he was replaying the memory in his head on loop. He paused it every time the screen filled with Sarah's face, cheeks flush and lashes wet. He thought, *This was us in the beginning.*

HE WRAPPED A towel around his waist and brushed his teeth. When the fog in the mirror cleared, he did a double take. He looked . . . *handsome* was too generous a word, but maybe some hint of it. His face and neck had a golden hue from all the hours he'd spent outdoors of late. Boyish freckles sprinkled the bridge of his nose. And there appeared to be a trace of definition along the line of his jaw that wasn't there before. Implausibly, the patch over the right eye evoked ruggedness, not infirmity. The left eye—and this was truly wondrous—projected confidence, purpose, and a whisper of mischief. Who was this guy?

David was still on the bed when he came out of the bathroom, only completely nude now and reading the Gideon Bible. The roach smoldered in the corner of his mouth. Popeye had retreated to a far corner of the room.

"Whoa," Mayer said.

"Why don't you take a picture? It'll last longer."

"Sorry, it's just . . . I figured you to be a lot hairier."

"Oh yeah?" David lowered the Bible.

"When we were twelve you were already sprouting like a Chia Pet."

The elder brother laughed. "I used to go to the beach and people thought I was wearing a sweater vest."

"So what happened?"

"Laser, bro. I got the citywide package—uptown and downtown."

"I can see that."

David snapped shut the Bible and tossed it beside him. "You gonna call Sarah?"

"Yep."

"Tell her everything?"

"Yep."

David swung his legs off the bed. He started toward the bathroom, then stopped and turned around. "When you're done with that, there's something I've got to tell you. Something to do with Sarah."

"What?"

"After." He went into the bathroom and closed the door. Mayer put on clean chinos and a plaid cotton shirt, leaving it untucked. He found his phone and sat on the bed. Popeye hopped up next to him. He ran a hand up the grain of the dog's coat, the short hair bunching between his fingers like paintbrush bristles.

"Here goes nothing."

He dialed. The first ring broke midway through—then silence. He checked the screen. They were connected.

"Sarah?"

He checked the screen again.

"It's Mayer." He laughed self-effacingly. "Of course it's me."

The shower came on. David started humming "Walk with You."

"Sarah, there's something I need to tell you."

He checked the screen a third time. He needed a prompt from her. Anything. He recalled the time he froze up on their first date, and she came to the rescue with questions about his childhood. There were no questions this time.

He said, "It says in Tehillim, 'He who speaks lies shall not stand before my eyes.'"

His wandering eye landed on the front cover of the Gideon. He flipped it over. "In light of recent events, I prefer 'He who shall not stand before my eyes speaks lies.'"

On the wall facing him hung a framed photograph of an old man with a knotty wooden stick walking through a tunnel of overhanging leaves. His back was to the camera, but Mayer would have put money down that the look on his face was seraphic.

Two roads diverged in a wood, and I—

Something wet swabbed his arm. He looked at Popeye, whose eyes seemed to ask, *You hanging in there okay, pal?*

He gave the dog a reassuring tug on the jowls. "Let me explain," he said. And he did.

DAVID KEPT THE shower running for the duration of Mayer's phone call. When he came out of the bathroom, he resembled a steamed yucca. After getting an eyeful of his brother's stricken face, he tiptoed to the far side of the bed. He put on a pair of white Levi's and a Cuban collar shirt with palm trees on it, all the while stealing apprehensive glances at the back of his twin's head.

He put on his watch. "Guess we should go to the doctor now."

Mayer nodded and got to his feet. He scooped his laundry off the floor, wadded it into a ball and stuffed it into a plastic bag.

"It's gonna be okay," David offered.

"I know," Mayer said.

"What's that thing Rabbi Kugel always used to say?" He ran a hand over his bald head. "'This, too, is for the best'?"

Mayer turned around. He was grinning. "*Gam zu l'tovah.*"

"That's the spirit," David said, grinning back. "Listen, you come live with me, alright? I'll take care of everything. I'll arrange to have all your stuff packed and shipped from New York. You don't have to see Sarah again if you don't want to."

Mayer's smile expanded until the corners of his mouth touched the back molars.

"Ese?"

"I told her the whole story."

"And?"

The smile stretched to what seemed like the limits of human capacity. David felt himself wanting to look away.

"And . . . she wants to keep me."

WELL, NOT THE *whole* story.

He'd redacted gratuitous details like the impromptu topless show on Bourbon Street, and the two nights he'd lain—albeit not in the biblical sense—with another woman.

"So what *did* you tell her?" David asked. "About Charlayne, I mean."

They were at Willoughby Eye Clinic on West Main Street. None of the three other patients in the waiting room raised so much as an eyebrow at the urn on David's lap, or the squinty-eyed dog at his feet.

"Nothing, really," Mayer said. "Why make her suffer more than I had to?"

"Well, you had to tell her something; she knew about Char from the Café Du Monde video."

"I just said she was some woman my crazy brother offered a ride to," he said. "Which is basically true."

"Uh-huh. And Sarah kept quiet the whole time you were talking?"

Mayer's eye burned like he'd rubbed cayenne pepper into it, but he was too giddy to care. "I kept checking my screen to make sure she hadn't hung up on me."

"Well, what did she finally say?"

"That's the weird part."

What Sarah finally said—after an interminable delay—was "Where are you now?"

At first Mayer thought she meant it in a metaphysical sense, given all he'd been through. But Sarah was nothing if not literal. "In a hotel room," he said. "In a town called Blue Ridge. We came here to shower and change clothes. Then I'm going to the eye doctor."

"And your *giyur* is Sunday?"

He said it was.

"Better make it Tuesday."

He looked at the screen for the umpteenth time.

"My father has eyes all over Brooklyn," she went on. "I don't need him ask-ing what you're doing back in town when you're supposed to be sitting shiva."

"I thought you never told him my mother died."

"I didn't—but he knows. And he for sure knows this *Dayan*. Slomowitz is his name?"

"Yes."

"I'll call him right after we're done talking."

"I don't understand."

"To tell him to move your *giyur* to Tuesday, and to make sure he keeps quiet. *HaGaon HaRav* will have a heart attack if he finds out his *eidem* is a goy."

Mayer grabbed a handful of bedcovers to steady himself. "Sarah, what are you saying?"

"I just said what I'm saying."

"Yes, but—how do you react to everything I told you?"

"I react that I'll meet you at the *beis din* Tuesday. You'll get your *giyur*, then Slomowitz will marry us."

Now he was the silent one.

"Mayer?"

"Then and there?"

"Then and there."

He had so many questions, but knew not to ask. He closed his left eye and imagined he'd open two eyes and be back in the *beis medrash* at Ohr Lev, having just come out of a hallucination of a dybbuk whispering provocations in his ear.

"ISN'T THAT SOMETHING," David said.

"*Hashem* works in mysterious ways."

"What did she think about our adventures through the Deep South?"

"She expressed no opinion."

"What did she say about you getting plugged in the eyeball by a firework?"

"We talked about important things," Mayer said testily. "Us. My *giyur*. Protecting her father."

"I see." David picked up a *People* magazine from a table, the cover featuring Dominic Day raising a fist. The headline was "Tragedy and Triumph: My Story." A young female receptionist who sat behind a counter shouted at a patient old enough to be her great-grandfather, "Your appointment is this time tomorrow, Mr. Oakley!"

"What's that?" the man said, cupping an ear.

"You came a day early, Mr. Oakley!"

"Don't take that tone with me!"

Leafing through the magazine, David said, "I guess this means we get an extension on our adventure."

"That reminds me. I should call Yossi, let him know what's going on."

David closed the *People*. "Hey, Ese?"

"Yeah?"

"Are you happy?"

Mayer beamed. "Only on my wedding day was I happier."

"Then I'm happy too."

Together they watched a tot in OshKosh overalls and thick glasses play with a wooden bead maze. "By the way," Mayer said, "what did you have to tell me?"

"Hmm?"

"At the motel, you said after I got off the phone with Sarah you'd tell me something that had to do with her."

"Oh, yeah. Not relevant now."

The receptionist called out, "Belkin," and they followed her to an examination room. A few minutes later, a stern-faced woman of about forty-five entered. Both Belkins had the same thought: Almira Gulch from *The Wizard of Oz.*

"You must be the fella who knew better," she said to the man in the exam chair. "Margaret Willoughby."

She even sounded like Almira Gulch. She plunked down on a rolling stool and scooted over to her patient. With a practiced hand, she peeled the dressing off his eye. "Well, that doesn't look good. What the heck happened?"

"We were at a fireworks store a couple of nights ago, and basically—"

"I mean how'd it get so red?"

"I may have forgotten my ointment once or twice," Mayer admitted abashedly.

"No shit," she said. "Let's hope you don't have endophthalmitis."

"Infection?"

"Big time. And trust me, you do *not* want that."

She dilated his pupil with a drop that stung so badly he thought he might scream. After twenty minutes, she had him put his chin on the chin rest of a slit lamp, and flicked a switch that beamed light directly through the pupil. He groaned at the fresh wave of pain.

"It's bad, alright," she said, looking through the scope. "I'm not saying you've got endophthalmitis, but I'm not saying you haven't got it either."

Mayer felt like his eye was being cauterized. Tears ran down his face in rivulets. After an eternal wait, she flicked off the light and moved the slit lamp away.

"Sorry that took so long, but I needed to be sure."

"And?" David said.

She looked incredulous but pleased. "No endopthalmitis, but you've got a nasty case of conjunctivitis, plus inflammation inside the eye."

"Post-traumatic iritis," Mayer said.

"Aren't you a regular Gregory House," the doctor said.

She prescribed him eyedrops for both maladies, to be applied four times a day. She washed the wound with saline, medicated and dressed it. "And don't screw it up this time."

"No, ma'am."

"You're not the first guy to come see me who didn't take his medicine, but you may be the luckiest."

"What would've happened if he hadn't been lucky?" David asked.

"Partial blindness, maybe. Amputation. I've had a couple of patients die."

She offered her hand to Mayer. "I'd consider paying alms to whatever higher power you believe in, 'cause somebody up there loves you."

OUTSIDE THE DOCTOR'S office, the Belkin boys squinted into the sunlight. Popeye chased a scent until his leash went rigid. A windblown supermarket circular wrapped around David's ankle. He kicked it free.

"Close call, huh?" he said.

"What's a close call?"

David looked at his brother. "Your eye, dummy."

"Right. So I've been thinking: we should head north."

David put on his sunglasses just as a meadowlark flew past his head and on toward the mountains. He watched it until it was a freckle on the horizon.

"Hello?" Mayer said.

"I'm listening."

"I know my *giyur* isn't for four days, but we've got a lot of ground to cover between here and Brooklyn. I think it makes sense to be close to home with time to spare."

The elder Belkin kept his eyes on the blue yonder. In these breezy elevations, one could almost forget he was in the middle of a historic heat wave.

"We could get a hotel in New Jersey, maybe Staten Island, and just relax, use the pool and wait this out," Mayer said.

"Really makes you think, doesn't it?" David said.

"What does?"

"The big old sky."

Mayer looked up, a hand visoring his brow. "What about it?"

THEY DROVE TO a CVS in the center of town. David and Popeye ran in
while Mayer stayed in the car and dialed Yossi.

"*Shalom aleichem*, boychik," the rabbi said.

"You're not going to believe what happened."

"I believe it. Itzik called me a little while ago."

"Really?"

"He said he had the honor of a phone call from the daughter of *HaGaon
HaRav* Yaakov Drezner, who was, shall we say, insistent he bump your *giyur*
back to Tuesday."

"And what did he say?"

"He said sure. Mazel tov! A happy ending after all, *Baruch Hashem*."

Mayer thought he detected a note of disingenuousness in the rabbi's tone.
"You don't sound entirely happy," he said.

"I'm happy, I'm happy. How often in life do you get exactly what you
want, particularly when the odds are stacked against you?"

"Not so stacked after all. I should have given her the benefit of the doubt."

"Never mind should have. What's important is she stood by you, as any
good wife would."

"*Baruch Hashem.*"

"I am curious, though. Why Tuesday? She didn't give her reasoning to
Itzik."

Without going into the particulars, Mayer explained Sarah's wish to keep
the matter low-key. As he talked, a dirty pickup with a broken axle pulled into
the next parking space. Thick exhaust spewed from its tailpipe.

"I see," Rabbi Kugel said. "On the bright side, you and Dovid can extend
your adventure back to its original timetable."

The truck doors opened and a family of three got out. The father resembled, to an uncanny degree, one of the obese motorcycle twins from *The
Guinness Book of World Records*. The mother was skeletal in a dirty tank top
and cargo shorts, her eyes vacant and her chin cratered with red blemishes.

The son, about nine, appeared determined to match, if not surpass, his father's heft.

"The adventure can't end soon enough," Mayer said.

"It can't be that bad. By the way, your suitcase came. I was there to sign for it this time."

"*Baruch Hashem.* Can you ship it to my house?"

"Of course. What's your address?"

Mayer gave it to him, and promised to mail a check to cover costs, along with a repayment of the three-hundred-dollar loan and a donation to Chabad of Moab.

"*Shkoyach*," Yossi said. "That's very kind of you."

"It's the least I can do after what you did for me."

"It was my pleasure. You'll stay in touch, yes?"

"Of course," Mayer said—though he couldn't imagine why he ever would.

AFTER HANGING UP, he reclined his seat and daydreamed he was back in the *beis medrash* at his coveted corner spot, picking up in the Gemara where he left off. At issue, he recalled, were the supplies a priest needed for the leper's atonement ritual: a cedar branch a cubit long and a quarter the thickness of a bedpost, a hyssop plant no shorter than a handbreadth, a crimson strand weighing a shekel, and a sparrow.

In the daydream he wore blacks and whites, the tips of his tzitzis brushing the floor and a big velvet yarmulke beneath a fedora. His actual fedora was still at Ida Mae's house, never to be retrieved. His yarmulke had disappeared somewhere between the Gulf of Mexico and the Blue Ridge Mountains.

On a whim, he checked the glove compartment. The yarmulke wasn't there. Nor was it in the center console or the passenger door compartment. He checked the floor by his feet and under the floor mat. Then he decided why not, and climbed into the back to look under the passenger's seat.

Content that he'd tried his best, he was about to shimmy back to shotgun when he glanced at David's overnight bag on the seat beside him. He looked out the window. No one was coming. He considered the bag for a moment. He unzipped it.

Inside were the usual travel essentials—shaving kit, underclothes, toothbrush—and some unusual: a nylon case with a powerful herbal piquancy, a box of glow-in-the-dark prophylactics, a tube of K-Y Jelly, an unspeakably vulgar two-pronged object made of polyvinyl—and, wedged in the crotch of the thing, a black velvet yarmulke.

He gave out a pained whimper and freed the yarmulke. He pressed it to his face. It smelled of artificial strawberries. He mounted it on his knee and massaged the creases like a wildlife worker rubbing dish soap on a petroleum-soaked pelican. "I'm so sorry," he bleated to it. "So, so sorry."

He heard a familiar voice singing a familiar song and saw David and Popeye coming up the walkway. He zipped closed the overnight bag, put the yarmulke on his head, and squirmed back to his seat just before the rear door opened and the dog hopped in.

David opened his own door and passed his brother a paper bag. Inside were the eye drops, a box of adhesive eye patches, gauze, surgical tape and an oblong piece of black fabric the size of a half dollar with a loop of elastic string attached at two sides.

"I had to get it," David said as he turned the ignition. "You've been bitching about the sunlight bothering you, so I figured this'll kill two birds: protect your eye and bring out your inner Plissken or whoever—Fury or Cogburn or—"

He saw the skullcap on Mayer's head and closed his mouth.

"Go on," Mayer said.

"Dayan."

"Good one."

"Look, Ese, I was gonna give it back to you. I thought we'd be spending more time in New Orleans than we did. I was afraid if you walked around with that thing on your head it would, you know, cockblock me."

"Cockblock you."

"Well, yeah," David said.

Mayer's mouth curved into a chilly smile. "So you got me to take it off. Then you hid it."

"You make it sound so diabolical. Remember in Biloxi when I ran to the car to get Doritos for Popeye? I saw it on the seat and I just grabbed it and stuffed it in my bag. It was a split-second decision that I never thought about again."

"Except for all the times I asked if you'd seen it and you said no."

David looked out his window at the dirty pickup.

"Ever since Mom died," Mayer said, "you've been on a nonstop crusade to take me off the *derech*."

"What's the *derech*?"

"Path, you ignoramus. The path of good."

The family of three came up the walkway in single file. The boy was in the lead, twirling a Toblerone like a baton. Next came the father, his work boots on the brink of splitting open from ankle to heel. The mother shuffled in the rear, scratching at a scab on her arm.

David looked from the trio to Mayer. "Jesus, will you stop looking at me like that? I said I was sorry."

"No you didn't!"

"Well I am, okay?"

"You couldn't let it go, could you," Mayer said.

"What?"

"Me leaving you behind in New Moab."

A look of bewilderment came to David's face, followed by comprehension, then indignation. "Wow. You've got some ego, my friend, if you think—"

"Mom died, and you finally saw your chance to get even."

"Right, I got even by giving you an all-expenses-paid adventure of a lifetime. Talk about amateur hour. I should introduce you to the guy who put a dent in my head with a crowbar."

The dirty truck started up with an unhealthy hammering sound. As it reversed out of the spot, it shuddered like an off-balance washing machine.

"Look me in the eye," Mayer said. "Tell me that every step of this 'adventure of a lifetime' wasn't designed to lead me astray."

"For example?"

"These clothes," he said, pulling at his plaid shirt like it was a mucous membrane. "Bourbon Street. The dog."

"So now you have it in for Popeye too." David laughed without humor. "Way to thank him for saving your life."

"From the fire that you started."

"Which you laughed about in hindsight."

"Because I smoked your pot."

"Because you forgot your medication in the car."

"*Chad gadya, chad gadya,*" Mayer said. "I'm not laughing about it now, okay? I'm not laughing about any of it, especially—*Ribono Shel Olam!*—the woman you brought to my bed in New Orleans."

A smug expression fell over David's face, and Mayer seethed at having just handed his brother the win. "Deny it!" he shouted. "Deny that you haven't been trying to sabotage me since Tuesday."

"You got me," David said, waving an invisible white flag. "I've been waging covert psychological warfare on you from the start. Every step was meticulously planned, every possible outcome accounted for. I even helped Mom put the finishing touches on her suicide note. And I would've gotten away with it if not for you meddling kids."

David vamped a look of contempt, but his good nature got the best of him. "I'll confess to one thing," he said. "I did see an opportunity when Mom died—to reconnect with my twin brother, whom I never stopped loving. That's all I ever wanted, I swear. I never wanted to lead you astray. I just wanted to have fun with you, to show you the world a little bit. Has it not been great—at least at times?"

"You stole my yarmulke."

David threw up his hands. "I was going to give it back to you!"

"Fine. Let's not go in circles. In a few days I'll be a Jew again, God willing."

"And in another couple of years, me too, God willing," David said.

"No."

"No?"

"Never happening."

"Why?"

"A dedicated Jew is selfless and humble. You are an egomaniac, a degenerate and a glutton. You aren't fit to be a Jew."

David took a sharp breath and held it. His mouth tightened and his cheeks reddened. He looked as if someone lit a match in the center of his head. Then, all at once, the light in his eyes went out and his face turned haggard. His chin sagged into his chest.

Mayer wasn't sorry; better his brother accept the truth now than make a fool of himself before the *beis din*. He'd make a perfectly adequate Noahide by sticking with what he was good at—spending money, smoking pot and chasing women.

David grabbed his phone off the mount and started typing.

"What are you doing?" Mayer asked.

"I had big plans for us for Shabbos, but fuck that."

Shabbos! Mayer had forgotten all about Shabbos, which started tonight at sunset. A week and a lifetime ago, he and Sarah ate their traditional meal of broiled chicken, potato kugel and poached pears. After the meal they had their weekly intercourse. It was, like dinner, hurried, hushed, and without eye contact.

"We couldn't have done Shabbos anyway," he said.

"Oh no?" David asked, still typing.

"Jewish law forbids a goy from keeping the Sabbath."

The elder opened his mouth like he had a retort, then swallowed it. "Just as well, because it's not happening." He remounted his phone, started the engine and shifted into reverse.

"Where to?" Mayer asked.

"Charlotte."

"What's in Charlotte?"

"The airport."

"We're flying?"

"You're flying. Your ticket's being issued as we speak. First class. My wedding gift to you."

The first pangs of regret metastasized behind Mayer's rib cage. "Well, what about you?"

"I'll probably spend a couple of days in Charlotte. I've got friends there—you know, people like me."

"David."

He said nothing.

"David."

Nothing.

"David!"

The elder Belkin braked so abruptly that the younger grabbed the dash.

"I'm sorry for hiding your yarmulke, Mayer. Now shut the fuck up."

— CHAPTER 15 —

THEY STOPPED AT A FILLING STATION ON THE
OUTSKIRTS OF BLUE RIDGE, WHERE DAVID TOPPED OFF DAISY'S TANK
and bought a chicken salad sandwich and a miniature pecan pie from the
convenience store. He didn't ask Mayer if he wanted anything; Mayer didn't
ask for anything.

A half hour later they were in North Carolina. David put on a Joan Baez
retrospective, starting with "The Night They Drove Old Dixie Down." After
just three songs, he was Baezed out and switched to The Band. When "The
Weight" came on, he crooned to the chorus, as people in cars do; Mayer, who
still knew the song by heart after all these years, sang not a verse.

At Bryson City, David detoured off the I-74 for the scenic route into the
Great Smoky Mountains. But first he stopped in downtown Cherokee, whose
log cabin aesthetic brought to mind a Davy Crockett movie set. He pulled up
to the Pow Wow Gift Shop, and without saying anything, went inside. The
others stayed in the car. Down the block, a crowd had gathered to watch a
Cherokee man in a buckskin breechcloth and leggings perform a traditional
dance. He spun and stomped as another man banged a water drum and sang
a war song.

Then everything went to hell. A silver Mercedes-Benz G-Class with
tinted windows tore out of the parking spot in front of Daisy. It had one of
those gutted exhaust systems that, at full throttle, made it yowl like a Le Mans
race car. The dance troupe lost its audience instantly. Not fifty feet ahead, a
young woman with black braided hair was pushing a stroller across the street.
She saw the Benz coming and froze. Mayer grabbed the dashboard and cried,

"Look out!"

At the last possible moment, the vehicle swerved, dodging the stroller by inches. From under its hood came a locomotive honk so galvanizing that anyone within a hundred feet either screamed, ducked or leapt in the air—or any combination of the three. The young mother leaped, taking the stroller with her. The infant nearly bounced out on the landing. Its horn still blaring, the Benz tore a path toward the mountains.

David burst out of the gift shop. He saw the hysterical woman and ran to lend a hand. She didn't want a hand; she wanted a rocket launcher. Her expression was that of someone chewing a ghost pepper and defiantly refusing to expectorate it. She gesticulated wildly, screaming obscenities that would make Samuel L. Jackson blush. David tried to calm her, but quickly deduced that his aid wasn't needed or desired. He walked back to the car.

"Did you see that? That was insane," Mayer said.

David said nothing. From a shopping bag, he took out a dream catcher made of willow wood, sinew and owl feathers. He hung it on the rearview mirror.

"Dave, I—"

David referred his brother to the flat of his palm.

THEY ENTERED THE Great Smoky Mountains National Park by way of an oscillating two-lane that hugged the Oconaluftee River. After nine miles the river capillaried into creeks, and the road rapidly gained elevation. The air sweetened as hardwoods displaced conifers as the dominant tree. At five thousand feet, the road leveled out on a ridge along which the boys caught glimpses of ravine between the trunks on either side.

Just shy of the Tennessee border, David turned onto Clingmans Dome Road, where they got their first unobstructed bird's-eye of the Smokies. The mountains' namesake vapor rose from the gorge like the breath of a sleeping dragon. After six miles or so, the road came to a parking lot. David grabbed

Ida Mae and let Popeye out. The dog bounded up a steep paved trail to a circular observation tower. David followed without looking back.

Mayer unbandaged his eye and looked in the rearview mirror. It was still a mess, but the redness had taken on a promising pink tint. He medicated and redressed it, then got out of the car and took a solitary walk uphill.

At 6,643 feet, Clingmans Dome was the highest point in the Great Smoky Mountains. On a clear day, one could see Tennessee, Kentucky, Virginia, North Carolina, South Carolina, Georgia and Alabama. Forearms resting on the tower rail, Mayer imagined he'd died and entered the Garden of Eden. *"Baruch atah adonai eloheinu melech ha'olam she'kacha lo be'olamo,"* he said, thanking the Almighty for his wondrous creations. He wished he could thank David too.

There were dozens of other sightseers, and several dogs whose butts Popeye appraised before offering his own. Near Mayer stood two young hikers using a trail app to identify peaks to the northeast—Mount Love, Mount Collins, Sugarland Mountain. He heard one hiker mention to the other that the Appalachian Trail was practically under their feet.

Since reconciling with Sarah at the Blue Moon Inn, Mayer had managed to banish Charlayne to the outskirts of his mind. But at the mention of the AT, he could smell her lemongrass lotion, feel a phantom coil of her hair on his chin. He was curious as to what trail badges she'd earned so far—a skinned knee, a bruised buttock, a blister on her heel. He wondered how many days and hours would pass before she stood right here, and whether she'd think of him.

Then he heard a high whistle from the southwest that made his whole body tingle. Could it be? He rushed to join the awe-stricken crowd at the other side of the tower. A bald eagle hung in an updraft perhaps thirty yards away. Its mighty wings were seven feet from tip to tip, its emblematic crown stark white against the green mountains. It was magnificent, everything Mayer had hoped for—and more, for in its talons was a rattlesnake. The feeling was akin to an elderly widower cleaning out his wife's closet and finding her long-lost engagement ring in the finger of an old glove.

He reached for his back pocket to finally check off *Haliaeetus leucocephalus*. What he pulled out wasn't his bird book but *A Grief Observed*. He stared at its tattered cover. He opened it, brought it to his face, inhaled—and put it away.

HAD HE GONE to Clingmans Dome but not seen the eagle, *dayeinu*—it would have been enough.

Had he seen the eagle but not the snake in its talons, *dayeinu*.

Had he seen the snake but not what came next, *dayeinu*.

It all happened so quickly. They were driving back toward Cherokee. Mayer was staring at the blue strip down the center of the leafy overhang in hopes of another eagle sighting. No luck, but he did spot a northern flicker, a belted kingfisher and a field sparrow. They rounded a sharp bend at a steep incline, and David braked hard to avoid hitting two cars stopped in the middle of the road. There were two more cars idling in the oncoming lane.

"What the hell?" he said.

A man and woman exited the Subaru in front of them and jogged up the road without shutting the doors. David looked ahead and caught a glimpse of what they were jogging toward, and his eyes bugged. He opened his door, got snagged on his seat belt, cursed, unbuckled the seat belt, got out of the car and ran. Popeye clawed his way over the center console and ran after him. Mayer grabbed Ida Mae and ran after the dog.

What he saw proved that "breathtaking" wasn't strictly a euphemism.

Two black bears stood in traffic on their hind legs, performing a sort of forward-back dance step. They were about five feet tall and well fed, flanks jouncing as they plodded along. The eleven spectators circling the pair— Mayer made twelve—watched in awed silence. Even Popeye had a faraway look, intuiting something miraculous was afoot. The crowd soon doubled in size, but everyone kept quiet to avoid spooking the animals.

Mayer first read the bears' play as a game of Gladiator Hands, the object being to throw each other off-balance. He soon realized this wasn't so; the object was to stay upright, yes, but both bears seemed to know that neither could succeed without the other. Now and then, one would pitch forward and the other would teeter. Then the fallen one would rise and they'd steady each other and get back to it.

He searched for David in the crowd, expecting he'd be filming the spectacle like everyone else. To his surprise, David wasn't watching the bears at all; he was watching Mayer. Tears streamed down his face. His nose ran. The younger hadn't seen the elder cry since they were kids, and suddenly he wanted to cry too. He managed a smile instead. David did the same. They started laughing silently. The younger stepped toward the elder, and the elder toward the younger. As they reached for each other, the earth exploded.

Or seemed to anyway, as an Amtrak-caliber air horn blasted from behind them. The reverb felt like a slap on the side of the head. Half the spectators leapt in the air and the other half ducked. Personal effects clattered to the ground, including Ida Mae, who bounced across the road. The forest came alive as hundreds of thousands of birds, mammals, amphibians and insects fled en masse. The bears reeled. One threw back its shoulders, tipped back and overcompensated with a lurch that knocked the other flat on its back. Then both were on all fours, bounding into the brush.

All heads turned to the perpetrator, a silver Mercedes-Benz G-Class with Secret Service–tinted windows that veiled its occupants completely. While technically an off-road vehicle, the posh car was as harmonious with nature as a pair of Louboutin heels. Mayer heard a wet, predatory growl that he first thought to be coming from the Benz. But no, it was Popeye—shoulders squared and hair upright on the back of his neck, snarling through clamped jaws.

Mayer moved to retrieve his mother where she'd come to rest on the yellow lines in the middle of the road. As he reached for her the horn blasted again, and he jumped back empty-handed. The crowd hurled angry epithets at the Mercedes, their voices drowned by the prolonged blast. After an eternity, it ceased. David, his face the color of eggplant, got the first shot. "You fuckhole!"

The motorist leaned on the horn a third time. Popeye had had enough. He charged the three-ton vehicle like a pain-maddened toro bravo, saliva strings fluttering from the corners of his mouth. The Benz leapt into the oncoming lane and the game of chicken was on. The dog stayed the course—he was too furious to do otherwise—and the driver swerved, hooking a hard left onto the east embankment. Popeye ran a post route, beating the bumper by a hair to get to the driver's side. The driver spun the wheel, and the Benz fishtailed. When it cleared the shoulder, the dog was gone.

The vehicle roared past the crowd. One of its wheels nicked Ida Mae, pinwheeling her into the west embankment. Mayer didn't think. He picked up a piece of shale the size of a lacrosse ball, took three steps and fired. It sailed in a perfect line drive, punching a fist-sized hole through the rear window with a satisfying crunch.

"Great shot, Ese!" David crowed, leaping up and down. "Fuckin' A!"

The Mercedes's wheels locked, and it screeched to a stop. Mayer grabbed another piece of shale and stood on the yellow lines. The only sound was the throaty rumble of eight pistons. David picked up a rock and got next to his brother. The Benz's reverse lights came on.

A hiker with a half-shaved purple 'do grabbed a hunk of shale. A platinum-haired family of four on holiday from Austria armed themselves, and now it was a militia of seven. Some college kids from Gainesville, here for a week of camping and fishing, made it twelve. A Nashville couple celebrating their fiftieth wedding anniversary were next, followed by the couple with the Subaru. They all waited—hoped—for an excuse to fire.

They never got one. The Benz's white lights flicked off and the wheels spun, kicking up gravel and dust. At the first curve, it accelerated when it should have slowed, and the port side went airborne. Ears pricked for a crash, but all they got was the ebb of its oversized engine as it made for the foothills. Mayer found Ida Mae in the embankment, dinged up and scratched but puncture free. David ran across the road to where Popeye was last seen. That he'd been struck was a foregone conclusion—but how hard?

"Popeye!" he called, hands cupped around his mouth. "Popeyyyyyyyye!"

He slid-ran down the steep dirt hill into a gully. Mayer followed and promptly fell on his ass, sliding most of the way to the bottom. They scanned the forest floor for the mangled body of their lionhearted friend. David called the dog's name again, netting neither bark nor whine. He called out until his voice cracked. Mayer cast his eye groundward so he didn't have to see the look on his brother's face.

"I think I see him!" a woman shouted from above. It was the hiker with the purple hair, pointing down the gully at her two o'clock. The boys ran across a fern bed and hurtled over the broad trunk of a fallen tree. Mayer's shirt got caught in a blackberry bush and he tore it free. They came to a dry creek bed where a furry gray mound pitched about, tail stub rotating like a satellite dish.

"He's alive!" David shouted, and a great cheer erupted from the road. "He got stuck in a foxhole!"

The boys each grabbed a hind leg, and on the count of three pulled hard. The dog slid out like a backwards birthing calf, and they all fell back in a tangle of limbs. Popeye, covered with mud and dead leaves, looked none the worse for wear. When he was done steamrolling the Belkins with love and affection, they were as dirty as he was—and just as happy.

"OKAY, LET'S HEAR these Shabbos plans."

"I thought goyim can't do Shabbos," David said. He started the car but kept it in park, waiting for the two cars ahead to pull out.

"Well," Mayer said, "there's a loophole."

"Of course there is."

"If the goy wants to partake in Sabbath rituals, he has to purposely commit a Sabbath prohibition to set himself apart as a non-Jew."

David studied his dirt-encrusted fingernails. "For example?"

"Going for a walk while carrying something—his car keys, say—to violate the law against carrying outside of a fenced-in area."

"That's it?"

"That's it. So why don't you go ahead and cancel that flight. See if you can get that Shabbos reservation back."

David grinned knavishly.

"You never booked the flight," Mayer said. "You never cancelled the reservation."

The grin held steady and Mayer broke eye contact lest he grin too. He wouldn't admit it, but he was pleased for once to have been played. He needed a break from all the driving; what better excuse to do so than celebrating the glory of the Fourth Commandment—in what minimal capacity he could.

When traffic cleared, David pulled onto the shoulder. "Here's the deal. Remember yesterday when you and Charlayne were having that heart-to-heart at the gas station?"

"Yeah."

"Well, I was on my phone looking for something up our alley for Shabbos. I didn't have anything particular in mind, just something to, you know, feed our souls and our bellies. Not two minutes on Google, I found this Shabbos retreat, and it's almost too perfect. The itinerary, the food, the location—this didn't just fall into our laps."

"What do you mean?"

"The Man Upstairs personally ordered it."

"Don't get carried away," Mayer said.

"People normally book a year in advance for this thing."

"So you greased some palms."

"False. There just happened to be two last-minute cancellations."

"Just happened?"

"Just happened. But if you still think divine providence has nothing on us, I'm okay shacking us up at a Motel 6 on the Jersey Turnpike. I think they have HBO. I could have us there in eleven hours if I step on it."

The road was quiet now, save for the occasional passing car. Most of the forest creatures who'd fled had come home as if nothing had ever happened here. Mayer pointed where to go and David made a U-turn. They headed north to Tennessee.

A WEEK AGO, Mayer had only ever been to Georgia, New York and New Jersey. Now he had eight states under his belt.

Two miles into Tennessee, the road met a river tributary called Walker Camp Prong, and they ran parallel for a while. Through the trees, Mayer saw rafters and kayakers pitching through rapids. In calmer waters downriver, anglers in fly fishing waders cast for brook trout. He glimpsed in the thicket what was almost certainly a swallow-tailed kite, rare in this area, and sought the bird guide—again, in vain.

"I wonder how Charlayne's doing," he said.

"Great so far," David said.

"How do you figure?"

"She posted something about hitting her tenth mile a couple of hours ago."

"Oh yeah?"

David tapped his iPhone screen a few times and handed it over. Charlayne was doing Rosie the Riveter, a hair-thin line of dried blood on her flexed forearm, her jaw set and her eyes exuberant. Her rucksack framed her face and filled most of the background. The caption said "10 down, 2,180 to go. See you in Maine, boys?"

"Think we'll ever see her again?" David asked.

"No," Mayer said, and sighed through his nose. "Not me, anyway." He pulled A Grief Observed out of his pocket and opened it to a random page.

There were no notations and only two underlined sentences: "There is one place where her absence comes locally home to me, and it is a place I can't avoid. I mean my own body."

AT AROUND SEVEN they entered the town of Sevierville in the foothills of the Smoky Mountains. This was God's country, abounding with cow pastures flecked with buttercups, horse ranches, vineyards and chapels standing by their lonesome in grassy fields. David detoured through downtown to get a look at the bronze likeness of Sevierville's hometown heroine Dolly Parton.

In the Queen of Country's honor, he selected "Traveling Man" as the last song of the day. It was a sublime few minutes, the hilly road shaded by old spruces and oaks, the woody air sweetened by azaleas, rhododendrons and black-eyed Susans, the sky an electric early-evening blue. Seconds after Dolly made her final lament to her traveling man, David pointed ahead to a sandwich-board sign at the base of a sloped driveway and declared, "We've arrived."

Mayer read the sign and said, "Stop the car."

David did.

"You're goofing on me," Mayer said.

"What?"

"You wanted to see the look on my face."

"What are you talking about?"

Mayer reread the sign. *Welcome to the Annual Smoky Mountain Shabbaton, hosted by United Reform Congregation of Atlanta.* David lifted his foot off the brake, and Daisy started to roll.

"I said stop the car."

"Jesus, why?"

"I don't do Reform. I can't do Reform."

"Why the hell not?"

Mayer could feel his temperature rise. "How do I explain this diplomatically? Look, the foundation of Judaism is its laws, right? Its commandments.

To practice Judaism is to maximize one's time carrying out those command-ments. That's the fundamental mission."

"Okay."

"Imagine there were no laws and no consequences. You were free to do basically whatever you wanted. You could marry a non-Jew, eat nonkosher food, drive your car on Shabbos."

"Anarchy," David said, dryly.

"The Reform movement is a body without organs. A book without words. Trivial folk traditions. Potato knishes and matzo ball soup."

"Klezmer music and horah dancing."

"Oy vey and shalom."

"Dude," David said. "It's a spiritual retreat, not a seminary. Meditation circles and yoga, one-on-one counseling, gourmet vegan cooking. The rabbi is some kind of wellness guru who's written a bestselling book series. I've seen her on *LIVE with Kelly and Mark*. She's—"

"She's a she?"

"Yes, and *she's*—get this—Sienna Garza's rabbi."

"Who is Sienna Garza?"

"A former Miss America who's now a fashion influencer slash actor who's romantically linked to your favorite pop phenomenon, Dominic Day."

"The 'Walk with You' guy."

"Uh-huh."

"Do me a favor," Mayer said. "Let's go somewhere else. Please. This doesn't work for me."

"Tough titties, Ese. I'm wiped out. I need some R&R."

"I bet there are beautiful old mountain hotels around here."

David bared his teeth and pantomimed strangling his brother. "Can't you get out of your own head for once and just roll with it? God!"

"It's demoralizing, okay?"

"No, not okay. There's no refund on the cancellation."

"Really? How much did you pay?"

"Four figures apiece."

Gawking, the younger Belkin looked away. For all of David's sins, he'd been a remarkably good sport through all Mayer's protests, pieties and condescension. Could he not be a team player just once?

"I didn't know it wasn't refundable," he begrudged. "I guess that changes things."

The driveway was long and serpentine, its terminus hidden from street view. They drove through a thicket of trees that opened to a sprawling alpine lodge atop a grassy hill. It was a splendid building with a prow front, log roof, towering windows and a wraparound deck. On the western side was a pergola with black-eyed Susans, hydrangeas, and climbing roses the color of orange sherbet. On the eastern side was a firepit encircled by Adirondack chairs. To the south were the Smoky Mountains, moss-colored in the waning light.

"Stupendous," David said.

As they continued along the driveway to the eastern side of the lodge, a low growl sounded from the back seat. Mayer turned around. Popeye's teeth were bared, the hair on the back of his neck standing at attention. His opaque eye brought to mind the *Village of the Damned* kids.

"What's with him?" David asked.

"Don't know."

The driveway ended at a small parking lot in the back. There were six other cars lined up facing the building: a Hyundai Sonata, two Teslas, a BMW 8 Series convertible, a Jeep Wrangler—and a silver Mercedes-Benz G-Class with a hole the size of a grapefruit in the back window.

"No," Mayer said in disbelief.

"Oh boy," David said.

"No, no, no," Mayer said.

Popeye, deducing the Benz was unoccupied, stopped growling and started yawning. David parked beside it and turned off the car.

"What are you doing?" Mayer said.

"Parking."

"What? We have to get out of here."

"Are you joking?" David asked.

"Aren't you?"

"If this isn't *hashgacha pratis*, I don't know what is."

"Divine intervention, exactly," Mayer said. "God might as well have put up a sign that says 'I'd turn back if I were you.'"

David shook his head reproachfully.

"Don't give me that look," Mayer said.

"I watched you stare down the barrel of a Nazi's shotgun."

"Only soldiers and fools walk into danger deliberately."

"Right," David said absently. "Right." Without warning, he plucked Ida Mae off his brother's lap and got out of the car.

"Where are you going?" Mayer said.

David let Popeye out and the two headed to the south side of the lot, which ended at a grassy strip edging a bluff. A minute later, Mayer got out of the car and joined them. He peered down the ninety-foot drop at a shelf of boulders and scrub brush, then to his left at a freestanding rear deck jutting over the abyss. David kept his eyes on the serrated panorama. "Do you really not feel it?" he asked.

"Feel what?"

"Never mind."

"No, tell me."

David wavered. "Look, I know you think we're just a couple of pills in God's roulette wheel, but—"

"That's not what I—"

"Just listen. Some of the hardest lessons I ever learned were at casinos, and I'm telling you: this is no roulette game. It's poker. The hand's been dealt. Do we raise or do we fold?"

Mayer put his hands on his hips, belly jutting slightly, and scanned the horizon. The sky was azure to the east, marmalade to the west. The air smelled of aspen and stone. With two fingers, he plucked the phantom Chesterfield from between his lips and flicked it into the ravine.

THE INJURED MAN administered his eye drops and swallowed three Tylenol. David got the luggage out of the trunk and put Ida Mae in his overnight bag. He filled Popeye's bowls with water and kibble and set them on the ground next to the car.

"Not this time, pal," he said when Popeye made a face. "Can't have you turn Mr. Mercedes into Salisbury steak. But we'll check up on you every couple of hours." The dog sat on his haunches and whined for all he was worth—but stayed put. The boys came around the side of the lodge to a cozy wraparound porch with wicker rocking chairs and a log rack full of firewood. David was about to lift a brass knocker on the heavy oak door when his brother told him to hang on.

"If it comes up in conversation," Mayer said, "which it definitely will, don't mention our situation to anyone."

"Which situation?"

"The whole ordeal. Finding out we're not Jewish. Just pretend we're a couple of lifelong goyim with a Jewish surname—which is true. We're here because we're curious about Judaism."

"What do you care? You don't know anyone here."

"Because someone might debate us on the definition of a Jew. They might say if our father was Jewish then so are we."

"So?"

"I won't be able to stomach that."

"Whatever." David raised the knocker and let it drop. "You might want to remove your yarmy, then."

Mayer whisked the yarmulke off his head an instant before the door opened to reveal a woman of distinct beauty. She was around the same age as the twins, with large green eyes accented with flecks of brown, high cheekbones, full lips and October-red hair that cascaded to her waist. Barefooted, she wore a tunic patterned with gold-and-blue interwoven rectangles.

She put a finger to her lips, stepped onto the porch and closed the door gently behind her. "There's a Vipassana circle," she explained in a hushed voice. Her eyes roved the boys' sodden garments and Mayer's bandage. "You must be David and Marty. Welcome."

"And you must be Rabbi Teitelbaum," David said. "I recognize you from TV."

"My father is Rabbi Teitelbaum. You can call me Debbie."

Mayer thought he heard a faint New York inflection in her speech. Her face looked familiar, though he was certain he'd never seen her before.

She extended her hand. David shook it, Mayer left it hanging. "I'm so happy you were able to join us," she said. "We booked months in advance, but two of our guests cancelled yesterday. Before I had a chance to tweet out the availabilities, you grabbed them."

"*Hashgacha pratis*," said David.

Mayer gave his brother a black look. Debbie gave a startled smile. "Indeed. Now, why don't you come in, freshen up and have something to eat before *Kabbalat Shabbat*."

"Sounds great," David said.

"My one request is that you leave your devices in my care during your stay."

The Belkins made identical bemused expressions.

"In the spirit of Shabbat," she said. "You'd be amazed how liberating it is to lock your screens in a drawer for a day or two." She looked askance, circling a toe on the deck floor. "And if I'm being completely honest, one of our more, um, prominent guests requested it for privacy purposes."

Her subtle embarrassment disarmed the boys. They handed over their phones without further objection. Debbie opened the door and led them through a vestibule to a cavernous room of modern rustic design with vaulted ceilings, walls of exposed oak beams and a floor of repurposed walnut planks. The furnishings were tasteful: wooden rocking chairs, terra-cotta papasan chairs, and couches of supple leather. Cinemascope windows wooed eyeballs to the Smokies on one side and the foothills on the other.

Consciousness-expanding music played from in-wall speakers. A circle of seven guests sat lotus-style on a Turkish rug, wearing white linen pants and tunics, and nothing on their feet. The boys took off their shoes and followed the rabbi to a spiral staircase, passing the other guests on the way. They included a redheaded woman of about thirty wearing a Bukharan-style kippah; an older white man with snow-white hair tied in a ponytail; a slender white man in his early twenties with face scruff and a pompadour, flanked by two heavily muscled men, one Black and one Asian; two young Asian women; and an ambiguously gendered individual about fifty with a buzz cut.

The trio climbed the stairs, then crossed a balcony to a corridor. Debbie opened the fourth door on the left to a sun-drenched bedroom with two queen beds, a vase of fresh flowers and a balcony with a gorgeous mountain view. On each bed was a neatly folded set of clothing identical to what the other guests wore.

"Why don't you guys get washed up and changed?" she said. "When you're ready, come down—quietly—and make your way to the dining room, which is just below where we're standing. I'll have a snack ready for you."

"Sounds good," David said affably. But as soon as she closed the door, his eyes went so wide they looked like they might roll out of their sockets.

"What?" Mayer said.

David held a finger up, waiting for Debbie's footfalls to fade to silence. "I'm freaking out, Ese. I'm freaking the fuck out."

"Oh no. Did you drop acid?"

"Did you not see the kid with the haircut out there? With the two commandos?"

"He did look familiar. Is he famous?"

David palmed his bald dome. "This is incredible. Now I *know* this was preordained."

"You knew that earlier."

"No. Now I *know.*"

Mayer sat on the bed and kicked off his shoes. "Well, who is he?"

David sat next to him. "Are you ready to have your mind blown?"

"I guess."

"Dominic freakin' Day."

Mayer looked at him.

"Two fools breaking rules skinny-dipping in the pool?" David said.

"He looks different without the wheelchair."

"Bro," David said. "He's Mr. Mercedes."

"No!"

"He's got to be."

"But his legs," Mayer said. "How could he drive that thing?"

"They rig cars for disabled people. Or maybe one of his guys was driving."

"Okay, but . . . no. He's wholesome. He'd never—"

"Wholesome my baby-smooth ass," David said. "His public image was manufactured in a boardroom and bleached and starched over fifteen rounds of focus groups."

Mayer chewed his lower lip. "We should get out of here."

"Fuck that. We're staying."

"What about those two gorillas with him? They know what we look like. They'll tear us apart."

"I still say we let this play out."

"But why? What's the point?"

David grinned. "I don't know, Ese. I don't know."

— CHAPTER 16 —

THEY SHOWERED, PUT ON THEIR MEDITATION
CLOTHES AND MADE THEIR WAY BAREFOOT TO THE FIRST FLOOR. AS
they passed the Vipassana circle they stole glances at Dominic Day. To their
immediate horror, his eyes were open—but he appeared not to see them,
so fixated was he on the woman in the gold-and-blue tunic sitting directly
opposite him.

They found the dining room without difficulty. It was a large, airy space,
one corner taken up by an open kitchen where three chefs prepared a vegan banquet. Two bowls of red lentil soup seasoned with lemon and parsley
awaited them at a rustic wood table, along with a platter of toasted quinoa
with chopped apples and cinnamon, a chard salad tossed with vinaigrette, a
wheel of cashew brie, a steaming basket of nut bread, a pot of warm goose-
berry jam and a decanter of Riesling.

The earthy fare hit the spot, though David, not a lentil fan, didn't touch
his soup. The boys masticated so contentedly that neither heard the rabbi tip-
toe in until she was standing right in front of them.

"The *bubbe* in me is kvelling right now," she said.

"Dynamite grub," David said, "and that's no small praise from a sworn
carnivore."

Debbie glanced at a young chef at the counter who was slicing bok choy
with blurring speed. "You heard that, Eduardo?"

Eduardo nodded without missing a beat on the cutting board.

She took a wine glass out of a kitchen cabinet and poured herself some
Riesling. David pulled out the chair beside him.

"So tell me," she said, "what brings you to Tennessee? Or are you boys local?"

"Regional," David said. "We're on a road trip from Georgia."

She swirled her wine. "Did you just set out today?"

"Tuesday, actually. It's been a . . ." He snickered sophomorically. "Wayward journey."

"Evidently," she said, eyeing Mayer's bandage. "What happened to you?"

With his tongue he dislodged a grain of quinoa from between two molars. "Fireworks mishap."

"You're kidding."

His silence was answer enough.

"Are you okay?" she asked.

"Yep, yep, fine. Just a graze. Looks worse than it is."

"Thank goodness." She sipped some wine and observed the brothers. "At first glance, I'd say we've got ourselves a farce about two grown men who set out to reclaim their boyhoods and wound up in the ER."

David chuckled into his glass of ice water. "You wouldn't be far off."

"Only, you've gone off script."

"How's that?"

"By coming here. Not exactly the Delta Tau Chi house."

"We needed peace of mind for a change," David said. "It's been a long few days."

"And we have a general interest in your faith," Mayer added.

"Fascinating faith," David said. "Actually, our father was a Jew."

He got a kick in the shin from across the table.

"Interesting," Debbie said. "But you don't consider yourselves Jews?"

"No."

She frowned slightly. "I've hung out with members of just about every religion under the sun, but you might be the first gentile I've ever heard say *hashgacha pratis.*"

"Just something we picked up along the way," David said, not quite looking at her.

"I'm intrigued. How did that happen?"

"It's a long story." David glanced apologetically at his twin, then at the door. "Say, haven't you got your flock to see to?"

"I'll pop in on them soon, but they're pretty much on autopilot for now—most of them, anyway. Besides, you're my flock, too, for as long as you're here."

"That's very kind. Your hospitality knows no bounds," David said. "The food alone made the trip worth it."

"I'm so pleased you liked it . . . though nobody comes just for the food."

David glanced at his brother, who issued a cease and desist with his one eye. Debbie touched his forearm and their eyes locked. "Forgive me if I'm being intrusive," she said, "but from the moment you showed up at my door I've been getting a really compelling energy from you guys. I'd love to know your story, if you're willing."

David gave Mayer a look that said *Ball's in your court, pal.*

The younger twin's shoulders sank. Travel-worn and spiritually barren, what he needed now was an early night's sleep—and a pre-dawn departure before Dominic Day and his probably 'roid-boosted associates found out they were ever here. Instead, he was once again playing the role of grinch, courtesy of David. Would he never learn?

"Whatever," he said.

JUDGING BY RABBI Teitelbaum's myriad reactions—enchanted, somber, horrified, in stitches—David hit all the right notes narrating their adventure. The only details he redacted pertained to Dominic Day. By the tale's end, her eyes had a liquid sheen and she was well into her second Riesling.

"First off, here's to Ida Mae," she said, raising her glass. "May her memory be a *bracha.*"

"Amen," the Belkins said.

"I'd also like to say—"

"Don't," Mayer said.

She gave him an inquisitive look.

"Don't say that since our father was a Jew, we're Jewish. I can't."

She smiled quizzically. "What kind of rabbi would I be to impose my theology on you?"

His chin doubled. "Sorry. Please go ahead."

"I was just going to say how guilty I feel that your story so entertained me."

"And I feel guilty at how tickled I am to hear you say that," David said.

"I've actually pondered your exact situation as a hypothetical, more than once," she said. "But I've never heard of anyone who actually went through it."

"Lucky you," Mayer said.

"Indeed. You must be traumatized. David, you're maybe not too affected, but poor Mayer, how do you cope with such a loss?"

Mayer rubbed his good eye wearily, thinking, *If I had a nickel.* "I don't know. I guess the only way to answer that is to point out the inherent flaw in your question. A loss implies I owned something that was taken from me. But I was never Jewish. I owned nothing, so I lost nothing."

"Interesting take," Debbie said. "But you identified as a Jew. That's a form of ownership, no?"

"Not by my definition. And even if so, it doesn't matter. What matters is I'll be a Jew, *im yirtzeh Hashem*, Tuesday morning. Tuesday afternoon I'll be back in the *beis medrash*, picking up where I left off."

"Like nothing ever happened."

"Like nothing ever happened."

Debbie crossed her legs, leaned forward and cradled her chin in her hand.

"I suppose you'd handle it differently," Mayer said.

She shrugged. "It's my nature to look for meaning in things. Your experience begs to be picked apart and analyzed piece by piece. People write memoirs about this kind of thing."

"I don't see the point."

"I could recommend some books, kabbalistic works. I think they'd help you see the point."

"Thanks, but not interested."

She tapped her chin a few times. "I just can't believe you're not the least bit curious why God did this to you."

"Like he'd tell me," Mayer retorted with more ire than he intended—but he'd had this discussion enough times in the past few days to last several lifetimes. "You have to understand that what happened to me—to us—wasn't an act of God, but the opposite: an inaction by God."

Debbie arched her brow. "An act of neglect?"

"No."

"Then what?"

He pressed the back of his neck to relieve the pressure knot there. "Please, with all due respect, can we not? You're a . . ."

"Reform rabbi."

"Yes," he conceded, "and I believe in God's revelation on Mount Sinai. We're different—and that's okay. But—"

"I believe in God's revelation," she said. "But I also believe the Torah evolves over time. The Torah originally reflected Jews' understanding of God's revelation 3,300 years ago. As our people have advanced through the ages, so has our interpretation of the revelation."

"The Progressive Era," David trumpeted, like he'd just discovered uranium.

"Very good, David," Debbie said. "We now believe in what's called the progressive revelation, which essentially means that God entrusts his people to interpret his word as suits the times."

"It's too bad your movement commandeered the word *progress*," Mayer said. The clergywoman appeared unfazed by the slight.

"Humor me," she said. "What did you mean by 'inaction by God'?"

"I'd really rather not."

"You're with friends."

Mayer drew a long inhalation in through his nose and released it. "I'm with friends," he repeated. "Fine. It's very simple. David and I aren't Jews. We don't matter."

"Speak for yourself," David said.

"Okay, *I* don't matter. There's no divine providence that steers me one way or the other. There is no question of 'Why did God do this to me?' God didn't do anything to me, because he couldn't be bothered. And I wouldn't have expected more of him."

"Do you really believe that?" Debbie asked.

Mayer watched the last glint of gold sink behind the mountains. "At this point, it's what I'm going with, okay?"

"Just like that."

"Look," Mayer said, "in another few days I'll be, God willing, a Jew. I'll be married to my wife, living in my house, learning in my yeshiva. It's the life I had and the life I want. What else matters?"

Just then a sharp female voice from the living room severed the thread of their discussion. Debbie hurried out to investigate. The Belkins heard a hushed conversation dominated by women's voices—then a petulant male voice uttering the only words they could make out clearly: "I'm sorry. *Damn.*"

When Debbie returned, her face was flushed.

"Trouble?" David said.

"All sorted out." She plunked herself down and drained her wine glass.

"Another?" David said, lifting the decanter.

"Two's my limit on the job." She took a long, meditative breath. "Where were we? Ah yes, your yeshiva. I gather from the subtext of your story that you guys weren't brought up Orthodox."

"Our mother raised us without religion," Mayer said.

"Or food," David added.

"But you, Mayer, became Orthodox anyway."

"That's right."

"May I ask why?"

He glanced at the kitchen clock, which said eight thirty-three. "I don't think we have time."

"There's a little time," Debbie said. "Humor me. Then we'll light Shabbat candles and have dinner."

"Dinner!" He patted his stomach and laughed. He had to admit he liked the woman, despite her appropriated honorific. She was courteous, personable, inquisitive, empathic, smart . . . and, okay, easy on the eyes. And so he wet the roof of his mouth with some ice water and told her about the day he and David came upon the big menorah outside the yellow house on Virginia Avenue, and later encountered the house's owner on their front stoop talking to Ida Mae—who picked that moment to disclose that they were Jewish.

"*Hashgacha pratis*," Debbie said with a half smile.

Mayer grunted a laugh.

"And that's what started it all," she said.

"Every event leading to this moment, yes. David had the good sense to shrug it off, but I was absolutely certain that God put me on a mission that day."

"I'd argue that your intuition was correct, just as David's was correct for him."

"Please, a talking menorah?" Mayer said. "And a few hours of research would have exposed our mother as a fraud. Her grandfather was a Nazi, may his memory be erased."

The rabbi's eyebrows shot up.

"Just a little aside Mom tossed in her letter."

"Well," she said, "I'd argue that if God had intended for you to research your mother's lineage, you would have."

"No. I was negligent. And I got what I deserved."

"What do you mean?"

"What do you mean what do I mean? I desecrated God."

For the first time, Debbie looked genuinely perplexed. "How did you desecrate God?"

"By studying Torah, of course."

The confusion in her eyes gradually gave way to clarity. She uncrossed her legs and leaned back, and for a long moment stared out at the mountains. "You're referring to the prohibition against gentiles learning Torah."

"Correct."

"I'm not sure the prohibition is so cut and dried."

"It's right there in Deuteronomy," Mayer said. "'Moses commanded us the Torah, the heritage to the congregation of Jacob.' The Talmud interprets this to mean that the law, i.e., the Torah, is exclusive to the children of Jacob and forbidden to gentiles."

"And in fact," Debbie said, "in *Masechet Sanhedrin, daf nun tet*, the Gemara equates a gentile who studies the Torah to either a thief or a rapist, depending on how one interprets '*Torah tzivah lanu Moshe, morasha kehillat Yaakov*.' In any case, a gentile who studies Torah is liable for the death penalty, according to Rabbi Yochanan."

Mayer blinked.

"But," she continued, "the Gemara then brings forth a seemingly contradictory statement by Rabbi Meir, which basically equates a gentile who studies Torah to a high priest. Which begs the question, is he a high priest or a felon? The Talmud settles the issue by ruling that a gentile is permitted to study certain portions of the Torah, so long as they pertain to the seven Noahide laws."

Mayer got the disorienting sense that a trap door had opened in the seat of his chair and he was sinking through it. "The Rambam," the rabbi went on, "says the prohibition of a gentile studying Torah is like the prohibition of a gentile keeping Shabbat. The concern in both cases is that the gentile might corrupt these mitzvot by integrating them into his pagan religion."

David touched a fist to his lips to hide a grin.

"But the Rambam appears to contradict himself when he states in the *Mishneh Torah* that a gentile who wishes to perform a mitzvah in order to seek a reward from God is allowed to do so. Not everybody agrees with him on this point, notably Radbaz and Rav Moshe Feinstein. Nonetheless, the Rambam ultimately looked favorably on the gentile who performed mitzvot out of love of God—including the mitzvah of Torah study. And correct me if I'm wrong, but Rabbi Menachem Ha'Meiri took this approach as well in *Beit HaBechira*."

Mayer could only stare at her now in owl-eyed wonder.

"I'd argue that even if you were prohibited from learning Torah, God would forgive you because you made an honest mistake," Debbie said. "Even if you'd done it deliberately, though, the Rambam himself would commend you. But desecrate God? I don't think so."

She fell silent, and for a time the only sound was the muted clang of buffet platters being set atop heating pans.

David finally said, "Who *are* you?"

Debbie laughed, a sweet, high sound. "Just another Jew with a story. Mine goes something like this: when I was a lot younger, I was considered quite a scholar in my community. Not everyone approved of a woman studying Talmud, and long story short, I haven't spoken to my father in twenty years. But the foundation of who I am was laid in my youth, just like you. Just like everyone."

Suddenly Mayer knew why her face looked so familiar. The summer he was fifteen, when many of the *talmidim* went on vacation and those who stayed took lighter workloads, he read every Holocaust book he could get his hands on. Some had photos taken in ghettos and concentration camps, and he discovered something ubiquitous in the faces of the victims—a world-weary resignation rooted in two thousand years of exile. Debbie had the exact same look.

"You and I share a common love, and that's the Torah," she told Mayer. "We don't know why we love it. We just do."

Mayer felt a lump rise in his throat and swallowed it.

"Maybe you ought to consider that God made all this happen to you for a reason, because God does everything for a reason."

He looked through the window at the night sky. The stars were coming out like fireflies. "But what—" His voice became hobbled and he started over. "What possible reason? I mean, who *does* that to a person?"

"That's the question you've got to keep asking if you ever hope to find the answer."

He realized he was squeezing a table leg so hard that the corners of the wood dug painfully into his palm. "What if I never find out?"

"You will. The Kabbalah teaches that even curses are blessings. The Baal Shem Tov, founder of the Chassidic movement, said that every occurrence, down to one blade of grass blowing in the wind, is an essential function of the universe—and is therefore good, no matter how bad it seems."

"*Hashgacha pratis*," David said.

"Exactly. There's a story in which the Baal Shem Tov was walking with his students and he pointed out a leaf falling from a tree. The leaf landed next to a worm that was on the brink of death unless it ate something. God had assigned the leaf to save the worm."

"I remember that story," David said. "Rabbi Kugel used to tell it in his sermons."

"The concept predates the Baal Shem Tov," Rabbi Teitelbaum said. "As Rabbi Akiva famously said in *Masechet Berachot*, 'Whatever the merciful one does is for the good.'"

Mayer knew the maxim. The Talmud told a story about the Rabbi Akiva traveling with a donkey, a chicken and a candle. He sought lodging in a town one night, and was refused. "Whatever the merciful one does is for the good," he said, and slept in an open field. Overnight, a wind blew out the candle, a fox ate the chicken and a lion ate the donkey. The same night, brigands came and carried off the people of the town. Had the innkeeper given Rabbi Akiva lodging, or had the brigands come through the field and seen the candle or heard the animals, he would surely have been lost.

It was a good anecdote, but it had a bleak postscript: years later, Rabbi Akiva was one of the ten martyrs the Roman emperor Hadrian executed. His men flayed him alive with metal combs.

"Okay, but that was Rabbi Akiva," Mayer said. "For unexceptional guys like me, the pieces never fall into place so perfectly. God's intentions are ambiguous."

"Yes, but I believe God delights in us contemplating his intentions," Debbie said, "especially nowadays, when fewer and fewer people give God any thought at all. But here's some practical advice that I sometimes offer to friends going through hard times: ask yourself what change you might make in your life to turn this negative experience into a positive one. Picture a future in which, looking back on it, this was the moment things took a turn for the better. Then chase after that future."

"That's what Yossi told us at Mom's!" David exclaimed. "He said our mission should be to figure out how Mom's letter actually made our lives better in the long run."

Mayer had only the vaguest recollection; in the apocalyptic aftermath of Ida Mae's posthumous revelation, he could hardly process—let alone retain—instruction. How surreal, he thought, that a Chabad rabbi and a Reform rabbi should give the same counsel.

"I'm sorry, but I don't see how I could ever reach that conclusion," Mayer said.

"I bet you'll reach it sooner than you think," Debbie said. "Look back on the events of the past three days. Have they opened your eyes to something in your life that needs to change? Something you struggle with disproportionately—that zags whenever you zig?"

Mayer fingered a burl in the walnut tabletop. David watched him soberly, bouncing his leg. Debbie looked at the clock. "Oy! We've gone overtime. Let me rouse the lambs and we'll get *Kabbalat Shabbat* and dinner going. Be right back, guys."

As soon as she was gone, David grabbed his brother's forearm. "I've gotta tell you something, Ese. It's about Sarah . . . Ese?"

Mayer had a funny grin on his face. "You know what I was just remembering?"

"What?"

"The night those women pulled up their T-shirts on Bourbon Street."

David laughed uneasily. "An odd moment to talk smut, but I'm always down."

Mayer's grin flatlined. "I was devastated."

"I know. I was there."

"Do you want to know why—why specifically?"

"Go ahead."

"Until that moment, I'd only ever seen one uncovered woman in my life. I felt like I'd betrayed Sarah by seeing another."

"I get it. My bad. You wanted Sarah to be your only one."

"No. Mom was my only one."

David blinked. "Mom?"

"Remember that pink bathrobe she always wore, how the belt always came loose?"

Comprehension bumped aside the confusion on David's face. "You're telling me you never saw . . ."

Mayer shook his head.

"Not even during . . ."

"It was always in the pitch dark, always at night. Blinds drawn and everything."

"Sorry in advance for asking, but . . . isn't that pretty typical among the Orthodox?"

"There's some debate on the issue, but typical? No. What's even less typical is that Sarah and I never . . . We never even once . . ."

"You never what?"

Mayer thumped his chest to dislodge the word. "Kissed. On the mouth, anyway."

David made a little noise. He reached across the table and touched his brother's cheek. Just then, the dining room door burst open and Debbie came in, hands balled and pressed to her thighs. Her posture had the rigidity of a bodybuilder flexing every muscle at once.

"Debbie?" David said.

She looked up, but appeared not to see them.

David stood. "What's wrong?"

"Nothing." She took two more steps, halted, took another step, halted again. "Actually, something. I just got . . . I can't believe I'm saying this . . . goosed."

"What?"

"They were all in deep meditation . . . at least I thought they were. Re-emergence can be disorienting, so I always like to be the first person people see when they open their eyes."

She faltered. David urged her to continue.

"I was just starting the process when I felt a hand grab my . . ." She barked a brief, disbelieving laugh. "He got a real handful too. Up the skirt and everything. I felt like one of the secretaries on *Mad Men*. Worse, actually. I'm sure I'll be black and blue."

Mayer shot to his feet and said, "That son of a bitch." David gaped at him.

"So, I spun around," the rabbi said, "and he had this shit-eating grin on his face, all smug and entitled. He actually wiggled his eyebrows."

"What did you do?" David asked.

"Nothing. I felt like I was back in the eighth grade. I just walked out."

"That little motherscratcher," David said. "Goose a woman, you're a scumbag. Goose a woman of God, suffer the wrath of Kushiel."

Rabbi Teitelbaum poured out the last of the Riesling and quaffed it in two swallows. "He was cobra-quick, too, for a guy whose legs don't work. I can't figure out how he got back to his seat so fast."

"You have every right to call the cops," David said.

"Oh, I'll do something. I just need some time to think."

"What's to think about? Just call the cops and let them handle it."

"It's not so simple. As soon as I call the authorities, it's public record, and public records have a way of getting in the wrong hands. Next thing I know I'll have TMZ at my door. It wouldn't be the first time, and I'd like to avoid going through that again. Also, I'm very close with Dominic's girlfriend. In fact, she was the one who got him to come this weekend. She thought it would—"

She cut herself off, pantomiming zipped lips.

"What do women even see in this fraud?" David asked.

Debbie raised her shoulders. "He knows how to make every girl—and quite a few boys—feel like his songs are about them. The wheelchair works in his favor, believe it or not; the women most drawn to him are the ones who've had bad experiences with men. They think he's safe."

Both Belkins had the same flashback to Ida Mae's letter: *And oh God, that dream machine Dominic Day, who even though he's in a wheelchair, that song of his makes me feel like I'm 17 and in love for the first time.*

Mayer went to the window overlooking the parking area below. Popeye saw him and trotted over, tail stub fluttering like a folding fan.

"Rabbi Teitelbaum?" he said.

"Yeah?"

"See that silver Mercedes right there?"

She joined him at the window. "I do."

"I just want to confirm—is that our man's car?"

"It is. Why?"

IT TOOK FEWER than six minutes for the Belkins to pack their bags and change into street clothes. Debbie, meanwhile, roused the others and ushered them to the kitchen to light Shabbat candles and conduct an abridged *Kabbalat*

Shabbat service. She then bid them enjoy the buffet and said she'd be right back.

She met the twins at the foot of the spiral staircase. She handed over their phones and led them out a side door, where an ecstatic Popeye ran to greet them. As the quartet made their way to the parking area, Debbie touched Mayer's elbow.

"What's with the pirate patch?"

He adjusted the piece of black fabric covering his right eye. "Just a new look I'm trying out."

She studied him critically before nodding her approval. When they reached Daisy, she said, "I wish you guys weren't cutting your visit so short. Won't you take even a partial refund?"

"We got our money's worth and then some," David said. He unlocked Daisy and put Popeye's food and water bowls on the rear floorboard while Mayer unzipped his brother's overnight bag and took something out.

"Rabbi Teitelbaum, I'd like you to meet our mother."

"It's a pleasure, Mrs. Belkin," she said. "You should be proud of your boys."

Mayer looked at the night sky. The stars were dimmed by the light of the waxing moon, but still dazzling. Debbie and David looked up as well. Popeye gave a whine and started walking figure eights.

"Rain's coming," Mayer said, observing the dog.

"I don't think so," Debbie said. "There's nothing in the forecast."

"That's what they told Noah."

He glanced at the dining room window, through which he could see guests carrying plates of food to the communal table. "Better go back to your flock."

"May I hug you?"

He extended his arms and she stepped into them, then into David's. She looked from one brother's face to the other. "I can hardly tell who's who."

"*Zei gezunt,*" Mayer said. Be healthy.

"*Zei gezunt.*"

Casting them a final glance, she turned and went back the way she came. The boys waited until they heard the side door click shut.

"Now what?" David said.

"Try the door."

David pulled the door handle on the G-Class's driver's side. "Holy shit," he said. "How'd you know?"

"What's that I see in the cupholder?"

David leaned over the seat, saw the key fob, gawked at it, then at his twin.

"Go ahead," Mayer said.

David climbed into the Benz and made himself cozy in the captain's chair. He put his foot on the brake and pushed the start engine button. It chugged wetly to life. He tapped the gas, revving it a couple of times.

"Pipe down!" Mayer said. He checked the dining room window to see if faces were crowding the glass. None were. Someone in there was strumming a guitar and singing. David was examining the driver's console with curiosity.

"What are you doing?" Mayer asked.

"Looking for the hand control."

"Isn't that it?"

"That's the gear selector," David said. "I'm talking about the hand control that disabled drivers use."

"What do you need that for?"

"I don't."

"Then let's get this show on the road."

David put the SUV in reverse. As he was about to back out of the spot, he saw a straw Stetson cowboy hat with a flared brim on the back seat. He picked it up and put it on his head. It fit perfectly. He reversed, turned the wheel and backed up until the rear wheels touched the driveway. He parked and got out. Mayer arrived holding Ida Mae in two hands.

"Now that the time has come, I don't know what to say," David said.

"How about, 'She died doing what she loved'?"

This cracked both brothers up, but they got serious in a hurry. Mayer circled his thumb around the dent where the Benz clipped Ida Mae on New-found Gap Road. "I never gave the eulogy I'd planned for you, Mom," he said, "and it's just as well because it was crap. Here's a better one: you didn't have an easy life, but you made the best you could of it. If not for you, I'd never have discovered my love of Torah—and I wouldn't be where I am right now either. Which makes you the most influential person in my life."

He passed the urn to David, who reflected on it for a second. "Who'd have thought it possible, but in your crazy-ass way you got the Belkin boys back together. We'll do our best to make it up to you, Mom."

He kissed the urn and put it in the back seat.

"Hang on," Mayer said. "Pass her here one sec." He unscrewed the lid and tossed it away. In a nimble motion, he upturned the urn so that the rim was flush with the leather upholstery. He lifted it carefully, leaving a four-inch mesa of gray ash on the back seat.

David got behind the wheel and shifted to drive, letting it roll without gas. Mayer and Popeye followed on foot, their heads lowered in solemn reverence, as if this lampoon of a funeral procession were the real deal—which, when you got right down to it, it was.

As they neared the dining room window, Mayer became hyperconscious of the SUV's humming engine, the grating crunch of gravel under its tires. He stared anxiously at the window, anticipating a gaggle of oglers swarming it all at once—Dominic Day, the hitherto sensitive artist with a heartrending backstory, now fogging the glass with the call to jihad.

Shockingly, the window remained spectatorless, and Mayer uttered silent thanks to Eduardo and his talented kitchen crew, whose irresistible offerings were a heaven-sent decoy.

The brake lights came on and the Benz stopped. David put it in neutral, hopped out and joined his brother and Popeye in the back. He looked uneasily into the darkness beyond the grassy embankment on which they now stood.

"This is fucked up, even for me," he said.

"Oh, grow a pair," Mayer said. He planted his hands on the bumper and waited.

"You grow a pair," David shot back. He got in position.

"This one's for Debbie," Mayer said.

"And for all the innocent hearts stolen by that knockoff Bobby Sherman," David said. "I'll bet five bucks he's not even disabled."

"I'll take that bet and raise you five."

They pushed. The six-thousand-pound monster rolled without a squeak of resistance, as if resigned to its role as biblical scapegoat. At the point of no return, the boys released it and stepped back.

"*Bitachon*," Mayer said. In God we trust.

For a heartbeat and a half, the air went absolutely still, as if the planet had halted on its axis. Then a tremendous crash rocked the earth ninety feet below and echoed through the ravine. The boys looked over the cliff's edge. The Benz was on its roof, the headlights and taillights still on, the wheels spinning lazily. Tendrils of Ida Mae snaked out from many gaps, the ashes floating like dust motes in the rays of light.

"What the *fuck!*"

The Belkins' heads jerked to the left. Dominic Day was on the rear deck, leaning so far over the railing that one of the bodyguards had to grab him by the hips lest he perform a high bar. The other bodyguard came onto the porch pushing an empty wheelchair.

"Wait a minute," Mayer said. "How did he—"

"I knew that fucker was a fraud!" David hooted, his face aglow. "You owe me ten, Ese!"

He aimed his iPhone at the ambulatory Dominic Day, the deck light exposing him like a prison high beam, zoomed in and started filming. The bodyguard with the wheelchair shoved it against the back of Dominic's thighs in an effort to collapse him, to no avail.

Seconds later, the other guests crowded around Dominic, peering over the rail and gaping. But as the pop sensation continued shrieking into the void, the others realized that a better spectacle stood—literally—right in front of them. Several reached for their pockets before realizing they didn't have pockets, or phones. The desperate bodyguard finally grabbed Dominic in a bear hug and forced him into the chair.

Debbie was the last on the scene. She took one look at the upside-down Benz and clapped a hand over her mouth. Her dismay was no front; the Belkins had never specified the punishment they'd had in store for the ass-grabbing divo.

"You two! Stay right there!"

This order came from one of the bodyguards after he spotted the cowboy, the pirate and the one-eyed dog at the cliff's edge.

"I figure it's time to hightail," David said.

"I figure you're right," Mayer said.

They ran for Daisy, David struggling to extract the key fob tangled in his jeans pocket. He yanked hard, tearing the pocket and losing the thing. It landed in the dark with a plastic clatter.

"What are you doing?" Mayer hissed.

David saw the flicker of the fob in the moonlight. He scooped it up and thumbed the unlock button. Mayer flung open a rear door, scooped up Popeye and threw him in the back seat, then slid in next to him. David got behind the wheel. He put Daisy into reverse and skidded out of the parking space.

"Hit it!" Mayer said.

David shifted into drive, spun the wheel and floored the gas. Daisy went briefly airborne where the driveway angled sharply down. She came back to earth with a clatter and hurtled down the hill.

At the foot of the driveway David hooked a sharp left, veering into the opposing lane as Mayer and Popeye swooned to starboard. He rolled down the window and let out a lusty "Yeehaw!" that ruffled the feathers of a barn owl perched high in an ash tree. The owl twisted its head all the way around to watch the car fade into the night. The taillights constricted to pinholes. They dimmed. They flickered. And they were gone.

— EPILOGUE —

IT WAS AN ARCTIC DAY THE LIKES OF WHICH BROOKLYN
SELDOM FELT ANYMORE, THE WIND SO COLD AND DRY IT SINGED THE
lungs and petrified the eardrums. A Dodge Charger—orange, circa 1969—
parallel parked with inches to spare between two gray minivans on Foster
Avenue. The driver looked at his phone, then up the block at a hardware store
called G & Sons Distributors. He scratched his stubbled cheek.

"This can't be right."

"It's on the second floor," Mayer said, indicating a paper sign in Hebrew
taped to the door with an arrow pointing up.

"That's what you people call a courthouse?"

"No one calls it a courthouse. It's a *beis din.*"

"Whatever," David said. "You sure you want to do this alone?"

"I think it's for the best."

"How long do you figure you'll be?"

"Hour and a half," Mayer said.

"Shit. I guess I'll take Popeye for a walk, maybe get a blintz or something."

Mayer got out of the car, pressing down his black fedora—purchased just
for this occasion—to keep it from blowing off, and hurried into the building.
The *beis din* of Kensington was in a converted apartment whose living room
functioned as a courtroom. The whitewashed walls were lined with book-
cases of Jewish legal texts. A long wood conference table monopolized most
of the floor space. Around it sat three rabbinic judges, two male witnesses, one
scribe, Sarah and her father.

Half a year ago, around the time the Belkin boys completed their wayward passage across the Deep South—and around the time Mayer decided to post-pone his conversion for a few months to do some deep-dive soul searching—Sarah launched a campaign to win his hand in marriage. She was indefatigable, proposing thirty-three times—and getting thirty-three nos. Finally, she threw in the towel and demanded an annulment; in her world, the only way out of a faux marriage was a faux divorce. Mayer was happy to oblige. Wanting to kill two birds with one stone, he'd scheduled his conversion to Judaism for the next day so that they could get out of New York as soon as possible. If he'd ever felt affection for the Big Apple, he lost it somewhere in the Smoky Mountains.

He took a seat next to the scribe, a Chassid, and stole a glance at Sarah. She looked good—great, actually, a poster child for the "age is just a number" gospelers. Rav Drezner, on the other hand, looked every one of his seventy-one years and then some.

The chief judge commenced the proceeding by grilling Mayer about his intentions. Was he giving Sarah a *get*—bill of divorce—of his own free will? Was his consent wholehearted? Had he ever said anything in the past that might render the get null and void?

The scribe composed the get using the tools of his ancestors—quill, ink-well, parchment. This painstaking process took some forty-five minutes. The witnesses inspected the document and signed it, and the chief judge peppered Sarah with questions echoing those he'd asked Mayer.

At last came the moment of truth. Mayer handed Sarah the get and stat-ed, in Hebrew, "This is your get and accept this your get and with it you shall be divorced from me, from this very moment, and you are untied and permis-sible to anyone."

Sarah raised the parchment above her head. She gave it to the witnesses, who read it again, this time aloud. After asking one last time whether either party wanted a stay of divorce, the chief judge declared the marriage dissolved. Ending on an upbeat note, he wished Mayer and Sarah mazel tov and a bright future, and dismissed them.

The exes had been advised prior to the ceremony to have little or no contact after its conclusion. Mayer uttered a blanket thank-you to all present, then beat heat out the door and down the steps. The outdoor temperature seemed to have dropped five degrees, but Mayer welcomed the shock to his system.

As he beelined up the block toward the car David had christened Daisy II, Sarah came up beside him, keeping pace. He prayed she was just hurrying to her father's SUV to escape the cold, but she grabbed his arm, drawing him to a halt.

"Now that there's no going back," she said bitterly, "do me a courtesy and explain yourself."

"Explain what?"

"Why you rejected me. Did your time as a goy go to your head? Did you meet someone else—the woman in the video from New Orleans, maybe?"

"Sarah, don't do this."

"It makes zero sense. I'd have forgiven and forgotten everything, married you discreetly and pretended nothing had happened. You turned down a life most men would give their right arm for—and for what? To putz around with your good-for-nothing brother in *Atlanta?*"

She said *Atlanta* like it was Mogadishu. He searched her lovely face for a thread of self-awareness, a sliver of cunning—anything to suggest a method to her madness. But all he saw was perplexity and wounded pride, and his heart flooded with sorrow, for he realized she was as much a stranger to herself as to him. It was all he could do not to wrap his arms around her slender shoulders and whisper, falsely, that everything would be alright.

A shadow, long and lean in the docile winter sun, appeared at their feet, and suddenly Rav Drezner was standing with them. "What is this?" he said.

"Just saying goodbye, Ta," Sarah said.

"No goodbyes," the Rav said. "This man is a stranger to you."

"He's not a stranger. He's my—"

"He's your nothing. Get in the car."

"In a minute, Ta. Please."

He sank his fingers in her shoulders, spun her around and shoved her toward his black Escalade. She staggered two steps, caught her balance and turned to her father, her eyes glowing like fire-forged ball bearings. He stared right back. Alas, she blinked first and her face dropped, her body slumped. The driver appeared, opened the rear passenger door and helped her in. Mayer could scarcely make out her silhouette through the tinted glass.

The Rav got into the front passenger's seat and closed the door without so much as a *zei gezunt* to the man he'd brought into his inner circle long ago. The SUV pulled away from the curb, leaving a vapor cloud in its wake. Mayer watched it turn a corner and disappear.

Such a moment merited a reaction, he thought. But what reaction? Resentment? Relief? Bittersweet nostalgia for the good times he could count on one hand? For better or worse, all he felt was elation—for reasons that had nothing to do with Sarah and everything to do with an email he'd woken up to this morning. He'd read it nine times, and each time felt like grabbing the nearest lamppost and bursting into "Singin' in the Rain."

A sub-zero gust of wind streamed up the block and he hastened toward Daisy II, eager to salvage his ears before they broke off like icicles. "How'd it go?" David asked once Mayer was snug in the car's toasty womb.

"As divorces go, pretty smooth sailing."

"Well, I'm glad."

David got on Ocean Parkway toward the Prospect Expressway. Manhattan awaited. Mayer was game for whatever his brother had in store for them tonight, within reason; he was to become an honest Jew tomorrow. He took out his iPhone and pulled up the email he could read a hundred times and never get sick of:

Hawkeye, you sweet, wonderful man. I'm so sorry for leaving you in suspense these past few weeks, but I've been recuperating in New Hampshire for frostbite on three toes, not to mention hypothermia, dehydration and malnutrition. The doc-

tors say I'm lucky that the only (potentially) permanent damage is loss of sensation on the tips of my toes. Mayer, I couldn't do it. I couldn't finish the AT. I almost died trying. Up through October I'd been burning trail like the Tasmanian Devil. I was in the White Mountains when the cold came. I'm a Minnesota girl. I thought I knew cold. Turns out I'd never even heard of cold. I went from covering sixteen miles a day to two. Every other day, I had to get off the trail to resupply and dry my clothes. But I wouldn't give up. I would not give up. I've never been so deter-mined to finish something. Then came the blizzard, and I had to bivouac. It was the longest forty-eight hours of my life. I couldn't get warm. I had very little food. I had visions of hikers finding my body like Chris McCandless. When the snow let up, I packed and made my final descent. I feel like I should be in mourning, but I'm euphoric. Maybe it's knowing I pushed myself to my absolute limit and lived to tell the tale. Of course, I'll be back to finish what I started, thru-hiker or not. This journey changed me in ways that will take me a lifetime to unravel. I have so much more to tell you, and so much to ask you. Are you in New York? Atlanta? When I get my strength back, I'll book a ticket to wherever you are.

MAYER WOULD LIKE to have said becoming a Jew—again, for the very first time—was as visceral a sensation as losing one's virginity. In reality, he felt nothing. Prayer felt the same. Shabbos felt the same. Kosher food tasted the same. It was as if he'd been Jewish, or Jew-ish as Ida Mae put it in her sui-cide note, his whole life.

His muted reaction had a precedent. On the last day of Moses's life, God told the children of Israel, "And not only with you am I making this covenant and this oath, but with those standing here with us today before the Lord or God, and with those who are not here with us today." The Talmud clarified that "with those who are not here with us today" referred to the souls pres-ent at Mount Sinai that would inhabit the bodies of future converts. In other words, Mayer's Jewish soul had been on deck all along.

A week after converting, he and David were back home in Atlanta, watching *Raiders of the Lost Ark*. They were bone-weary from a surprisingly long day cleaning and stocking the place for Charlayne's arrival tomorrow. Mayer had grappled with the prudence of sleeping in such close proximity to a non-Jewish woman he felt deeply for. He'd even asked David about putting her up in a nearby hotel, but David quashed the idea. In the end, he decided to leave it up to God.

As the film ended with the apathetic warehouse worker dollying the Ark of the Covenant into a labyrinth of wooden crates, David said, "Ese?"

"Yeah?"

"I was thinking. What if you and I had a—what do you call it?—Jewish study group."

"A *chavrusah*."

"Yeah." David clicked off the TV. He had the awkward bearing of a twelve-year-old summoning the nerve to ask a girl out. "I really want to join the tribe myself one day."

"That's good."

"I can't do it on my own."

"It's a process," Mayer said. "The *beis din* will instruct you on what you have to do."

"Right," David said. He turned the TV back on and stared absently at the rolling credits, tapping his foot to Indiana Jones's triumphant theme music. Suddenly he got up and left the room.

Mayer rolled his eyes. He got up and found his big brother on the master bedroom terrace overlooking downtown, contemplating humanity's answer to a mountain vista. Mayer's eye had completely healed since it got blasted with a firework, so he, too, could admire the towers in all their prismatic glory. Who knew how many tens of thousands of surplus dollars David had shelled out for this privilege, asking not a dime from his brother with whom he shared it?

"It's just, I've never been much of a team player," Mayer said. "In my yeshiva days I tended to study alone, against my rabbis' advice."

"No need to explain," David said. "You teaching me would be like Robert Oppenheimer teaching ninth-grade physics to the dumb kids."

Mayer watched his brother's profile, the circular motion of his jaw as he worked his lower lip between his teeth. "I'm not even sure where we'd start," he said.

"Well, I'm no savant," David said, "but last I checked, people start at the beginning."

"Right."

A beat of silence.

"Well?" David said.

"Well what?"

"Are we gonna do this?"

"You mean now?"

"Why not?"

Another beat.

"What the hell."

Leaving the terrace, Mayer meandered into a multipurpose room David had outfitted into a study, with custom shelves for his Talmud, *Code of Jewish Law* and the myriad other primary texts and responsa he'd collected over the years. He scanned row after row of titles, many of them staples of any Jewish home library, others obscure, a few out of print.

On a shelf just above the floor, he found The Five Books of Moses, a gift from Rabbi Kugel when Mayer left for yeshiva at thirteen.

Squatting, he slid out the book of Genesis. Its spine creaked when he opened the cover, the interior scrawled with *Property of Mayer Belkin* in a bar mitzvah boy's handwriting. He brought it to his face and smelled the pages, and felt an emotion from childhood that made him close his eyes and prolong the inhalation for as long as he could. He exhaled, and the feeling vanished like steam rising from a cup of tea. It had been enough.

David was waiting patiently on the living room couch, stroking Popeye's neck. The brothers' knees knocked as Mayer sat beside him.

"Do you know what this is?" he asked, holding up Genesis.

"No."

"It's the first book of the Torah. Everything that exists, all events leading to this very day, this very moment, started with the first page of this book. Do you believe that what I'm saying is true?"

David thought about it. "I'm not sure."

"Do you believe it's *possible* what I'm saying is true?"

The answer came right away. "Yes."

"That's a start," Mayer said. He examined the plain brown cover. "I'm ashamed to say I haven't studied this book in more than twenty years—not in depth, anyway—so I'm a little rusty. But if we help each other along, I think we'll be okay. How does that sound?"

David replied, voice cracking with emotion, "It sounds good."

"It sounds good to me too."

He opened to the first page and brushed his fingertips diagonally across the Hebrew words that were the bedrock of his people.

"In the beginning," he said.

— NOTES —

Bible Verses - Translated by the author

- Chapter 2, Genesis 9:5; Leviticus 20:23; Shulchan Aruch (Yore De'ah 345)
- Chapter 3, Psalms 77:2
- Chapter 4, Psalms 133:1
- Chapter 6, Genesis 25:27
- Chapter 7, Isaiah 1:16
- Chapter 10, Deuteronomy 11:19; Genesis 18:19; Matthew 22:39 (from the American Standard Version Bible)
- Chapter 13, Psalms 19:1; Song of Songs 6:3
- Chapter 14, Psalms 101:7
- Chapter 16, Deuteronomy 33:4
- Epilogue, Deuteronomy 29:13–14; Genesis 1:1

Song References - Paraphrased

- "Back in Baby's Arms" (performed by Patsy Cline) by Bob Montgomery
- "Chimes of Freedom" by Bob Dylan
- "Fortunate Son" (performed by Creedence Clearwater Revival) by John Fogerty
- "Lookin' Out My Back Door" (performed by Creedence Clearwater Revival) by John Fogerty
- "Take Me Home, Country Roads" (performed by John Denver) by John Denver, Mary Catherine Danoff, Taffy Nivert Danoff, William Danoff
- "Thank God I'm a Country Boy" (performed by John Denver) by John Martin Sommers
- "The Groom's Still Waiting at the Altar" by Bob Dylan
- "Traveling Man" by Dolly Parton
- "Willie and Laura Mae Jones" (performed by Dusty Springfield) by Tony Joe White

Book References - In the public domain

- A Grief Observed by C. S. Lewis, first published in 1961
- "The Road Not Taken," by Robert Frost, originally published in 1915

—ABOUT THE AUTHOR—

Photo: Robert Miller

Reuven Fenton has been covering breaking news for the
New York Post since 2007, and has earned national recognition for his
exclusive reporting on myriad national stories. He is a graduate of Yeshiva
University and Columbia University School of Journalism.
Goyhood is his debut novel.